THE BODY
IN THE
BALLROOM

ALSO AVAILABLE BY R. J. KORETO

ALICE ROOSEVELT MYSTERIES

Alice and the Assassin

LADY FRANCES FFOLKES MYSTERIES

Death at the Emerald

Death Among Rubies

Death on the Sapphire

THE BODY IN THE BALLROOM

AN ALICE ROOSEVELT MYSTERY

R. J. Koreto

CROOKED
LANE

NEW YORK

Published in the United States by Crooked Lane Books, an imprint of The Quick Brown Fox & Company LLC.

Crooked Lane Books and its logo are trademarks of The Quick Brown Fox & Company LLC.

Library of Congress Catalog-in-Publication data available upon request.

ISBN (hardcover): 978-1-68331-577-3
ISBN (ePub): 978-1-68331-578-0
ISBN (ePDF): 978-1-68331-579-7

Cover design by Andy Ruggirello
Book design by Jennifer Canzone

Printed in the United States.
www.crookedlanebooks.com

Crooked Lane Books
34 West 27th St., 10th Floor
New York, NY 10001

First Edition: June 2018

10 9 8 7 6 5 4 3 2 1

At the time this book takes place, more than a third of New York City's residents were immigrants. This book is dedicated to them.

If you haven't got anything nice to say about anybody, come sit next to me.

—*Alice Roosevelt*

CHAPTER 1

St. Louis wasn't half bad. I met some fine people there, but my job being what it was, I met a lot of bad ones, too. The Secret Service said they had found some funny business with money, and as St. Louis was a lively town, it was as good a place as any to plot something like that. Mr. Wilkie, the Secret Service chief, said I could make myself useful in St. Louis, and I suppose I did. Alice wrote me one letter from Washington, filled with backstairs gossip along with complaints about her stepmother and cousin Eleanor. She told me not to write back because it was too hard to hide, and she didn't want to make it difficult to get me back home, but I was in her thoughts, and she hoped to see me again soon. In the small hours, when I was really honest with myself, I admitted I sometimes missed her.

Everything was wrapped up in May, and they gave me a warm handshake and a train ticket to Washington, where they said I'd get my next assignment. I figured it was a good sign I wasn't being sent further West, so I packed my bags and bought some presents for Mariah, my older sister, who followed me East when I first got the Secret Service job. Then I caught the next East Coast train. It was getting warm, and I was feeling good getting on the move again. There wasn't much to see as we traveled, but I met a couple of salesmen who had some good tobacco, and I was free with my bourbon, so the time passed quickly.

I had been told to find Mr. Wilkie at the White House, and so I headed there directly. I knew a couple of the boys, and they waved me in. They were smiling, as if they knew a secret joke I wasn't to be told, but I could make a pretty good guess.

However, a servant intercepted me before I got very far and told me the president wanted to see me first. That surprised me, but I made my way to the executive office where I met with George Bruce Cortelyou, the president's private secretary. He came from one of the old Dutch families, like the Roosevelts, here since before the British, and I watched him take in my long riding coat, cowboy boots, and Stetson.

"Mr. St. Clair?" he asked, as if I could be anyone else.

"Yes, sir," I said.

"Go right in," he continued, with a tone that said if it had been up to him, I wouldn't have been admitted.

The president was sitting behind the desk in his executive office and stood the moment I walked in. He grinned and stepped away from his desk to shake my hand and slap me on the back so hard I almost staggered.

"St. Clair, great to see you again."

"A pleasure to see you, too, sir. Glad to see you looking well."

"I've had a report about St. Louis. Damn fine work, I heard. Very nice indeed. Mr. Wilkie and I were both impressed, and he is putting a letter of commendation in your file."

"Thank you, sir."

"But you're probably wondering what we have in mind for you next. Pull up a chair, and we'll talk."

We sat at a small table, and it took the president a moment or two to gather his thoughts, which was unusual for him. "As you know, St. Clair, my sister, that is, Mrs. Cowles, thought it might be best for Alice to get to know the Washington scene, so to speak, and with her under the protection of the Washington office, you were assigned to the St. Louis office." Which was another way of saying Mrs. Cowles had lost patience with Alice and my inability to rein her in, so I was exiled, and she was sent to the capital.

"But while it's been good having Alice close to me, she's spirited, as I don't need to tell you, and is chafing under the necessary restrictions." Now he was saying that even the entire Washington Secret Service office wasn't able to restrain her, and I hid a smile.

"Anyway, to get to the point, Mrs. Cowles went back a week ago to open up the Caledonia apartment again. There are some political events where she will represent me and introduce Alice. Also, with the spring season, there are some significant social occasions for Alice to meet other young people. So basically, St. Clair"—he took a deep breath and continued—"I'd like you to travel back to New York and resume your old position as Alice's personal bodyguard."

I thought that might happen, and when he actually said it, I realized I was pleased.

"Of course, Mr. President." I smiled, and Mr. Roosevelt laughed, in relief, I think. A moment later, the office door opened, and Mr. Wilkie walked in. I stood to greet him.

"St. Clair. Glad to see you're back. Very pleased with the way it went in St. Louis." He turned to the president. "Have you spoken to him yet, sir?"

"Yes, and he's agreed." Wilkie looked relieved, too.

"Very good then. If you're done, sir, I'll take St. Clair to her. My understanding is that arrangements have been made for Miss Roosevelt to leave tomorrow afternoon."

"Exactly. We're all done then. St. Clair, thanks again. And I'll be up in the near future, so I expect to see you again soon." We shook hands, and I followed Mr. Wilkie out the door.

"Is she smoking on the roof again, sir?" I asked. That's what happened the first time I met Alice in the White House.

He grimaced. "No. My understanding is that she is in the basement indulging a new hobby of hers. But you'll see." He led me downstairs, and that's when I heard the unmistakable sounds of gunfire. Mr. Wilkie didn't seem worried, however. "Miss Roosevelt somehow got hold of a pistol and has set up her own private firing range in a storage room. We launched an investigation to figure out how Miss Roosevelt obtained such a weapon but were unable to reach a formal conclusion, I'm sorry to say."

No wonder they wanted me back.

And just as when Mr. Wilkie had sent me to get Alice off the roof, he once again cleaned his glasses on his handkerchief, shook my hand, wished me luck, and departed.

I heard one more shot, and that was it. She was probably reloading. The sound came from behind a double door at the end of the hallway. I carefully opened it, and she didn't notice at first. I watched her concentrating on the pistol, her tongue firmly between her teeth as she carefully focused on reloading. It was an old Smith & Wesson single-action, and she was damn lucky she hadn't blown her own foot off. She was shooting at a mattress propped against the far wall, and from the wide scattering of holes, it was clear her marksmanship needed a lot of practice.

"A little more patience, Miss Alice. You're jerking the trigger; that's why you keep shooting wild. And that gun's too big for you."

It was a pleasure to see the look of shock and joy on her face. She just dropped the gun onto a box and practically skipped to me, giving me a girlish hug. "Mr. St. Clair, I have missed you." She looked up. "And I know you have missed me. They say you're back on duty with me. We're heading to New York tomorrow, and we'll have breakfast together like we used to and walk to the East Side through Central Park and visit Mariah."

I couldn't do anything but laugh. "We'll do all that, Miss Alice. But I'm on probation from your aunt, so we have to behave ourselves. *You* have to behave yourself."

"I always behave." She waved her hand to show that the discussion had ended. "Now there must be a trick to loading revolvers because it takes me forever."

"I'll teach you. Someday." I made sure the revolver was unloaded and stuck it in my belt. Then I scooped up the cartridges and dumped them in my pocket.

"Hey, that's my revolver," said Alice. "It took me a lot of work to get it."

"You're not bringing it to New York, that's for sure, Miss Alice."

She pouted. "I thought you'd relax a little after being in St. Louis."

"And I thought you'd grow up a little being in Washington. You want to walk into the Caledonia like a Wild West showgirl? Anyway, don't you have some parties to go to up there?"

"Oh, very well. But promise me you'll take me to a proper shooting range in New York and teach me how to load and fire your New Service revolver."

"We'll see. Meanwhile, if you don't upset your family or Mr. Wilkie between now and our departure tomorrow, I'll buy you a beer on the train." That made her happy.

We walked upstairs as she filled me in on White House gossip. "Oh, and I heard you were in a fast draw in St. Louis and gunned down four men." She looked up at me curiously.

"A little exaggeration," I said. I hadn't killed anyone in St. Louis, hadn't even fired my revolver, except for target practice.

"You didn't kill anyone?" she asked, a little disappointed.

"No. No one."

But then her face lit up. "Because your reputation proceeded you, and they knew there was no chance of outdrawing you."

"That must be it," I said.

"But look on the bright side," she said, still full of cheer. "New York is a much bigger city. Maybe you'll get a chance to shoot someone there."

CHAPTER 2

That night, I made myself comfortable on a cot in the back of the guard office and woke up early the next day, as usual. I wasn't expecting much to happen until Alice and I were to catch our train to New York. But there was a little fuss after breakfast, which I might not have even remembered, except it became important later.

There were a lot of people working at the White House or just passing through, and for all of us, they served a real nice breakfast downstairs. That morning, one of the visitors was an army sergeant in a well-pressed suit, and from his talking—and he talked a lot—I found out that he was some sort of aide to a general who was visiting with the president. He was very proud of his home state of Georgia, and for a while, he was just boring, and I wasn't really paying attention because they have the best biscuits there, and plenty of gravy.

But then the sergeant got into politics and said, "You know, I can't believe who they're serving upstairs here. None of us back home could believe it." The president had invited a man named Booker T. Washington to have dinner with him last year, and this Washington was apparently a very important leader among colored folks, and lots of people, especially down South, got upset that a colored man was dining with the president. The sergeant used a very unpleasant word for colored folk, and that's when I spoke.

"Sergeant. First of all, we don't criticize the president here because this is his house. And second, I don't like words like that, not ever, and especially not around other colored folks." Because a lot of the kitchen staff were colored.

Mariah would've been unhappy with me because she'd know I was provoking a fight I couldn't lose with someone who didn't know my background. So as everyone watched and listened, the sergeant said, "Listen, Cowboy, it's not your job to teach me manners."

And I said, "I agree. General Sherman apparently failed to teach you Georgia boys manners, so what chance do I have?" Sherman's march through Georgia was not that long ago, and they still hated him for it. Words went back and forth, and then we were taking off our jackets and stepping outside. It enlivened everyone's morning, and we had quite an audience for the ten seconds it took to me to leave him flat on his back with a black eye that he'd be explaining to his boss.

I leaned down next to him. "I don't want you using that word." He just nodded.

I went back inside and finished my breakfast. When I put on my coat, I felt something in the right pocket. Someone had wrapped some biscuits, still warm, in a napkin. I stuck my head into the kitchen and smiled at the cook, and she smiled back.

★ ★ ★

The president's chauffeur drove us to the train station. Alice couldn't be more excited, skipping down the steps. There were some reporters on the street, and she waved to them, and they waved back, and there were more reporters at the station. She told them that she was looking forward to going to the Rutledge ball where her dear friend Philadelphia was a making a debut. She talked about her new dress and said there would be pictures, but that was all. Mrs. Cowles had warned her about telling too much to the press, and Alice knew just how far she could push her aunt.

As the president's daughter, Alice merited a compartment just for the two of us, and we sat back and watched Washington fade away as we headed north.

"So everyone is talking about how you got into a fistfight on the lawn this morning, Mr. St. Clair, and sent some army sergeant home with a black eye. I want all the details."

"How it God's name did you hear?"

"The White House is the biggest gossip machine in the country. My maid couldn't stop talking about it." She paused and looked a little shy, almost uncertain. "She said . . . she said you hit some Georgia soldier because he insulted the colored staff. And because he said my father shouldn't have invited Mr. Washington to dine."

"That's about it," I said.

"Why? Why did you care so much?"

I shrugged. "He was impolite, and you know I'm always polite." Alice snorted. "Also, I knew colored soldiers when I was in the army, and they were good and brave men."

Alice looked at me skeptically. "Very well. But there's more to that than you're saying." She tossed her head. "We'll come back to that later. Meanwhile . . ." She produced a deck of cards. "Deal me in, Cowboy."

It wasn't a long trip to New York, and the time passed quickly between card games and Alice's chatter about her plans for New York—the upcoming debutante ball, other parties and formal dinners, riding in the nice little runabout I drove, seeing shows in the Broadway theaters, picking up knishes on the Lower East Side. "And I want to go back to that German restaurant—the Rathskeller. That's the name, right? With the sharp sauerkraut."

"Looking forward to it. And maybe this time we can have strudel before getting involved in gunplay." I remembered what happened the last time we were there. Alice just laughed.

We pulled into Grand Central Station right on time. I was never happy when we were surrounded by crowds. It was too hard to watch both them and Alice as she just strode among the people and flashed smiles at those who recognized her. Alice loved being recognized. Once outside, we grabbed a cab uptown to the Caledonia. It was a huge building, a block square and ten stories tall, uptown and just off the west side of Central Park. It was divided into apartments for the best people, and the Roosevelts kept a large suite for when they were in town. I had a cozy room in the half basement.

"Welcome back, Miss Roosevelt," said the doorman. "And you, too, Mr. St. Clair." I always got a look of sympathy from the building staff, who knew how hard my job was. "Mrs. Cowles is upstairs."

My heart sank a little at that. I hadn't spoken with Alice's aunt since she had told Mr. Wilkie to send me packing to St. Louis. I wasn't sure what kind of greeting I'd get.

"It's good to be back," said Alice, sweeping into the elevator. Upstairs, a maid was already at the door.

"Mrs. Cowles is talking on the telephone, miss, but will be out shortly." She turned to me. "And Mrs. Cowles said she'd like a word with you, too, Mr. St. Clair."

Alice snickered. "I bet she does. Thank you. I need to change, anyway. I believe we're having guests for dinner." Alice flashed me a smile. "Mr. St. Clair. Bright and early tomorrow at breakfast, as usual." When I had first been assigned as Alice's bodyguard, I'd get my own breakfast or wheedle one from the Roosevelt's cook, Dulcie. But Alice had wanted to talk over her day with me first thing so had invited me to join her for bacon and eggs in the breakfast room. Mrs. Cowles didn't seem thrilled with that, but I always stood when she entered and always said "ma'am," so I was tolerated. Now, I'd see if I was still tolerated

Alice gave me a wink and disappeared toward the bedroom. I cautiously pushed open the kitchen door. There was Dulcie, cutting up meat with a cleaver, focusing on the task at hand. She turned her red face to me but didn't put down the cleaver.

"You again," she said. "Never thought you'd be back."

"Oh, come on, Dulcie. You missed me. Admit it." I smiled broadly. She didn't respond and just kept whacking away at the night's dinner. I knew she could easily split me with that cleaver.

"Any chance of some coffee?" Again, no response for a few moments, then she put the cleaver down. The Roosevelts had the very best coffee, and I had really missed it.

She got me a cup and said, "And you know the rules. That flask of yours and your tobacco stay in your pocket."

"Yes, ma'am." I leaned back in my chair. If Alice behaved, this might work out. And then I remembered she had stolen a revolver for unauthorized target practice, so that was a pretty big "if."

I had coaxed a second cup out of Dulcie, which she slammed on the table with unnecessary force, when a maid stepped into the kitchen and said Mrs. Cowles wanted to see me in the parlor. Dulcie laughed at my evident discomfort.

I combed my fingers through my hair, smoothed my suit, and stepped into the parlor. Mrs. Cowles smiled at my arrival and told me to take a seat opposite her. She was not what you'd call a beautiful woman, but there was a lot of character in her face, and you knew for sure that she was the president's sister. She was married to a naval officer who was at sea much of the time.

"So here we are again, Mr. St. Clair. Starting fresh."

"Yes, ma'am."

"I trust you had a full conversation with my brother?"

"Yes, ma'am. The president and I discussed my taking up the assignment as Miss Alice's bodyguard again."

"I'm glad. As I'm sure you know, Alice has rejected any thoughts of additional schooling. Nevertheless, she's reached an age where she has to take on more responsibility on behalf of the family. She needs to learn more about mixing in Society, to work with me and her stepmother in representing the president.

Essentially, she needs an informal but still rigorous education in becoming a political hostess with an eye to someday becoming a political wife. I shall guide her in that. And you shall see that she goes nowhere . . . inappropriate. I was thinking of going into detail, but behind that fake stupid cowboy persona you present to the world, I know you are intelligent and even shrewd. So further discussion won't be necessary."

I wasn't sure if that was a compliment or not, so I just thought for a moment and said, "I understand, ma'am. I'm looking forward to taking Miss Alice to the better homes, museums, and theaters and leaving it at that."

Mrs. Cowles smiled again. "Very good. I'm so glad we understand each other."

Then Alice strode into the room. "What are you two talking about? Whatever it is, we have more important things to discuss. Aunt Anna—" Alice gave a quick glance at me. Knowing Alice as I did, that particular look sent a chill down my spine. "I need an escort for the Rutledge ball tomorrow. I thought it would be most efficient if Mr. St. Clair served in that capacity. He would be able to keep me safe, and we could easily rent evening clothes for him."

Alice gave me a quick smirk. But Mrs. Cowles gave me a look that spoke volumes before turning back to her niece. "I don't think that we pay Mr. St. Clair enough for that kind of work, Alice," she said. "I daresay he can guard you safely enough from downstairs. I doubt if you are under immediate threat from any of the invited guests. I already spoke with my friend Mrs. Lesseps, and her nephew Stephen will be delighted to escort you." Alice pouted. "He'll pick you up, and you and Mr. St. Clair will drive in his family's coach."

Alice sighed dramatically. "Stephen Lesseps? I'm not sure how entertaining he'll be. Oh, very well. And I suppose I'll have to make a show out of drinking that disgusting Rutledge punch?"

"It would be polite," said Mrs. Cowles.

Seeing my confusion, Alice turned to me. "Some Rutledge ancestor brought over a recipe for a ghastly punch from Holland some two hundred years ago, and it's become a sort of ritual that everyone has a single cup at their parties. It's considered rude not to. For them, it's a tradition. But it's really a waste of good gin."

"I'm not going to ask how you know whether or not gin is 'wasted,'" said Mrs. Cowles. "I'll simply tell you to behave yourself. This isn't just a party. Philadelphia Rutledge is making her debut, and she's their only child. Most of the leading people in this city will be there."

"Why aren't you going, then?"

"You'll represent the Roosevelts there, and that's representation enough from a presidential family. Indeed, that's why you're back in New York. I'll be having a quiet dinner with some old friends here who are too aged for elaborate debutante balls."

"You just don't want to drink that god-awful punch," snapped Alice.

"That's part of it," said Mrs. Cowles with a bland smile. "And don't say 'god-awful.' It's vulgar."

"It is god-awful. And it's a miracle it hasn't killed anyone. But very well. Anyway, Philly Rutledge is a good sort, and I missed her when I was in Washington." Then Alice looked up at the clock and brightened. "It's earlier than I realized. We still have some time today. Mr. St. Clair, I do believe we have time to go to a shooting range and have you teach me how to load and fire your Colt New Service revolver."

So much for "taking Miss Alice to the better homes, museums, and theaters and leaving it at that."

CHAPTER 3

The next day started pretty smoothly. We had a cheerful breakfast with waffles and sausages. Dulcie was torn between being pleased I was out of her kitchen and sullen that I was getting above myself, eating with my employers.

"So you'll just be spending the evening in the Rutledge kitchen with coffee and a free dinner?" Alice asked.

"Yup. We might get a card game going."

"Ooh, a card game? What kind of pot?"

"You can't join us. You'll be upstairs drinking Rutledge punch."

"It's boring to be rich sometimes," she said, and I laughed. She fixed a quizzical look at me. "And you'll be flirting with maids?"

"If they're not too busy," I said. Alice didn't like that answer.

"Remember, you're there to protect me," she said. "That's your primary responsibility."

"Protect you from what?"

"What if Stephen Lesseps leads me into a dark hallway and tries to have his way with me?"

I choked on my coffee. "Yes, I'm very worried about that. In any fight, I'd have to protect Mr. Lesseps from you."

"That's an unfeeling comment. And I was going to bring you a glass of Rutledge punch."

"From what I've heard, I could do without it. Anyway, I'm well provided for." I slapped my jacket pocket where I kept a flask. For emergency purposes.

"You still keep it filled with bourbon. Can't you carry something civilized like brandy or scotch?"

"When you're all grown up, you'll appreciate a good bourbon."

"Don't patronize me, Cowboy."

"Learn to behave yourself, Princess." She just rolled her eyes, and I had another waffle.

★   ★   ★

The rest of the day was quiet. Alice spent most of her time unpacking and working with a seamstress for last-minute adjustments to her dress. Since I knew she was safely inside, I took a few minutes to head over to the garage a few blocks away. The Roosevelts had a little runabout suitable for two passengers, three if you squeezed, and I used it to drive Alice around town. I usually kept it in the Caledonia garage, but right before I left for St. Louis, I left it with a service garage where they could give it a good cleaning and run it every now and then.

Peter Carlyle was on duty there, and he and I liked talking about motorcars. I had picked up a fair amount over the years, but Peter knew a whole lot more than I did. A lot of people had trouble imagining a colored man could handle anything as complicated as a car engine, but smart motorcar owners all over Manhattan had learned that to keep their machines running, they made sure Peter took care of them.

He grinned when he saw me. "Welcome back, Cowboy. I heard you were returning. The engine is humming, and I put in some fresh oil."

"Good to be back, Peter, and thanks. But who told you I was coming?"

"It's all over town," he said. "One of Mrs. Cowles's maids told her friend who works in the Caledonia laundry, who told the delivery guy, whose truck I just fixed." He lowered his voice. "I also heard you taught some manners to a Georgia cracker who didn't like who the president invites for dinner," he said. He seemed very pleased at that. As I had noted, Mr. Washington was a big man among colored folks.

"Word travels fast," I said. "Let's drink to good manners." I pulled out my flask, and after making sure the boss wasn't around, Peter took a healthy swig.

"Thanks, Joey. Well, good luck keeping watch on Miss Roosevelt. Give her my regards." Peter once let Alice drive the motorcar around the garage on a slow day, so she had a soft spot for him. "The car's all ready. Should be purring like a kitten. But if there are any problems, just come back, and I'll put you at the top of the list."

I gave the car a quick crank, and as Peter had promised, it started right up. I drove the car back to the Caledonia and cleaned myself up a bit. I got upstairs in time for a quick coffee in the kitchen before a maid said Miss Roosevelt was ready in the parlor. They had done her up nice in an elaborate dress, and what they had achieved with her hair was an engineering marvel.

"You sure clean up nice, Miss Alice."

"Thank you. I do look grand, don't I?" she said loftily. "Parties like this usually have a lively enough young set, and Philly is fun. Anyway, I'll *make* it lively."

"No doubt about that, Miss Alice," I said, and she bowed in acknowledgment. We heard the maid admit someone, no doubt Stephen Lesseps, and a moment later, a young man stepped into the parlor. He looked like most of those Society men, pale and fair-haired and a lot more comfortable in evening clothes than I could ever hope to be.

"Dear Stephen, good to see you again."

"Alice, you look lovely." He took her hands in his. "Washington obviously agreed with you, but I'm glad you're back in New York."

"I'm glad to be back. Stephen, this is Joseph St. Clair of the Secret Service, who is in charge of making sure nothing terrible happens to me. Also, to make sure you don't take any liberties on the drive to the Rutledges'."

Stephen didn't seem to know if that was a joke or not, but after a pause. he reached out, and we shook hands. He smiled briefly but didn't say anything. Alice waved her hand like a queen. "But enough talk. We should be off."

The Lesseps had a grand coach with matched horses. I thought about my little runabout and wondered when coaches like these would disappear entirely. A crack of the whip, and we were off. Alice and Stephen made small talk about people I didn't know as I sat opposite them on the short ride downtown to the Rutledge townhouse. Stephen eyed me occasionally. I knew he wished I wasn't there. I wanted to say, "Don't mind me; I'm a bodyguard, not a chaperone." Alice would've loved that, but I decided to say nothing.

I saw the couple through the front door, and Alice gave me a wink. Two cops walked a beat outside, as was typical whenever prominent people like the Rutledges held a party. I had a word with them and then walked down the stairs to the servants' entrance. I knocked and heard a bolt drawn back before I was admitted—good, they were careful. I introduced myself to the maid and took off my hat. They seemed to be expecting me— also good. I could smell the food on the stove and realized the evening was going to be an easy one.

Indeed, not only were they liberal with food and coffee, but there were a few chauffeurs around, and it didn't take long to get a card game going. I was doing pretty well—I cleaned out the Irish boys quickly, but there was one German, and they're impossible to read. I had a solid hand, and we were eyeing each other

closely when I heard quick footsteps on the landing, and the butler appeared at the table.

I knew there was a problem as soon as I heard the running.
One thing I had learned taking Alice from house to house is that
good servants never run. I was already reluctantly putting down
my cards and standing when the butler started talking.

"Miss Roosevelt?" I asked.

"What? Oh, no, she's well, but there's been an . . . incident.
Mr. Rutledge would be greatly obliged if you could come immediately." So nothing had happened to Alice. My next thought,
not a very nice one, was whether Alice had done something and
I was being called to fix matters.

"Can you tell me what Miss Roosevelt did?" I asked.

"I don't believe Miss Roosevelt did anything," he said.
"Except to recommend your, uh, involvement, sir. It's . . . but
Mr. Rutledge will explain."

I thought we'd be going to the ballroom, but the butler led
me directly to the bedrooms upstairs. Two men were talking in
the hallway. One I knew as Rutledge, elegantly attired and a
little portly, but with a strong face and touches of silver at his
temples. The other man I didn't recognize, although he wasn't a
guest because he wasn't in evening clothes.

Alice was in front of them both, arms crossed and quivering
with impatience. "It took you long enough to get here," she said.

"I had to finish my hand, and then we got lost on our way up
here."

"Very funny," she said. She turned to the two men.
"Mr. St. Clair is here. I'm sure we can count on him."

Rutledge stepped forward and held out his hand, and I realized there must be a big problem because men like Rutledge
didn't usually shake hands with men like me. "We've had a little
problem . . . an illness."

"I don't know what you were told, sir, but I'm a government
agent, not a sawbones."

Alice sighed audibly. "For heaven's sake, both of you. You're here because you carry a badge, Mr. St. Clair."

Rutledge glared at Alice. "Miss Roosevelt, this must be very upsetting for you. I'll summon young Lesseps to take you back down."

"That won't be necessary. But we're wasting time." She waved her hand to show that Rutledge's words, perhaps Rutledge himself, were being dismissed. "Lynley Brackton had a drink of Rutledge punch and got sick and just died. I'm sure he was murdered."

CHAPTER 4

"It could be an accident . . ." said Rutledge.

"I don't see how," said Alice. She glanced to the stranger in the suit who was hanging back and summoned him imperiously. "This is Dr. Henrick, the Rutledge family physician. Please tell Mr. St. Clair what you told me and Mr. Rutledge." Rutledge had the look of someone who saw all control being taken from him, and he didn't like it.

The doctor glanced quickly at Rutledge before speaking. "I was summoned here for what seemed to be some sort of stomach ailment. The patient, Mr. Brackton, had been taken to a guest bedroom, and he was almost dead when I got here. I know a little bit about poisons, and I strongly believe he had taken a massive dose of aconite, or wolfsbane, as it's commonly known."

"How can you be sure?" snapped Rutledge. The doctor, although about a head shorter than Rutledge and a lot more pleasant looking, stood on his dignity. "I made a study of various pathologies, sir, before taking my general practice, and although an examination will be necessary, the symptoms were consistent in every respect with wolfsbane poisoning."

"If you want my opinion, and I'm guessing that's why you called me, there appears to be a good reason to call the police."

"We knew that," said Alice impatiently. "But why make a

fuss? You're on hand, and Mr. Rutledge doesn't want a dozen city cops trampling through his party. I told him you'd handle it."

"Thanks, Miss Alice," I said.

"Couldn't you do . . . whatever is necessary? It must've been some kind of accident," said Rutledge

"Accident? How does wolfsbane end up in punch by accident?" I asked.

"Ha! That's what I said," said Alice. Rutledge gave her another look, but there was more than that. He was uncomfortable about something. He sighed and said, "I have a small greenhouse in the back—botany is something of a hobby of mine. And yes, we have wolfsbane. But I keep the door locked. Even my servants aren't allowed in."

"Is your hobby widely noted, sir?" I asked. Half a step behind him, Alice rolled her eyes, and I had a hard time keeping from smiling.

"I've spoken about it," said Rutledge cautiously. Which meant he was probably a bore on the subject.

"I don't know what I can do, but let me have a look at your greenhouse. Can you come with me?"

"I can't possibly see the need—"

"Oh, for heaven's sake," said Alice. "Give me the key. You gave me and Philly a tour last year, and everything is labeled. I'll take Mr. St. Clair, and you can see to Mrs. Brackton."

Again, with some reluctance, Rutledge reached into his pocket and gave me a key. "Anything you can do to keep this quiet. So far, everyone thinks Brackton was just a little unwell. His wife knows he died, but no one else knows. She's lying down in another room and has a friend with her."

I just nodded, making no promises.

"Alice, you are welcome to return to the other guests," said Rutledge. I heard a hint of desperation in his voice, but I could've told him it was no use.

"Mr. Rutledge, don't forget that my father was police

commissioner. I am sure I can be of great help to Mr. St. Clair." Without waiting for further comment, she turned, and I followed Alice toward the back stairs.

"Miss Alice, how did you get involved in this?"

"Oh, I was there when he got sick. A bunch of us were around the punch bowl, with Mr. and Mrs. Brackton off to one side. We all came around for a required drink of that horrible punch and were joking about it when he looked unwell. His wife summoned a servant, and Mr. Rutledge was there already. Anyway, I didn't see anyone dropping poison in his glass." She looked disappointed.

"I suppose everything was cleaned up," I said.

"Yes, and I was most annoyed at that. He dropped his glass, and it smashed. It should've been left for the police, but the maids swept in, of course. But it must've been his glass. We were all drinking from that bowl. Philly and I drank together. No one else got sick. But I told them everything else had to be left as is and had the butler stand guard."

"Glad you did that, Miss Alice, but still, this is all just guesswork. The doctor could've been wrong, and there's no proof of deliberate poison."

"You have another theory?" she asked.

"Maybe . . . he was taking some sort of medicine that was improperly made up."

Alice didn't think much of that. And when we got to the greenhouse at the back, we saw a clue she might be right. The lock had been forced. The door was glass in a metal frame, and the lock was a simple bolt. It wasn't designed to keep out anyone serious about getting in, just the casually curious or a child who had escaped his nanny. A good, solid pull, and the bolt would rip right out of the jamb—and that's apparently what happened.

"I think that makes it clear," said Alice with a tone of triumph, and I had to agree.

The room itself was impressive, with some beautiful plants

and shrubs and a winding walkway among them. Alice seemed to know exactly where to go. "Mr. Rutledge is rather well known in New York for this greenhouse, and when he showed it to Philly and me, he told us to be careful of the wolfsbane."

We came to a small plot, and that's where we found a second clue. Rutledge had neatly labeled each plant, and we easily found the wolfsbane. Or what was left of it. Someone had ripped out some stalks. We could still see the holes.

"So someone here broke in just to kill Lynley Brackton," said Alice. She could barely contain her glee.

"Miss Alice, there's a lot we don't know here. Let's not jump to any conclusions."

"Mr. St. Clair, just think. Someone wanted to kill Mr. Brackton and did so very quickly. A last-minute decision like this— they must've been desperate to kill him at a public place with snatched poison like that." She folded her arms and contemplated the broken plants.

"Quite a puzzle, Miss Alice, but not ours. There's definitely something here, but it's for the police to investigate, not us."

She sighed dramatically but let me lead her out of the greenhouse.

"Can I convince you to go back to the party?" I asked.

"It was beginning to bore me. Stephen Lesseps was beginning to bore me. What do we do now?"

"We don't do anything. I call Captain O'Hara, and that's the end of it."

"At least I can show you where the telephone is here."

There was a little closet near the front door, and I had the operator connect me to the Tombs with Alice leaning over me. I didn't expect Captain O'Hara would be in this late, but I reached an officer on duty who I knew would be able to find him. I identified myself as Secret Service and gave specific instructions for O'Hara and then made him repeat it back to me. No need to involve the low-level cops outside.

"O'Hara isn't going to do anything," said Alice sourly.

"You're wrong there, Princess. He's going to take this problem off my shoulders, allowing you to go back to your party and me back to my card game. Now let's find Mr. Rutledge." He was still in the hallway, muttering with the doctor. He seemed pleased to see me again but unhappy to see Alice was still with me.

"Mr. Rutledge. This looks like a homicide to me. I had to call the police. But I reached out to a friend of mine, Captain O'Hara. He's also a friend of the president's. He'll be as discreet as possible, come around the back with a few men in plainclothes."

"Thanks, St. Clair. I appreciate that and won't forget it. I'll let the butler know. The doctor here will be looking after Mrs. Brackton, who's very upset, of course."

"I gave her a sedative," the doctor said.

"Might we see Mr. Brackton's body?" asked Alice.

The doctor's jaw dropped, and Rutledge looked like Alice had delivered a roundhouse to his chin.

"For God's sake, Miss Alice," I said. I took her by her arm, but she shook me off.

"Captain O'Hara is going to want to see the body, and this way, we can give him a summary when he arrives." It was late, and the party would probably be breaking up soon, at any rate. I was hoping to give O'Hara a quick summary when he arrived and then make an even quicker exit with Alice and Lesseps in the family coach.

The doctor just glanced at Rutledge, still in shock, then shrugged and led us to the bedroom where they had laid Brackton out. Death hadn't been kind to him, but I could tell he had been a handsome man around forty. The doctor left us alone with him.

"Was he a friend of yours?" I asked Alice.

"Lynley Brackton? As unpleasant a man as I ever knew. Outwardly charming but always mocking someone. Gratuitously nasty. I can't say I'm sorry to see him dead. I'd imagine that almost everyone here had a reason to dance on his grave."

"A eulogy from a member of the Roosevelt family. What a send-off," I said, and Alice thought that was funny. "If no one liked him, why was he invited?" I asked.

"That's a silly question. He's in Society. Of course he was invited." She frowned then and stepped over to his right hand. "Look at this ring, Mr. St. Clair. It's rather odd." I sidled up next to her and peered in the dim light. He wore a heavy gold signet ring with XVII stamped on the front.

"A family memento? Or some sort of club, I'd guess, but I've never heard of it."

Alice gave me a sly look. "The odd thing, which you apparently didn't notice, is that Mr. Rutledge has the same ring."

"That would seem to indicate a club, then," I said.

"Perhaps. Anyway, nothing more to see here, but I suppose the doctors will take him apart and see how he died."

"How are you going to sleep with images like that in your head, Miss Alice?"

She looked surprised. "Mr. St. Clair, I always sleep very well."

With no more murder fun to be had, Alice decided to head back to the party.

"What are you going to tell Stephen Lesseps about why you were gone so long?" I asked.

"I am the daughter of the president. I have responsibilities," she said loftily.

"I am so proud of you, Miss Alice, for being able to say something like that with a straight face."

"That wasn't funny, Cowboy. Anyway, you have to stay until Captain O'Hara gets here, and I can't leave without you, but everyone here seems to enjoy my company, and maybe someone can get me a real drink instead of more Rutledge punch."

So Alice went back downstairs, and I returned to the kitchen. The chauffeurs were all heading out, so there was no chance for another card game. However, the cook gave me some coffee.

Eventually, O'Hara showed up at the back, as I asked, with half a dozen officers in plainclothes.

"What the hell is going on?" he asked me.

"One of the guests died, and I don't see how it could be anything but murder," I said and gave him a quick summary.

"Christ almighty," he said. "Who the hell would do that?"

"Your job, not mine," I said. "I don't envy you. Now, I know you can't cover this up entirely, but if you can continue to be discreet, Simon Rutledge will be very grateful." O'Hara brightened at that. "Anyway, most of the guests are gone, but I'm sure you can get a list to see if anyone saw anything."

"It'll probably turn out to be a crazy servant with a grudge. Oh well. Anything else you can tell me?"

"Yes. Don't have the punch. I hear it's disgusting."

CHAPTER 5

I made a half-hearted attempt to get Alice to go home, but I knew it was no use, and I figured O'Hara might want me around to speak with me again before the night was over. After the captain started with his investigations, Alice didn't seem to care where her escort was but wanted to find Philly, who seemed to have disappeared. "I know where she'll be. I've been here enough times to know where she'll go." We located her in a cozy little sitting room by herself. She stood as soon as we entered the room.

"Alice! You always know what's going on. Apparently Lynley Brackton is dead, and some are saying it was a heart attack, but there's a rumor going around he was poisoned. Is that true?"

"It would seem so," said Alice. "They always try to hush these things up, but it never works."

"That's some ending to my party," said Philly. She shivered. "I'm so glad you found me. I was tired of people soothing me. I just had to sneak away. You aren't going to say anything sensible, I'm sure."

"Of course not. I'm going to tell you how lucky you are. You and your party will be the talk of the town," said Alice. "Every debutante ball is the same, but we'll remember this forever."

That got Philly to laugh. "I like the way you look at things."

"I would've thought your mother would be all over you," said Alice.

"She was; dragged me away the moment they carried Mr. Brackton out then fell apart herself. You know my mother. She's got to have her dramatic moment, and then she took to her bed, where she'll probably stay for days. And Father is trying to minimize the police presence." Then she took a look at me.

"I'm being rude," said Alice. "This is Mr. St. Clair, my Secret Service bodyguard. He helped me when I was investigating."

"Yes, the servants were talking about a crazy young lady who was pretending she was a police detective, and I knew that could only be you, Alice," said Philly, and both girls laughed. Philly gave me an appraising look. She seemed to be one of those Society girls you came across by the dozen in Alice's social set, pretty enough with pale blonde hair that was beginning to slip out of its combs. She was freckled across the nose, and I could see just how young she was. But I also saw a certain shrewdness in those cool blue eyes as she took me in, and her chin was set, making me think this was a young woman who was never going to take to her bed at the first sign of unpleasantness.

"You're the lucky one, Alice, getting your own personal cowboy. How can I get one?"

"We're available in the Sears catalog," I said, and there was a moment of quiet before both women laughed.

"You get one automatically if your father is president. Mr. St. Clair was with my father on San Juan Hill, and as a reward for his heroism, he gets to spend his days with me."

"Yes, my reward," I said, and this time, only Philly laughed.

"Make yourself useful," said Alice to me. "Don't you have some tobacco with you? Philly and I would sure appreciate a smoke."

"Ooh, if you could?" asked Philly.

"All right, because I know you didn't show up here with your own supply, Miss Alice, but you owe me."

"Very well, but you owe me a trip to a firing range. You promised to teach me how to properly fire a revolver."

"You are lucky!" said Philly. I quickly rolled a pair of cigarettes for the girls, then struck a match on my boot nail and lit both of them up.

"Now, if we only had something decent to drink," said Philly.

"Mr. St. Clair only has bourbon in his flask," said Alice, shaking her head, and Philly wrinkled her nose.

"When you girls are older, you'll appreciate bourbon."

"Don't make your uncivilized taste in drink an excuse to patronize us," said Alice.

There was a knock on the door, and another man joined us, darkly handsome, almost exotic, with midnight black hair. With hair that dark and a complexion so pale, he probably needed to shave twice a day. He was wearing well-fitting evening clothes, and I guessed him to be just a little older than the girls. He grinned. "Is this a private party, or can anyone join?" he asked.

"It is private, but you're absolutely welcome," said Philly. "Alice, this is Abraham Roth. We met a couple of months ago at the Mortons'. Abraham, this is Alice Roosevelt, one of my dearest friends."

"The president's daughter? A pleasure, Miss Roosevelt."

"And this is Mr. St. Clair, Alice's Secret Service bodyguard. He was a Rough Rider."

"Were you now?" he asked, sitting down, and he seemed genuinely interested, not condescending the way so many of the young Society men were. "Can I interest a veteran in a real drink? I have some brandy." He produced a flask.

"I don't know about Mr. St. Clair, but you have two young ladies who would welcome something civilized. Mr. St. Clair only has bourbon," said Alice.

"Bourbon? That sounds inviting." So the girls got something besides Rutledge punch, and Roth and I did a quick change for his good brandy and my good bourbon.

"We were talking about the murder," said Alice.

"Murder? I heard only that Mr. Brackton had died. I assumed it was just some sort of sudden attack." He looked at me, and I nodded. Captain O'Hara could keep it quiet for now—keep the press away and cover up the worst details—but there would be no hiding it for more than a day or two.

"I'm sorry, Philly," he said. She just smiled and shrugged. "Is it just me, or are you two young ladies not particularly upset at the loss of Mr. Brackton?" asked Roth.

"He wasn't widely liked," said Alice. "Word gets around—about his cutting remarks, his womanizing. They said he and his wife had trouble keeping servants because of his temper and other behavior. Even his own household's maids weren't safe from him, it was said. Still, as long as his behavior wasn't too blatant, he still got on the lists."

"So, in Society, it would be more of a scandal to cut him off, so it's just easier to ignore him?" I asked. That's High Society for you.

"I'm afraid so," said Alice. "There are lines you can cross and lines you can't, and he knew the difference. At least up until now." She turned to Roth. "Did you manage to make his acquaintance?"

"No. I just heard him but didn't speak to him. I know that sounds strange. I was within hearing distance of him, as he well knew, and heard him remark to another guest that he remembered when you wouldn't find Jews invited in the better households." He smiled wryly, but Philly turned red.

"I am sorry you suffered such a discourtesy in my house. Party or not, I'm glad he's dead."

That sent a chill through the room. But then Alice complimented the band, and the conversation turned to safer topics for a while until there was another knock on the door, and a male servant entered the room.

"Excuse me, but Mr. Rutledge asked me to find a Mr. St. Clair. He would like to see you in his study."

"I'm St. Clair. Miss Alice, stay out of trouble. I'll be back."

"I'll be your lieutenant," said Roth, and he gave me a salute. I laughed and followed the servant.

I knew Alice was not happy about being left out of a conversation, but she realized she wasn't going to be welcomed into Mr. Rutledge's study so apparently decided to make the best of it with my tobacco and Roth's brandy.

It was Alice, when I was first assigned to her, who told me the difference between money that was made yesterday and money that was made a century or so ago. When I entered Mr. Rutledge's study, I realized right away what I was dealing with. Nothing was new, and everything was expensive. Any rich man can buy fancy paintings for his walls, but if you have fancy portraits of your grandfather and great-grandfather, well that's all the difference in the world.

"Mr. St. Clair, thank you again for your discretion and for arranging things with Captain O'Hara. Please, take a seat. Can I offer you a cigar?" Rutledge selected one from a wood box on his desk and lit me up from a gold lighter. A chair in his private study, a thank-you, and the best cigar I'd ever had. I was going to be asked for a big favor.

"Glad I could help, sir," I said.

"You seem like a cool-headed man. I've had a discussion with Captain O'Hara, and he agrees with me that it wouldn't be in anyone's interest to ask too many irrelevant questions." *That is, make an arrest without poking into the business of all the leading members of New York Society who had shown up that evening*, I thought. "But you're a federal agent, Mr. St. Clair. I was wondering if the Secret Service had an interest in an investigation beyond what the city does."

"I'm not that high-ranking," I said. "It wouldn't be my decision."

"But the nature of any report you made to your superiors would no doubt have some influence on their decision."

"I guess so," I said. "It doesn't sound like anyone is going to miss this Mr. Brackton, however. I never met the man myself, but word travels fast, and his death doesn't sound like a great loss."

Mr. Rutledge didn't pretend to be shocked at that. He just nodded slowly. "Can I ask you about your background? There's a reason for my question."

"I don't mind. Before I joined the Secret Service, I was a deputy sheriff in Wyoming. I was a sergeant in the Rough Riders and ran up San Juan Hill with the president."

"Good. Then you will understand what I mean when I say that Lynley Brackton had become unreliable. Think on that, Mr. St. Clair. As a lawman and a soldier, you know what it means to be unreliable and the depth of that criticism."

I nodded and thought about what Alice had said about crossing lines. Had Brackton crossed a line, and someone had been pushed to extremes? Had Rutledge done it and was warning me off? I doubted it. Poisoning someone at your daughter's debutante ball would be the act of a madman.

"Miss Roosevelt doesn't seem to have been under any particular threat. I won't report to my superiors that she was in any danger here, if that was your concern," I said.

That seemed to please him. "And speaking of Miss Roosevelt, she seems to have taken a deep interest in this evening's situation. I hope that won't continue. It would be embarrassing for everyone, her most of all. Could you discourage her?"

"I doubt it. Unfortunately, I'm her bodyguard, not her nanny."

Mr. Rutledge paused at that, as if he didn't understand if that was a joke or not. "Would it help if I called the president? Mr. Roosevelt and I have known each other for years."

"Again, sir, I doubt it. If he could control her, he wouldn't have packed her off to New York under my care."

This time, he decided to treat it like a joke and gave a brief chuckle. If nothing else, he realized that he had gone as far as he could with me. He stood.

"Thank you, Mr. St. Clair. I'm sure Alice is eager to get home, so I'll say good night."

A servant led me back to the little parlor, where Alice, Philly, and Roth were laughing about something.

"Where did you get that cigar?" asked Alice.

"I didn't steal it, if that's what you mean. Your father, Miss Rutledge, stocks an excellent cigar. I don't remember the last time I had one this good. Anyway, we should think about getting home. I'm sure Captain O'Hara is completing his initial investigation by now. Have you found Lesseps?"

"Oh, he came around while you were gone, something about needing to get the coach home, but Mr. Roth here offered us space in his motorcar," said Alice. "So I sent Stephen home with a promise of an invitation to Oyster Bay in the summer."

Philly was looking a little tired as we headed into the small hours. Alice gave her friend a quick kiss. "We will talk soon," she said, and we followed Roth out the front door. Rutledge had resumed his hosting duties and was saying goodbye to guests as they left. The Roth chauffeur pulled up in a big, elegant touring car, and a few moments later, we were on our way to the Caledonia. It was a quick trip home, and I spent it admiring the motorcar. It was the latest thing, and I knew Peter would love to take a look at it, too.

"If you don't mind my saying, this is an impressive machine," I said.

Roth laughed. "I don't mind. It's actually my father's. He likes motorcars." It must've cost a packet, and Alice seemed to read my mind.

"I don't think Mr. St. Clair is aware, but it's widely known that Roth & Company is probably the biggest name on Wall Street."

Roth gave a slightly embarrassed laugh. "We're among the top, at any rate."

"Are you in the family business?" asked Alice.

"I graduated from Harvard last year, and then my family sent me on a world tour. I'm settling into a related business, I guess you could say. My father has international interests, and that's my focus, importing items from Europe and the Far East for sale here." By then, we were at the Caledonia, and the chauffeur was helping Alice out of the car. We said our thank-yous, and Roth said, "It was a pleasure meeting both of you. I hope we meet again."

"I am sure we will," said Alice, and I led her into the Caledonia. The motorcar had barely pulled away when Alice grabbed my arm like she wasn't going to let go. "You're coming upstairs, Mr. St. Clair."

"Of course. I always see you into the apartment, Miss Alice. That's the rules."

"No, I mean you're coming in. We have a lot to discuss."

CHAPTER 6

"Can't it wait until morning?" I asked Alice.

"No, it can't. I want to tell you what I heard, and I want to hear what Mr. Rutledge told you."

We let ourselves into the apartment. Mrs. Cowles and the servants had already gone to bed. Alice dragged me into the breakfast room, as if she was afraid I'd run away.

"First, I'm going to tell you that I overheard an argument between Mr. Rutledge and Mr. Brackton early in the evening."

"Really? And how did you do that?"

"Don't use that tone with me. They had a photographer present, and no one knew where Mr. Rutledge was, so I volunteered to go find him."

"Why you? The Rutledges must have dozens of servants."

"You can't trust servants with something like that. They'd all be afraid to interrupt him. They needed someone who would grab him and drag him downstairs."

"So you found him."

"Yes, behind the closed door in his study. I heard yelling. Not 'angry that someone's been stealing my good brandy' angry but enraged. But what was more interesting was that someone was yelling back just as loudly."

"Why was that more interesting?"

"Because he's Simon Rutledge! He's head of one of the oldest families in New York and one of the wealthiest. I was trying to figure out who would dare to argue with him. People listen to Simon Rutledge; they don't argue with him."

"But you couldn't hear the words? Even with your ear pressed against the door?" I grinned.

"You have such a low opinion of me. Do you really think the president's daughter would demean herself to that level of eavesdropping?" I guess I looked a little doubtful because she glanced away. "Anyway, the door was too thick. But I can tell you who it was. I waited around the corner, and a few moments later, I heard the door open and saw it was Lynley Brackton—the dead man. I've been wanting to tell you ever since the murder, but we didn't have a private moment until now. I waited a minute so no one would think I was spying, and then I fetched Mr. Rutledge. He was all red in the face but calmed himself down."

"What about Mr. Brackton?"

"That's the odd part. He was smirking. As if he had pulled one over on Rutledge. Now tell me what Rutledge told you."

I gave her a quick summary. "So basically, it looked like he was just trying to avoid scandal. But it was what he said—Brackton was not reliable. A business deal? Or just something in Society? Had he crossed a line?"

"It can't be coincidence. The fight, the poisoning. The man was widely hated."

"But I don't see Rutledge killing him like that. I mean, maybe grabbing a letter opener in a rage and killing him in his study but not like that, staging a poisoning."

"You're right. There's a lot to think about. We have to decide what to do next."

"Next? We say good night, and then I go back to my room."

"You know what I mean," she said with impatience. "What about Brackton's murder?"

"O'Hara will get some detectives to nose around, and they'll find out what happened."

"But that's just it," said Alice. "What could have happened?

I mean, I was right there. On one side was me, Philly, and Mr. Rutledge. One of us would've seen someone dropping something into Brackton's drink. And who would do that, anyway? It was just us." She thought for a moment. "Let's think about that. Not just who wanted to kill him, but who had an opportunity. I was talking with Philly and her father on one side of the punch table. The Bracktons were on the other side—let me think—with whom? Just another woman; I can't recall her name right now. We'll sort it out later, but it was a small group, at any rate."

"Miss Alice, like O'Hara said, it was probably a servant."

Alice sighed dramatically and shook her head like she couldn't believe how stupid I was. "For God's sake, do you think a servant would suddenly get it into his head to break into a greenhouse, pull up some poisonous plants, and try to slip them to a guest? Mr. Rutledge said servants weren't even allowed in the greenhouse. We're going to the Tombs tomorrow to see what the police found out."

"Miss Alice, we just got back to New York. We're not going to upset things by going to the Tombs."

"Yes, we are. My aunt doesn't want you to take me somewhere unsafe. The Tombs are merely unpleasant. Breakfast at nine tomorrow. Good night, Mr. St. Clair." She swept out of the room and left me to let myself out.

I shook my head and headed to my room in the half basement. I gave myself a shot of bourbon and a final cigarette before crawling under the covers. I kept telling myself it wasn't my business, but Alice had a point. How did someone get poison into that glass?

★ ★ ★

I slept well and was upstairs promptly at nine, entering just as Mrs. Cowles was about to leave. "Good morning, Mr. St. Clair. I understand the party had a most unfortunate ending but that you stepped in and handled the situation with great tact."

"Thank you, ma'am. Is that what Miss Alice told you?"

She laughed. "Alice? Good heavens, Mr. St. Clair. What trouble I would be in if my information were filtered through the mind of my niece. No, I had other sources. News traveled fast. The official word is that it's under investigation, but it's an open secret it's a murder. I would not go as far as to rejoice in the death, but I shan't spend a great deal of time mourning Lynley Brackton. He was not a good man. He was not . . . reliable."

"That's interesting, ma'am. When I was speaking last night with Mr. Rutledge, he also said Mr. Brackton was unreliable. He made that sound like it was the worst insult in the world."

Mrs. Cowles gave me a curious look, and then her lips curved into a cool smile. "You've been among the most important and wealthy families in the most important and wealthy city in this country, Mr. St. Clair. I have no doubt that if you think about it, you will come to realize just how terrible an insult that is. We must rely on each other. It's what holds Society, any society, together."

I nodded.

"Anyway, I would be profoundly grateful if you could discourage what will no doubt be Alice's morbid obsession with the murder."

With that, she was gone. I went into the breakfast room, and Alice joined me a moment later. A maid came around with pancakes, bacon, and a pot of coffee.

"Your aunt doesn't want you to interest yourself in the murder," I said.

"She found out already? Good for her."

"By the way, she said Lynley Brackton was unreliable. Just like Mr. Rutledge said."

"That's fascinating. We'll remember that. First on our agenda will be calling on Captain O'Hara and getting the name of the detective supervising the case . . . but no, first we'll visit the Rutledges and see what I can find out from Philly."

"I think she may have been in a bit of a shock last night," I said. "In the cold light of day, do you think she'll want to continue dwelling on it?"

Alice rolled her eyes. "A lot you know about debutantes. Today, it will be even better. You hope that some young lady drinks too much champagne and makes a fool of herself so you have something to talk about. Now a death, a murder, that's something to mark your special day. Everyone in Society will be calling on her or inviting her to hear all the details. Heck, when her granddaughter is coming out decades from now, she can say, 'ah, but a man was murdered at my party.'" Alice then frowned. "No one died at my debut. Like I said, some girls have all the luck. But yes, we'll visit Philly first . . ."

I heard someone ring at the front door, and a moment later, a maid came in and handed me a note.

"Who's sending you notes?" asked Alice, half curious and half jealous. It was a cheap envelope with nothing but my name on the outside. I tore it open.

"It's from Captain O'Hara. Probably gave it to a beat cop to run uptown." I unfolded the note.

"Read it, Mr. St. Clair."

"I am."

"I mean out loud," she snapped.

"Oh, very well. 'St. Clair—Thanks for your help. Turned out to be easy. Brackton argued with some colored motorcar mechanic the day before, and we arrested him. Got him down in the Tombs. Expect a confession soon.' Goddamnit. Pardon my language."

"Goddamnit indeed," said Alice. "They arrested that nice mechanic who let me drive—that must be him, Peter Carlyle."

"Must be. Just spoke to him myself. He's pretty even-tempered, though. You said this guy Brackton started arguments as a rule."

"Nasty and arrogant. I'm sure it was entirely Brackton's fault and O'Hara was too lazy to really investigate."

It broke my heart to think of Peter in the Tombs. As bad as it would be for anyone, it would be worse for a colored man. I wondered if I knew of any lawyers who could take his case, but Alice was ahead of me.

"One final sip of coffee, Mr. St. Clair, and then we are definitely going to the Tombs to get Peter Carlyle released. And then O'Hara will tell us who's behind his arrest, and I will make them very sorry for what they did."

"Miss Alice—"

"Don't you want to get him released?" she challenged.

"Of course. I just don't see how you're going to do it."

"That, Mr. St. Clair, is the easy part. Grab your coat, Cowboy."

I felt a mix of hope that Alice could spring Peter and fear at what she'd do to get him out.

★ ★ ★

A few minutes later, we were in the motorcar heading downtown. Alice looked delighted with herself but almost exploded in impatience every time we got stuck behind a delivery van. I had barely parked near the Tombs when she jumped out of the runabout and marched up the stairs. I ran to keep up with her.

Alice barely stopped at the front desk. "Miss Roosevelt and Mr. St. Clair to see Captain O'Hara. Don't get up; I know the way."

"But Miss . . ." the officer was saying. Alice was already striding down the hall. I followed up and flashed my badge.

"Don't even bother," I said.

Alice did indeed know the way and just walked right in without knocking.

"What—Miss Roosevelt—how—why . . ." He was sitting behind his desk in his shirtsleeves, writing out a report, and he just stopped, the pen frozen right on the paper.

"How dare you. How *dare* you. We trusted you, and what do you do but lock up Peter Carlyle, who couldn't possibly be guilty. Get him out of his cell and up here. Right now."

He just stared at her for a moment, then looked at me over her shoulder. I shrugged. "She has a point, Captain."

O'Hara sighed. "Take a seat, both of you." We did, but Alice didn't get comfortable, sitting on the edge of her chair, no doubt so she could get up and grab O'Hara by his lapels if need be.

"I guess you know this Carlyle?" he asked.

"He's the mechanic for the Roosevelt car," I said. "And for most of the well-heeled uptown drivers. I've shared a smoke with him often over discussions about engines. I can't believe he killed Brackton."

"We asked around. Brackton had brought his motorcar around earlier in the week, and there was some disagreement about the extent of the repairs, and he accused Carlyle of being a lousy mechanic and a liar to boot. There were witnesses. Anyway, there is no one else even close to being a suspect. He hasn't confessed yet, but I'm sure he'll come around to realizing that it's in his best interest to admit it." He leaned back in his chair and looked very pleased with himself. Alice looked like she was going to explode.

"Even if you think Peter was capable of doing that, and I don't, did you give any thought to how Peter could sneak into the Rutledge mansion, into the ballroom, completely unseen?" she asked.

O'Hara seemed a little uncomfortable at that. "We're still working on that. But we have motive. And he easily could've broken into the Rutledge greenhouse. He also maintains the Rutledge motorcar, and either Simon Rutledge or his driver mentioned the greenhouse at some point. It's a well-known feature."

Alice sighed dramatically. "With your rather parochial background, Captain O'Hara, you may not realize it, but not too many colored citizens are invited to debutante balls. A black man would've stood out a mile away."

"Well, it was late, and maybe no one would've noticed. They were all tired and probably a little drunk." Alice and I could tell he didn't really believe it himself, and he saw the look of disappointment in our faces. "Oh, for God's sake, what do you expect? The best of New York Society was there. You want detectives to start questioning them? We asked everyone, especially those near the punch bowl table, and no one saw anything. You want me to bother all the great families of New York? This arrest made Simon Rutledge very happy."

"I don't think it made Peter Carlyle very happy," said Alice.

O'Hara rolled his eyes and looked at me. "Mr. St. Clair. You've been around. You know it's not a perfect world."

"I know. But it should be more perfect than this," I said. Alice turned and gave me a wink.

"Captain O'Hara," she continued. "I was by the punch bowl with Mr. and Mrs. Brackton. I was not inebriated." She stood. "I am going to visit District Attorney Jerome today. I will tell him that I will testify that I saw no colored men anywhere near us during the relevant period. I will be believed. Mr. Rutledge won't be so happy with you then, as he'll be wondering why you frittered away days after arresting an innocent man."

I could just imagine what Mrs. Cowles would say about Alice giving evidence in a murder trial.

"Oh, very well," he sighed. "I suppose we can keep looking around and see if we can find someone else who had it in for Brackton."

"And you'll release Peter Carlyle. Now."

He sighed again. "It's going to take a few minutes. You can wait in the lobby."

"I hope this won't take too long," said Alice. "We'll leave now so you can go about releasing him. Good day." And with that, she made a typical grand exit without even seeing if I was following.

O'Hara took a moment to speak with me before I followed Alice. "Just between us, was she really going to see the DA? Or was she bluffing?"

"Miss Alice never bluffs," I said.

CHAPTER 7

Alice paced like a caged tiger in the lobby while we waited for Peter.

"I'm glad you got him out," I said. "But it's only temporary. If they can't find anyone else, they'll arrest him again and make it stick. We'd best be gathering a few dollars and helping him get out of town."

"We are not going to see Peter chased away from his home and his job. What we are going to do is find out who killed Lynley Brackton." She glared at me. "Well? Aren't you going to try to talk me out of it?"

"Would it do any good?" I asked. She laughed at that. I did realize that she was right about one thing: I didn't see how anyone except a guest, all members of the best families, could've done it. So if Alice confined herself to the cream of New York, we just might get through this without violence. Of course, I was being optimistic.

O'Hara led Peter up himself, and the mechanic was looking a little worse for wear, blinking in the light. He seemed surprised to be released and doubly surprised to see us there.

"Joey . . . Miss Roosevelt, what . . . ?"

"It seems you have some powerful friends," said O'Hara sourly. "But this isn't over. Don't go too far. I'll probably be looking you up again." He gave us a skeptical look and left, shaking his head.

"You got me out?" he asked.

"Miss Alice swore you couldn't have been there," I said.

"Well, thank you very much, Miss Roosevelt," he said. "I'm still trying to find out why I was arrested in the first place. We just had an argument, that's all."

"We have much to discuss, and you look like you need something sustaining."

"I was woken up the small hours and was questioned pretty sharply by a team of Irish cops all night. Nothing to drink, and no breakfast this morning."

"Let me buy us all an early lunch and see what we can do. There should be someplace here we can get some sandwiches."

"I would appreciate that," said Peter with a grin. Alice stepped forward quickly, but Peter hung back to talk to me.

"What does she mean, 'see what we can do'?" he asked.

"She likes playing detective. And she isn't half bad at it," I said.

We easily found a restaurant not far from the Tombs. The waiter gave us a look, and although Alice didn't seem to notice, I did. And so did Peter. We were seated at a table, and a few minutes later, the manager came over looking a little flustered.

"I am terribly sorry, miss, but it is customary here, that is, regarding your guest . . ." His eyes darted to Peter, and that's when she figured it out.

"Do you know who I am?" she asked.

"Yes, of course, Miss Roosevelt," he said. Alice's photographs had been published far and wide.

"Then you must know that my guests are welcome at any establishment in this city. In this nation. You will see about getting us three beers and a plate of sandwiches." He looked like he was about to say something else, thought better of it, and left.

Peter looked a little abashed. "Sorry if I caused you any embarrassment, Miss Roosevelt," he said.

"Don't apologize," I said. "Miss Alice loves causing scenes." Alice gave me a dirty look, and Peter laughed.

"Then I'm glad I could oblige," he said.

He looked a lot better after he had eaten and drunk a little, and then Alice got down to work.

"So, Mr. Carlyle, I understand that the police accused you of poisoning Lynley Brackton. Tell me about the argument you had with him."

Peter shrugged. "It wasn't that much. He was always fussing about something. I had to do a lot of work on his motorcar. He had been running it hard and not bringing it in for care like he should. I was used to it. Nothing to kill him over. Anyway, the cops kept wanting to know where I was that night and if anyone could confirm it. But I couldn't tell them."

"Just between us here, where were you?" Alice asked.

"Private meeting," he said.

Alice sighed. "Don't be coy with me. What were you doing? Playing cards? Shooting craps?"

Peter laughed. "No, none of those things. I don't gamble. It was just a . . . private meeting."

"So were you with a woman? Were you at a bordello? As Mr. St. Clair will tell you, I am not as sheltered as people think."

He just looked away in embarrassment, and I felt the heat rising to my face. "For God's sake, Miss Alice, you can't talk about things like that," I said.

"There's a delightfully old-fashioned streak running through you, Mr. St. Clair. But we don't have time for old-fashioned niceties. We're dealing with the death of one man and the possible conviction of another. Mr. Carlyle, stop being silly. Where were you, so we can establish an alibi?"

But Peter just shook his head. "It's not that I don't trust you, either of you, and don't think I'm not grateful. But it's not just my secret. It's someone else's, as well. Anyway, it wasn't anything illegal, not in New York." He gave Alice a wry look. "And no, Miss Roosevelt, this isn't about being anywhere I shouldn't."

"Men are so silly," said Alice. "Very well, be that way. But we still need to proceed to find out who killed Brackton. I don't suppose you have any insight into who might've done that?"

Peter shook his head. "All I can tell you is that he was known for starting arguments. Proud as the devil. He was in the garage once, and one of the other mechanics dropped something on his foot, and Brackton laughed. He just laughed. A real joy in someone else's pain. I didn't kill him, but I won't pretend I'm sorry he's dead."

Alice nodded. "Yes, that sounds like Brackton. A range of motives. We have to winnow the suspects. I need a better sense of what happened at the party. We'll call on Philly Rutledge next."

"I appreciate all this, both of you," said Peter. "If there's anything I can do, just ask."

"It's possible we may need an investigative team for this before we're done," said Alice.

We finished the beer and sandwiches. Alice paid and took a moment to glare at the manager on the way out. We gave Peter a ride back to his garage, where he also had a room.

"Your boss going to be all right with this?" I asked. "Miss Alice and I can have a word with him if you want."

"Oh, he won't hold it against me, but thanks. J. Pierpont Morgan's driver brought in his car earlier, and I'm the only one who knows how to fix it. A few hours' sleep and back to work. Thanks again for getting me out, and for lunch."

"Don't thank her too much," I said. "You'll give her a swelled head. And she only did it so you'll let her drive in the garage again." Peter laughed at that.

"Mr. Carlyle, I confess I think less of you for making friends with someone as rude as Mr. St. Clair. I am pleased I could oblige, and we will talk again soon."

She waved her hand, and we were off to the Rutledge home.

CHAPTER 8

The Rutledge mansion was uptown from the Tombs. I remembered the address from the other night. Heck, everyone knew where the Rutledges lived.

"What do you think Peter was doing that he couldn't tell us?" asked Alice as we drove.

"He may just like keeping his private life private," I said.

"I don't see why. He needs an alibi. Surely whatever he was doing wasn't that shameful."

"Miss Alice, you may not understand, but it doesn't come naturally to men like Peter Carlyle to fully trust."

"Men like him?"

"Colored men. I know you did him a great favor. But still. He won't trust white people easily."

Alice started to say something, then thought better of it, and we rode the rest of the way to the Rutledge mansion in silence.

It must've been one of the biggest homes in New York. I couldn't see much of it the night before, but today, I could see just how impressive it was, how much effort had gone into the design, from the stonework on the walls to the oversize black door and bright brass fittings. Even the street in front of the house seemed cleaner here, which it may have been. The Rutledges employed a lot of people.

The door was promptly answered by the butler.

"We're here to see Miss Philadelphia. Please tell her Miss Alice Roosevelt and"—Alice slid her eyes over to me—"escort have called."

"Very good," said the butler. We were shown into a very nice parlor, the kind where the furniture looked too good to sit on. I liked a couple of paintings on the wall. From time to time, I got to briefly see some of the better rooms in the great houses, and the portraits were usually as exact as possible. But one of these was softer, a painting of a mother and children, and I found it really caught my attention.

"Mary Cassatt," said Alice, following my gaze. "She's an American artist but lives in France. I wouldn't have thought she'd engage you, Mr. St. Clair."

"You look at this, and it really makes you wonder what the people in the painting are thinking," I said. Alice cocked her head, as if she was considering that, too.

"Do you ever think about how difficult things are because you don't know what people are thinking?" she asked.

The butler came back into the room. "Miss Roosevelt, Miss Rutledge can receive you upstairs. Your . . . escort . . . can remain here."

"Oh, but I do want Philly to talk with you, too," she said to me. "She's probably just getting up. Debutantes always sleep in the next day, and she's no doubt eager to gossip some more. Anyway, I'll bring her down here when she's ready." With that, Alice followed the butler out of the room, leaving me alone. I thought the butler seemed a little worried about leaving someone like me by myself in a fine room, but maybe it was just my imagination. Still, it gave me more time to look at that painting, and I thought it was no easier to read Cassatt's characters than it was to read people in real life. I admired Cassatt for that. I admired Alice for realizing it.

The door opened, and a maid walked in. She was young,

probably around Alice's age, with a pale Celtic face and a strand of red hair slipping out from under her cap. She was no doubt Irish—there were Irish maids in every grand house in Manhattan.

She seemed a little surprised to see me. "Sorry to disturb you, sir. I was sent to clean." There didn't seem to be a speck of dust, but who was I to argue with her? She waved her feather duster over the figurines, fragile and expensive, and all the other little bits and pieces scattered around the room. Suddenly, her eyes darted to the door, and then she turned to me.

"Sir, are you a policeman?"

"Sort of," I said. "I'm Miss Roosevelt's bodyguard."

"Yes, sir. I saw you last night. But are you a policeman?" she asked again and sounded almost desperate, trying to find out who I really was. It seemed a lot more than idle curiosity, and I was sure maids weren't supposed to chat with guests. Even those like me, who weren't true guests. Being with Alice as I was, I guess she thought I was someone in authority, but in my Western riding coat and Stetson, perhaps I seemed less threatening than a city cop.

"I'm not a New York policeman, if that's what you mean." I took out my badge. "I'm a Secret Service agent, and my boss is the president in Washington, not anyone in the city."

The maid seemed a little confused, and I could see her struggling with what to say next. "It's just that, sir, I was wondering if you knew if they found out who killed the guest yesterday. I heard someone was arrested but let go." Again, she seemed worried about it, not just fishing for gossip. I was surprised it had already gotten around that Peter had been arrested and then released, but tales like that could fly fast.

"I can tell you they arrested someone, but he was released because it seemed clear it couldn't have been him." I smiled. "You're not worried he's going to come back and kill more people, are you?"

"Oh, no, sir. That's not it at all. I—I'm sorry to interrupt you. I just wanted to say that no servant could've done it, sir."

I heard footsteps in the hall outside, and I knew our conversation was coming to an end. I pulled a card out of my pocket. "Take this. It has my name and tells you where you can find me. I'll keep whatever you say secret from the city police. Can I have your name?"

"Cathleen, sir. Cathleen O'Neill."

"When do you have some time off, if I want to talk more with you?"

She paused. Cathleen didn't want to answer but clearly didn't want to lie to me, either. "Tomorrow afternoon. But I'm . . . I'll be busy."

Then Alice and Philly came in, and Cathleen slipped out the door.

Philly didn't look any worse for having been up late the previous night. She was dressed in a simple daytime dress like Alice. In the daylight, out of her fancy ball gown, I could see how young she looked. She was pretty much the same age as Alice, but I tended to forget how young Alice was, too.

"Philly, you remember Mr. St. Clair from last night. He has to come with me everywhere."

Philly extended a hand to me. "Of course. I didn't get a chance to say so last night, but I've felt I've known you for months. Alice has spoken of you frequently." Another woman might've said that with a wink and a smirk but not Philly, who spoke plainly. She didn't even notice that Alice, just a step to her left, had turned a little red. She glared at me, saying with her eyes that if I ever teased her about that she'd never forgive me.

"It's only because I am constantly having to explain why I'm followed everywhere I go by an armed cowboy. But we have more important things to discuss," said Alice. We took seats, and I said a quick prayer that the fancy chair could support me.

Alice turned to me. "I just gave Philly a quick summary of what happened at the party last night. I told her you had spoken with her father and that Lynley Brackton was heard arguing with him, as well."

"Mr. Brackton was always arguing with someone. Father didn't even like him very much. But it would've been awkward not to invite him."

"Philly, this isn't just idle gossip. A friend of ours was arrested last night. We got him out because there were no witnesses, but the police have to find someone, and they'll come back for him if they can't find out who really did it."

"Arrested someone? You mean a guest? It couldn't have been one of the servants, or we'd know by now."

"No, not a guest. Not someone who would ever get invited here. We'll discuss that later. Right now, I'm trying to figure out who hated Lynley Brackton so much that they killed him."

"Alice! You don't think my father—"

"Of course not, Philly. But do you know anything? Was your father involved in some sort of business? If there was bad feeling with your father, there may have been bad feeling with someone else."

Philly shook her head, but she seemed a little worried now. Maybe she was seeing the downside of having a murder in your house. "Father wouldn't discuss something like that with me, not with anyone."

"Not your mother?"

"Mother? Of course not. She's still in her bed."

Alice rolled her eyes. Roosevelt women didn't take to their beds when there was unpleasantness.

"Well, we're not going to let anyone's refusal to discuss it stop us."

"Stop us from what?" asked Philadelphia, now looking genuinely confused.

"I just told you. We have to find out who killed Lynley Brackton."

That only deepened Philadelphia's confusion. "You mean, Mr. St. Clair? He's Secret Service, I know, but I thought the New York City police would be handling this."

"Oh, good grief, the culprit would be dead of old age before the New York City police found him. They already made one wrong arrest, and they'll do it again and hang the first person they can just to end a case where someone from a leading family has been killed. So let's see what the three of us can do. Remember who was by the punch bowl table. It was you, me, and your father on one side, and Mr. and Mrs. Brackton by the other, with, oh, what was her name again? That rather striking dark-haired woman—"

"Delilah Linde."

"Right. You and I were discussing how many of the young men were incapable of dancing, and then your father was asking me about my father. And the Bracktons and Mrs. Linde were having their dutiful glasses of that punch. Someone made a joke about how late it was for us to take our one glass."

"Wait a minute," I said. "Who was keeping track of who had their glass? If this punch was so terrible—no offense, Miss Rutledge—why not just say you had it?"

Philly just shook her head, and Alice looked at me like I was an idiot.

"That isn't done," said Alice. "You can claim a medical reason, like the doctor banned you from strong drink, or you're one of those odd temperance ladies, but you'd better not get caught with anything else."

"Or you'd be considered unreliable," I said.

Now Alice looked at me like I was a good pupil.

"Your memory is the same as mine," Philly said to Alice. "You and I were talking to my father, and he was asking about your father, as you said, and none of us were really paying attention to what was happening at the other end."

"But I think your father was," said Alice. "I'm trying to

remember. It was just for a few moments. We were laughing about something, and then I saw your father just staring at the Bracktons and Mrs. Linde at the other end of the table. Remember, after we were done laughing, you looked up, and your father was looking at the three of them."

"I think that's when he noticed Lynley wasn't well," said Philadelphia.

"Perhaps. It's so hard to figure out the timing, though. Am I just imagining it, or was he noticing something *before* Brackton looked sick?" Alice frowned. "Things happen fast, and later, you don't realize it."

"It was a busy room," I said. "But Captain O'Hara said no one saw anything."

"But what if no one realized what they saw?" asked Alice. "I mean, someone must've dropped poison into Lynley Brackton's glass. It was just us around the punch bowl at that time." That made sense. If the punch was as terrible as Alice said, there would hardly be a line to get to it, especially as it was late, and apparently, most people had already taken their medicine.

"Servants," I said. "Both of you ladies grew up with servants. You're surrounded by servants. If a servant with a tray of food or glasses of wine passed by, you wouldn't have noticed. You wouldn't have thought about it or remembered."

Alice looked startled at that. But then she smiled. "You are correct, Mr. St. Clair. When you have servants all your life, you take them for granted. Waiters and maids were walking around, not only serving but cleaning up. One of them could've gotten close to Mr. Brackton. All the gentlemen were a little drunk by that point, spilling things on their suits, and one servant or another was coming by with a cloth to help clean up." She shook her head at the memory. "It would have been easy for a servant to get close, and no one would think twice."

"But our maids are good girls, most of whom have been with us for years," said Philadelphia.

"And I don't see why one of your maids would've taken such an immediate, murderous dislike to Lynley Brackton," said Alice. "But I'm sure your parents hired extra waiters for the evening. Perhaps one of them . . ." she mused.

"Not likely, Miss Alice," I said. "It may be that someone wanted to kill Mr. Brackton and snuck into the party to do it, but they would've come prepared, not wait to break into the greenhouse to steal poison."

Alice gave me a superior look. "I didn't say I had the solution. I'm just thinking out loud, trying to work through the possibilities. Police detectives do that."

Philadelphia looked a little stunned by the whole exchange. Gossip was one thing, but New York Society girls, Alice excepted, didn't discuss this kind of thing.

Alice waved her hand, ending that line of conversation. "We'll come back to logistics later when we know more. But we were talking about someone sneaking in to kill Brackton. Why would anyone want to? I mean, he wasn't the most likeable of men, but still . . ."

"Personally, I loathed him," said Philadelphia with a vehemence in that sweet face that seemed to take even her by surprise. Alice raised an eyebrow, and Philadelphia turned a little red, embarrassed by her own outburst. "I'll admit it. It was beyond the usual 'we just don't like him.' He had a nasty, sarcastic way of talking. I hated him for what he said about Abraham Roth. There was no call for that. I said last night I was glad he's dead, and I meant it."

"I don't blame you. Abraham was quite a pet. I rather liked him," said Alice. She looked at me hard to make sure I wasn't laughing at her. "But to the matter at hand. This has been useful. We clearly need to find out more about Mr. Brackton. Do you know anything about his widow?"

"Mrs. Brackton? My mother knew her somewhat before her

marriage. Her school nickname was 'Mouse' because she was so meek. Just the kind of woman to submit to a man like Lynley Brackton." There was a mix of pity and disgust there—if not a lot of compassion. But Philly and Alice were young, and the young see things in black and white.

"We're thinking of paying a call on her," said Alice.

"Do you think that's wise, so soon?" asked Philadelphia.

"It's a murder," said Alice, as if that explained everything. Philadelphia stood and placed a hand on Alice's arm. "You will be careful, won't you?"

Alice glanced at me and smiled. "That's Mr. St. Clair's job. He's an incredible shot."

"Oh, yes, I'm sure," said Philadelphia. "But I meant careful in what you hear. There are stories . . . Society gossip and all . . . things you don't want to get out." She looked at Alice meaningfully.

"Of course. I can be very discreet in my murder investigations. Certainly better than the police." Philly seemed a little reassured at that. As astonishing as it must have been to her that Alice was launching a full-fledged murder investigation, it was better than having a handful of Irish cops learning the secrets of a dozen of New York's best families.

"One more thing before I go. I noted Mr. Brackton wore a heavy signet ring with the number seventeen in Roman numerals. And your father wears one, too. Do you know what it means? Some kind of club or freemasonry?"

"I don't really know," said Philadelphia. "Father belongs to a variety of clubs, and maybe that's a reference to one of them."

Alice looked like she was going to say something, then changed her mind. "Just idle curiosity; nothing to do with this, I'm sure. Anyway, thanks for talking to us." They kissed goodbye.

"A pleasure meeting you again," I said.

"Thank you for coming," said Philadelphia, and she escorted

us out of the room. "I hope I was able to help . . . in whatever you're doing. You will be discreet, both of you?" She looked a little nervous, a little hopeful.

"Of course, dear Philly. And remember, the quicker we can find out everything, the less likely the police are to find out things we don't want them to. We'll talk again soon, and my regards to your parents."

The butler showed us out the door, and Alice just stood on the very clean sidewalk for a few moments.

"I like you friend Miss Rutledge," I said, "but I hope she never tries making a living as a card player."

Alice grinned. "You saw it, too? I figured you would. She was nervous about something. What could an innocent debutante be worried about someone finding?"

I snickered at that. "Oh, come on, Miss Alice. Look at you, for one."

"I am special," she said.

"Yeah, I know. But I've been kicking around with your set for a while now, too long to think that every debutante is quite as, oh, unsophisticated as people would like to think."

"I suppose you're right," she said. "Still, with Philly. I can't imagine."

"Yeah. And I'm still trying to figure out about Lynley Brackton being invited even though no one likes him. Just because he's one of you. That's a heck of a reason."

"Don't be so critical. I bet there were folks in Laramie whom no one liked but who still came to drink whiskey at the bar."

I nodded. "Yes. You're right about that. We had those who sooner or later offended everyone. I knew who they were when I was a deputy sheriff, guys who made themselves as hated as this Brackton guy. And one day I'd find one in a gully with a bullet in the back of his head. Did Brackton finally push someone here too far?"

"Did you ever find out who killed any of those men?" asked Alice.

"No one saw anything. No one heard anything. And anyone who might've done it had half a dozen witnesses who swore they were nowhere near the victim. After a while, I didn't even bother."

"People took care of their own," said Alice.

"In Laramie. And in New York. It's not going to be easy to get anyone to say anything."

"No one is going to care if his murderer is found," said Alice.

"There, you're wrong, Miss Alice. In Laramie, we didn't care. But men like Rutledge are going to demand a hanging."

"We're going to have to stop them, then. No matter what."

It was the "no matter what" that frightened me.

"One more thing," I said. "While you two ladies were upstairs, I had a conversation with a maid." I recounted the story, and Alice seemed fascinated.

"I wonder what that's all about? It sounds like she was afraid, or worried. Maybe she heard that the servants would be implicated. It's a pity you were interrupted. We'll have to come back to her. I don't suppose she'll be going anywhere. Meanwhile, I think we'll stop looking at the logic of the circumstances and think about who hated Brackton enough to kill him. What's interesting is that it was a last-minute decision, or they would've brought their own poison. Anyway, I think we need to call on the widow, Victoria Brackton."

"Miss Rutledge suggested you wait a day, and I'm inclined to agree with her. Should we wait until tomorrow, maybe?"

Alice sighed dramatically. "The police won't wait until tomorrow."

"The police aren't going to be questioning her at all. She would've told them last night she saw nothing and knew nothing, and I don't see Captain O'Hara and the other boys in blue showing up to ask more questions. Anyway, you're not the police."

"I'm better than the police. I'm a Roosevelt. And you carry a badge."

"Do you think that my boss, Mr. Harris, head of the New York office of the Secret Service, is going to be pleased with me running an unauthorized investigation?"

"You take things too serious, Cowboy."

"And you're getting in over your head, Princess."

"You're getting sidetracked. Back to the topic at hand. We need to talk with Victoria Brackton, but I suppose we can wait a bit. She'll be better rested, and I suppose one day won't make a difference. I also want to talk to Delilah Linde, who was with them, but not until I talk with Victoria. It seems improbable, but could Mrs. Linde have been the poisoner? It was so risky with people all around. Mr. Rutledge was looking over there; I'm sure of it. He was facing them, even while talking to me and Philly, and he would've seen something. I'm sure he did—I don't think it was just when Lynley Brackton got sick. I don't see how . . . but maybe this will become clearer the more we know about everyone involved."

"Why couldn't Mrs. Brackton have killed her husband?" I suggested. Alice thought about that.

"It happens. But why then such an elaborate, public killing? You'd have a score of opportunities to kill a husband at home and make it look like an accident." She discussed it so casually, as if she came across that every day. "But we need more details about everyone."

"You can get the woman's point of view from Mariah. She's invited us for dinner tonight."

"Really?" She grinned and clapped her hands. Alice liked my sister, and my sister found Alice endlessly amusing. "We have other things to do—buy some wine for her, and I want a hot dog and a knish and a beer, and I'm long overdue for a visit to my bookie."

"Excellent all around, Miss Alice."

"One more thing—remember that little gun you took away from that man who was stalking us in our last adventure?"

"It's called a derringer. And to answer your next two questions, yes, I still have it, and no, I'm not giving it to you."

Alice pouted and folder her arms across her chest.

"That wasn't what I was going to ask."

"Yes, it was."

"What if I promise to practice my marksmanship under your tutelage?"

"And what if you accidently shoot me? You'll call your father and say, 'I'm sorry, Father, I shot my Secret Service bodyguard. Can you get me another?'"

"I'll tell Mariah you're being mean to me," she said. I just laughed.

CHAPTER 9

We had a good afternoon. Alice enjoyed her hot dog and a knish, which apparently weren't yet available in Washington.

Alice's bookie worked downtown, off of Houston. He did business from behind a small table in the back of a barbershop. She always got a lot of looks when we went in. All the patrons were men getting haircuts and shaves and reading the *Police Gazette*, and not too many young ladies patronized the place.

As usual, we found Ike the bookie in the back. Viewing the proceedings with his sharp eyes, he wrote out slips from a pile of paper with the aid of a pencil he stored behind his ear. He collected cash in a series of envelopes, using a system known only to him, and paid out winnings from a stack of bills.

"Miss Roosevelt. A pleasure to see you again. I was afraid you were taking your business elsewhere." *How nice that she's recognized by bookies*, I thought.

"I've been out of town. But I'm back, and I've been saving my allowance." They held a brief discussion—apparently, the horses were running in Florida—and Alice placed her bets.

"Can I interest you in a wager, Mr. St. Clair?" Ike asked.

I shook my head. "I play cards, not the ponies."

"Mr. St. Clair feels he has control over his cards," said Alice. "He can't control a horse. Unless he's the one riding it." The bookie laughed.

Her business finished, Alice headed out the door at her usual double-time pace. But Houston isn't Fifth Avenue, and I didn't like her leaving the barbershop ahead of me.

"For heaven's sake, nothing is going to happen to us," she snapped.

But I beat her to the door, and taking a quick look out, I didn't like what I saw. Across the street was a man in a worn jacket that didn't match his pants. He also wore a cloth cap that shaded his face. He wasn't doing anything, just leaning against a lamppost. He was facing the barbershop door but quickly turned away so it would seem he was not interested. I glanced down the block, and there was a similarly dressed man who was also now making a big show of not looking at us.

Revolvers, even small ones, were heavy, and I could tell from the way his jacket hung that at least the closer man was armed. From their awkward behavior, it was clear they weren't professionals, but that didn't mean they weren't dangerous. Actually, amateurs can be even more dangerous.

"Back inside, Miss Alice," I said as she craned her neck to see what I was looking at.

"What's the matter?"

"A couple of men are interested in us. And we're not going outside until I find out why." I took her by the arm, and we headed back to Ike's table.

"If you let me carry a gun, it would be two against two," she said.

"Wouldn't that be a great headline in the *Herald*: President's Daughter Takes Out Three Windows, a Motorcar, and a Streetlight."

We waited for Ike to finish with his current customer and then had him alone.

"Change your mind, Mr. St. Clair? I can give you some great odds—"

"Not now. There are a couple of men outside waiting for us. Who do you run with?"

Ike laughed. "I don't 'run' with anyone. I pay the owner for the privilege of being here. This is small time. These are stacks of singles here, not twenties."

"Come on," I said. "You know what I mean. Someone owns this neighborhood. You pay someone else, too."

Ike looked unhappy and glanced between me and Alice. He was a man who had dedicated his life to making bets and was now betting on Alice. "Miss Roosevelt, have a heart. I've always been fair, gave you good odds, even gave you credit in a slow week. Why are you causing trouble for me?"

"It's not you, Ike. It's who you know. Just answer Mr. St. Clair."

He sighed and lowered his voice. "This is Irish territory. I give a cut to Liam Doyle's boys." Everyone knew about Liam Doyle. I had no doubt Ike was very careful about giving Doyle a piece of his take, in exchange for which Doyle would refrain from sending Ike to the bottom of the East River. "You're saying Doyle's sent a couple of guys to look at me?" Ike asked. The idea seemed to scare him. "I don't cheat him by a nickel. I'd have to be crazy. And there are two guys out there? I'm just small time—"

I shook my head. "Those boys don't look Irish. And maybe Doyle is having trouble with the Italians, but they don't look Italian, either. Any other business associates who may have an interest?"

Ike shook his head. "There are other gangs, but who's going to go to war with Doyle over my operation?" I had thought that maybe Alice's gambling activities, especially as she was always accompanied by a federal agent, had made one of the gangs nervous, but that didn't seem to be it.

"Is there a back entrance here?" I asked.

Ike pointed with his thumb to a door behind him. "There's an alley that runs behind here."

The door led Alice and me to a little storage area, then outside to an unpaved alleyway and the backs of neighboring businesses. "What now?" asked Alice.

"We think," I said. I knew the alley could lead us away, but I had no idea if there were more toughs in the neighborhood.

"The afternoon is turning out to be more entertaining that I had expected," she said.

"I'm so glad," I said.

Meanwhile, Alice was thinking, too.

"Mr. St. Clair, I remember my father saying the best defense is a good offense."

"So do I, Miss Alice, but I don't see what kind of offense we can mount, and no, I'm not getting you your own revolver."

"We'll discuss that another time. But what do you think those men are up to? Are they out to kill me?" I had to give Alice her due, coolly contemplating that possibility. But I shook my head.

"No. There are two of them. You only need one to kill. And they don't look crazy, like a couple of anarchists. I think they want to grab you. They could do it fast, and if they're both armed and coming from different directions . . ." If it was just me, that was one thing, but with Alice in the mix, it was complicated.

"But there are people in the street," said Alice.

"People don't react quickly. This could be over before any of them have time to come to our aid."

"They will if I tell them to," said Alice, grinning.

"So now you're a colonel, like your father?" I asked.

"No. I have no military training. But you will admit I am an expert in calling attention to myself. A good offense, Mr. St. Clair." She outlined her plan. I wasn't thrilled with it, but it did have the element of surprise, and I didn't want to wait in case the toughs had reinforcements coming.

So it was back past an increasingly bewildered Ike, then Alice headed straight out the front door with me right behind her. The guy across the street looked up, and the one down the block saw, too, and started walking toward us. They could both beat us to the motorcar. I made sure my coat was clear of my revolver. Alice turned to me, winked, and then more loudly than I could imagine, screamed "Thief!" Both men were startled. A couple of workmen looked up, along with a young shopgirl and a clerk.

Alice pointed to the nearer man. "Thief!" she cried again. "Someone call the police and grab him before he gets away." The men froze and began to panic. This was not what they had expected. Professionals would've handled it but not this pair.

Alice turned to the other one. "And that's his accomplice," she shouted. "Get them before they get away." She continued to shout, and a couple of barbers joined us. More people on the sidewalk turned to look at Alice and then at the toughs, and other people stepped out of the shops to see what was happening.

The plan worked. Whatever the toughs had planned to do was now in tatters. These men had clearly been given specific instructions and weren't used to thinking on their own. Everyone was watching them; a couple of men were moving toward them, and who knew when the cops would show up?

The man down the block turned tail and started to flee. Seeing he was now alone, the man across from us broke and ran, too. But I could get him. I pushed Alice back into the shop and took off after him. After half a block, he looked over his shoulder to see me gaining on him, and then he stopped, faced me, and reached into his coat pocket.

CHAPTER 10

"Son, you'll be dead twice before you can get that out. You don't want a shootout here, believe me," I said.

He gave that a moment's thought, then accepted defeat and put his hands up. I pushed him against the wall of the building and frisked him quickly, removing a small revolver. I cuffed him and led him back to the barbershop.

Alice was thrilled. "Nicely done, Mr. St. Clair!" And then she said to my prisoner, "A wise move not drawing your gun. I've seen Mr. St. Clair hit four dead-center targets in as many seconds from a longer distance than that." I may have pushed Alice back into the shop, but she had clearly stepped out again to watch.

He didn't seem to appreciate the compliment on his intelligence, and Alice and I walked him back through the barbershop, past some astonished barbers and customers, and once again past Ike, who, seeing this wasn't affecting his business, decided to ignore the whole thing.

There was a rickety old chair in the storeroom, and I pushed our prisoner into it. Now we got a proper look at him. He had a fair complexion and was clean shaven, with hair a little darker than mine, lightly built, but muscled. I had gotten a good feel for his hands when I cuffed them, and they were rough and calloused. This was someone who worked for a living. But he certainly didn't look Irish or Italian, or indeed, like any of the usual gang members. Still, I thought I'd sound him out on that, anyway.

"First, why don't we start with your name?" I said. He didn't say anything, just shook his head.

"If he isn't going to cooperate, you might as well have shot him," said Alice.

"Yeah, but think of the paperwork," I said. "I guess we're going to do this the hard way." I pulled him up, and he braced himself. I think he thought I was going to give him a beating, but all I was planning to do was empty his pockets. He didn't have much, just a little money, a couple of keys, and some paper, including a receipt from a boardinghouse in Brooklyn made out to Edwin Chester. I put them on a shelf next to bottles of hair tonic.

"You're a real amateur, Eddie. If you aren't going to give the authorities your name, you shouldn't be carrying around receipts with your name on them." He hung his head. "Now be a good boy, and tell me why you and your colleague were carrying guns and following the president's daughter around. You're one of Liam Doyle's boys, aren't you? He won't thank you for getting caught so easily."

That got him to talk. "Doyle. Like I'd have anything to do with that papist bastard. They're almost as bad as the Italians." So he didn't like Irish Catholics. In this city, he had a lot of company.

"And do you have any better opinion of the Negroes?" His look said it all.

"My goodness, you don't seem to like anyone. I wonder if this has anything to do with why we were being followed," said Alice. She had been sorting through his wallet. There was a little money and a single piece of cheap paper, which Alice began to unfold.

"That's mine," said Chester, and he started to get up, but I stopped him fast.

"There are two names on this card: mine and Abraham Roth's. Tell me why," demanded Alice.

Roth—the young man who had given Alice and me a ride home the other night.

Chester shrugged. "I was paid to deliver a message to each of you. We already delivered one to Roth. I just get my assignments. I don't know the name of the man who gives me the assignments, and that's God's honest truth. I'm just given cash by a man who pays me for certain tasks."

"You must be very stupid to need to write the names down instead of memorizing them," said Alice. He bristled a little at that. "Why don't you need to write down the message? Unless—" She smiled in triumph. "Unless it's the same message each time. I bet you've had to deliver it again and again, in fact." It was a good conclusion, and the look on Chester's face showed us that she was right. "Why threaten me and Mr. Roth? You must have some idea about who's holding the other end of your leash. You're clearly too stupid to be doing this on your own. You don't like the Irish. Is that what this is about? Some anti-Irish group? But the Roosevelts are Protestant, and the Roths are Jewish. Tell me. I mean to know." I thought she might hit him. "Now, tell me the message you were going to deliver and already delivered to the Roths."

But he shook his head at that.

"You're wasting your time, Miss Alice. He's done talking. Let's just take him down to the Tombs." Even the threat of a night in that cold and damp place was enough to wring a confession out of many suspects.

But Chester grinned at this threat. "I'll be out in a day," he said.

"No, you won't. I'm Secret Service," I said. "And you threatened the president's daughter. No city friends will get you out once I put you in. You'll speak in the end."

That panicked him for a moment, but then he gave a half-hearted shrug. "Do what you want. I'm just paid to deliver messages. You can't hold me forever. I didn't actively threaten anyone, and you can't even prove I was going to deliver a message. And there's no law against having names in your wallet."

"That's very clever," said Alice. "Is that something else your masters taught you to say? Perhaps you're right. But if the city police and the Secret Service can't threaten you, I bet I know who can." She turned to me. "Mr. St. Clair, even I've heard of Liam Doyle. My father mentioned him when he was police commissioner. He's a criminal of some means, and judging from Ike's fear of him, not a man you want to upset. Mr. Chester here doesn't like Catholics. I imagine Mr. Doyle despises Protestants, especially Protestants who carry guns into his neighborhood, making trouble near a bookie under his protection and bothering a customer of that same bookie. Maybe you and I will pay a call on this Mr. Doyle and give him Mr. Chester's name and address. I doubt if Mr. Chester's friends will have much influence with Liam Doyle."

Now that got him. He paled and licked his lips. "All right. If you promise not to give my name to Mr. Doyle. I can't tell you who hired me. Like I said, I just get certain instructions. I swear we weren't going to hurt Miss Roosevelt. We were just told to approach her, and Roth, too, and tell them they should mind their own business. I swear to God that's all I can tell you."

I picked him up by the lapels of his jacket. "A name. You're an incompetent fool, but I don't think you're so stupid as to go to work for someone without knowing who he is. No one is that stupid. You can't afford to upset the wrong people, so you'd know who your paymaster is."

"I work at a warehouse near the docks. There's a foreman there who gives some of us extra work sometimes, special assignments like this. We don't ask questions."

"Did this foreman let you know where this money was coming from?"

"For God's sake—" he said, and he was really frightened.

"Oh, let's just put him the car and drive him to Mr. Doyle's place of business," said Alice. "He doesn't know anything. I assume Mr. Doyle is a Democrat. If the president's daughter makes a gift of this man who is causing trouble in his neighborhood, we might even get him to vote Republican."

Eddie stopped being terrified for a moment to think about whether Alice was joking. So did I.

"All right," he said. I put him down. "You can't give me away, though. There's no point in saving me from Doyle if the boss finds out I gave him up. I'll be dead one way or another."

"Fine," said Alice. "Now stop wasting our time."

He looked around as if he was afraid of being overheard. "Brackton. Lynley Brackton. He owns a lot of property down there." He was sweating.

"Brackton is dead," said Alice.

"What? When? No one told me. I told you, I get my information from the foreman. He told me that Mr. Brackton would appreciate any work I was doing, that's all—wait, you don't think I killed him?"

Alice arched an eyebrow. "I only said he was dead. Why did you think he had been murdered?"

Eddie was in way over his head. I could see now that he was genuinely confused and we had taxed his limited intellectual skills to their utmost.

"For God's sake, everyone hated and feared him." He gave a humorless laugh. "No one ever thought that Mr. Brackton was going to die in his bed."

Alice thought about that for a moment. "When were you told to find me—you and your companion?"

"Last night. The foreman said that it was a special job. We were to find you and tell you to mind your own business." He screwed up his face. "But you said Brackton was killed last night?"

"It must've been the last thing he did," said Alice, more to herself than to either of us. Then she focused back on Eddie. "Weren't you told that I am always accompanied by an armed Secret Service agent?"

Eddie shrugged. "We were told it was some broken-down

cowboy put out to pasture and given the job as a bit of charity."
He realized what he said then. "I'm . . . I'm sorry. No offense."

"None taken," I said.

"This broken-down cowboy was a second away from putting
a bullet between your eyes," said Alice. Eddie had no response
to that.

"Why do you go about armed?" I asked.

"To protect ourselves from the Irish boys," he said. "It's a
rough world out there."

"So it is," I replied. "Miss Alice, do you have any more questions for this man?"

"I don't think so," she said, looking down at him as if she
was trying to decide what to do about him. He couldn't meet
her gaze.

"Here's what's going to happen," I said. "Maybe you're right
and can slip out of any charges here, but you won't get away
from the gangs. I don't think your masters are powerful enough
to protect you from them. Or if they are, they don't care. In one
week, I'm giving your name to Doyle. You'd be well advised to
be out of New York City and on the far side of the Delaware
River by then. Tell your friend, too, because Doyle will get it
out of you. And your boss, the foreman. Doyle isn't as kindly as
I am." I uncuffed him, and he looked like he was going to argue
the situation, but Alice shot him the steel-eyed glare that even
her father feared. We gave him back his few possessions—except
for the gun—and we watched him leave quickly through the
front door.

"That went very well," said Alice, looking a little smug. "Me
and Abraham Roth. We know Brackton doesn't like Roth,
doesn't like Jews in general, but why me?"

"Miss Alice, are you sure Brackton didn't see you eavesdropping last night? If he did, that would've been enough to get you
on his list."

She looked a little shifty. "He might've," she admitted.

"That's just great. So the last thing Brackton does in this world is send a couple of his boys to attack you. You're just lucky Chester was too scared to call your bluff. What if he had said, 'Go ahead, Miss Roosevelt, go call on Liam Doyle.' What then?"

Alice shrugged. "It wasn't a bluff. We'd call on Mr. Doyle. What's the harm in that? He has no reason to want to hurt me, and you never know. We really might've gotten him to vote Republican."

"He's a brutal criminal who employs dozens of violent street brawlers. I don't think city elections concern him, beyond the politicians he bribes. Miss Alice, that was quite a gamble. I couldn't bring you to him. What would your aunt say? Nothing gets by her."

"How do you go through life in such a constant state of worry? There you were, charging up San Juan Hill without a care in the world. And you fuss over calling on some petty Irish thief."

"Miss Alice, he's not . . . oh, never mind. Do you know that when your father first assigned me to watch over you, he told me after a month with you that I'd wish I were back in Cuba?"

Alice laughed. "He did? That's very funny. I like that." Then she gave me a quizzical look and became suddenly serious. "Do you? I mean, do you ever think you'd rather be back in the army than with me?" She looked a little nervous, like the answer was very important to her, and I felt a little bad about telling her what the president had said to me.

"And miss all this fun?" I said. "Anyway, I want to put my feet up and have a fine dinner. Let's go buy some wine and head over to Mariah's."

That restored her good humor.

CHAPTER 11

My sister greeted me like usual—with a kiss on the cheek and a light slap. She was looking good, with her smooth, dark complexion and hair falling in black ringlets.

Alice hung back for a moment, looking a little shy. She admired Mariah, and Mariah's good opinion seemed to be important to her. I think it was because Mariah didn't treat Alice as a child or the president's daughter, but rather as just another young woman, and Alice rather liked that.

"Hon, it's good to see you again," Mariah said, giving Alice an embrace.

"I missed you, too," said Alice.

Mariah stepped back and looked at Alice. "You're looking thin. Don't they have cooks at the White House?"

"Yes, but none of them are as good as you."

Mariah laughed. "Thanks. Well, I've got some good food on the stove. So find some glasses and open that wine you brought."

Roosevelts don't set their own tables, but Alice was pleased to help out. I uncorked the wine while Alice got the glasses and put plates and silverware out.

"Have you been doing well?" asked Alice.

"Yes, thanks." Mariah worked as a cook, not for any one house, but for special dinner parties or substituting for families between regular cooks. She liked the freedom and did well for herself. I would've thought she'd want a night off, but she always said she was happiest when cooking, and I wasn't complaining. She spoke about some of her recent jobs, and Alice shared some backstairs gossip from the White House, which amused Mariah. I refilled everyone's glasses, and soon we were sitting down to eat.

"Brunswick stew," said Mariah. "I've cooked it before with squirrel and possum, but this is with chicken. I don't make this for anyone I work for. Just friends."

"I'm flattered," said Alice, turning a little pink.

"So has my brother been behaving himself?" asked Mariah.

Alice gave me a sidelong glance. "Oh, yes, and he was very brave today, almost getting into a shootout down on Houston Street. But the plan was mine."

My sister just raised an eyebrow. It wasn't easy to shock my sister. I smiled and shook my head. Alice was eager to describe the event and did so with just a little exaggeration.

"Who are these men? What do they want?" asked Mariah.

"It's related to the murder we're investigating. I was at a debutante ball, and a man was poisoned. They arrested a friend of ours, a mechanic, but he's clearly innocent, and we got him out of jail. We think these threats are related to the murder. The men were paid by the dead man, who set them on us—and on another guest he didn't like. He seems to be a member of a group called the XVII, but we know almost nothing about them."

Mariah shook her head and grinned. "The pair of you, at it again. Joey, keep her safe, all right? And Alice, watch over my brother."

"I keep a close eye on your brother and take my duties seriously," said Alice loftily. "But I think I could do a better job of it if he'd let me have my own revolver. I bet you've carried a gun, Mariah."

"Yes, I have, hon. But that was in another time, in another place."

"It's hard being the president's daughter," said Alice. Mariah laughed, and Alice turned pink again. "Actually, Mariah, I do have something to report on Mr. St. Clair. He got into a fistfight on the White House lawn."

My heart sank. I saw where Alice was going with this, and there was no stopping her. Mariah glared at me.

"He flattened a visiting army sergeant from Georgia because he used a nasty word about colored people, and since Mr. St. Clair won't tell me why he goaded the sergeant into a fight he couldn't lose, I thought you could tell me."

Mariah just shook her head again and had some more wine.

"Miss Alice, was there ever a question you had that you didn't ask?" I asked.

Alice stuck out her chin. "Of course not. I'm brave. Like my father."

"The president also has a sense of diplomacy," I said.

"It's all right, Joey," said Mariah. "Alice is my friend, and after all, it's nothing to be ashamed of." She fixed Alice with a look, and Alice looked almost comically serious, seeing that she was about to learn something important. "You know that Joey and I have different mothers. His mother's mother came from the Cheyenne tribe. My mother's mother was what was called in New Orleans a free woman of color. She was a Negro."

Alice blinked and was quiet for a few moments. I could see her thinking carefully about what next to say.

"So you're a quadroon?" she eventually said.

"That's what they call us," said Mariah.

"Alexandre Dumas was a quadroon," said Alice. "He was a famous French writer."

"You don't say," said Mariah. "Anyway, Joey here"—she ruffled my hair, which I hated—"is a little protective of me and what people say. And he picks fights he shouldn't." That last line came out like she was a mother who just found her boy digging into the strawberry jam.

"Well, Mariah, you might be glad to hear that, according to my sources, your brother laid out the Georgia boy in ten seconds." Then Alice gave me the same look Mariah had, like I was a naughty boy. "The least Mr. St. Clair could've done was call me so I could've watched." That made Mariah laugh again.

"Anyway, this is all part of the problem," continued Alice. "That mechanic, Peter Carlyle, the one who the police think did it, is a Negro. And if we don't find out who did it, they're going to arrest him and convict him."

Mariah nodded. "New York isn't New Orleans, but I can see it being a problem if they're set to fix this murder on this Carlyle friend of yours. Did he have a reason to kill the dead man?"

"Everyone did," said Alice. "I think we have to talk to Simon Rutledge. What were he and Brackton arguing about? I bet it has something to do with his death. Brackton had it in for Roth and set men on me presumably because I had overheard him."

Mariah shook her head and looked at me. "You sure earn your keep, Joey," she said.

"What's wrong with my conclusions?" asked Alice.

"Miss Alice, nothing is wrong with your conclusions," I said. "But even if you know him well, you can't just ask him about a private conversation. He isn't going to tell you any more about Brackton. He doesn't even care Brackton is dead. At best, all he'll do is tell your aunt, and you'll be sent back to Washington."

"I suppose," Alice said with a sigh. "But I am right about one thing—we need to find out more about Brackton. Yes, everyone hated him, and they've hated him for a long time. But why was he killed that particular night? That's the big question. No one came prepared to kill him. They broke into the greenhouse to poison him there. What came out at the party? It must've been related to the fight he had with Simon Rutledge."

"I can't answer that, but I wish you luck," said Mariah. Then she looked a little mischievous and bent her head close to Alice. "You've been keeping busy, girl. Is Joey being cooperative?"

Alice gave that a moment's thought. "Yes. I'd have to say he is. And for my part, I am trying to behave a little more appropriately."

"So thus far you see yourself as being appropriate?" I asked, more than a little surprised.

"I'm just hoping that when all is said and done, you won't be sorry," said Alice.

"Miss Alice, I'm already sorry."

CHAPTER 12

All in all, it was a real nice dinner. Alice liked seeing Mariah again, and Mariah found Alice's backstairs White House gossip entertaining. But when we were back in the motorcar, I could tell something was bothering Alice.

"You didn't really mean that when you said you were sorry we got started with this, did you? It's for a good cause—helping Mr. Carlyle." She looked a little annoyed and a little uncertain.

"I'm not sorry I'm helping Peter. I'm sorry I'm involving the president's daughter."

"That's the most ridiculous thing you've ever said. You're useless without me." And her look told me I'd be in big trouble if I laughed, so I didn't. She folded her arms and looked pleased with herself.

I saw her inside the apartment, and she said, "Be ready to go right after our breakfast tomorrow. We'll be paying a call on Victoria Brackton. The first shock should be over, so it should be a most productive visit. Good night, Cowboy."

"Good night, Princess," I said. I headed downstairs. I realized that it was unlikely Mrs. Cowles would blame me for what happened outside the barbershop, and there was no harm in making a condolence call, so I was still on safe ground. At least, so far.

*   *   *

I had a good night's sleep, and Dulcie gave us eggs and bacon in the morning. Alice was all excited to get going.

"No need to rush," I said. "You don't want to wake the poor woman up to pay a condolence call."

"But I want to get her alone. And I'm sure she's delighted to be a widow. I can't imagine being married to Lynley Brackton was a picnic."

"Marriages are funny things, Miss Alice. He may not have been the best husband, but she may miss him, anyway."

"Since when have you become an expert in marriage?" said Alice.

"Not marriage. But people get used to the way things are, and a change, even if it's good in some ways, can be unsettling."

Alice frowned at that thought and then finished her coffee. "Let's go. I'm sure she's up by now." A few minutes later, we were in the motorcar heading downtown.

"How well do you know Mrs. Brackton?" I asked

"Hardly at all. Quick introductions at a few parties, talk about how warm the weather is for this time of year and the latest fashions in hats."

"She won't think it odd that someone who hardly knows her is making a condolence call?"

Alice shook her head, astounded at my ignorance. "If you don't know someone in Society, you still *know* them. We're all of a kind. Besides, everyone is always welcoming to Alice Roosevelt." She smirked. I could see her point. Even before her father became president, the Roosevelts were one of the best families in New York. Mr. Roosevelt's move to the White House only made them greater. Hardly anyone would question a visit from his daughter.

The Bracktons had a townhouse that wasn't as big and fancy as the Rutledge place, but it was still nicely set up with the brass all polished. A black wreath hung on the door. I was glad to see that Alice had managed to put on an expression that said, "I'm so sorry for your tragic loss" and not "I'm coming to investigate a murder."

A servant opened the door, and I noticed he was wearing a black armband.

"I'm Alice Roosevelt, here to pay a call on Mrs. Brackton." We watched the servant's eyes flicker to me. "Oh, and this is my bodyguard, Mr. St. Clair. He is not permitted to leave my side."

"Very good, miss. Please follow me." He showed us into what seemed to be a library, filled with leather-bound books that were probably dusted twice a week but never read. I looked around, but Alice seemed impatient. She had been in dozens of rooms like this before.

A few minutes later, Victoria Brackton joined us. I had hardly seen her the night of the party, so this was the first good look I got of her. I made allowances for the fact that she had just lost her husband and probably wasn't sleeping, but beyond that, she seemed hollowed out. I'd known plain women who became beautiful the more you knew them because there was a light, a fire, inside them. But I guessed Mrs. Brackton had once been beautiful, and that light and fire had gone out long before she became a widow.

A maid came right behind her with some coffee and cookies and then left, closing the door behind her.

"Victoria, I am so sorry," said Alice, and she stepped over to give Mrs. Brackton a hug and then led her to a chair. I thought Alice had overdone it a little, considering she hardly knew the woman, but Mrs. Brackton didn't seem to mind.

"Can I get you something?" asked Alice. "I mean, something besides these cookies and tea? I am at your disposal."

"Thank you, but my maid just . . ." She stopped, as if she couldn't be bothered to complete the thought. "Thank you for coming, Alice." She looked at me and seemed confused.

"Oh, don't mind him. That's Mr. St. Clair, my Secret Service bodyguard. He has to be here."

Mrs. Brackton frowned at that and kept looking at me. "You were there that night, weren't you? Simon Rutledge said you were very helpful." I thought maybe Mrs. Brackton was not as dazed as she first seemed.

"Yes, ma'am," I said.

"That's something like a policeman?" she asked. Just like the Rutledge maid, she was trying to find out who I was.

"Something like," I said. Alice looked both annoyed that this exchange was derailing any conversation she had planned and curious about where it was going. Mrs. Brackton nodded and turned back to Alice.

"I know you are still in shock," said Alice, "but I want to reassure you everything is being done to uncover whoever committed this crime. You know that my father was police commissioner here once, and Captain O'Hara, who is in charge of the case, was an associate of my father's and knows you and I and the Rutledges are all friends. The police will devote their full resources."

"I am sure you're right. That's very kind of you," said Mrs. Brackton. But it was toneless, as if she wasn't even aware of what she was saying. Her eyes wandered around the room and landed on me again. Alice seemed a little frustrated by the woman's vagueness and tried to pull her back.

"Of course, the police can be rather difficult. It can be a little awkward to talk with them. They can be hardworking and efficient in catching criminals, but for people like us . . . what I'm saying is that if there is anything perhaps a little delicate that you feel uncomfortable relating to a police officer, you can tell me, and I'll see it is submitted—discreetly—through the right channels."

That seemed to get Mrs. Brackton's attention, and she thought on that, nodding slowly. Then she turned back to me again. "And I can trust your discretion, too, Mr. St. Clair?"

"You can rely on me as you rely on Miss Roosevelt." I gave

her what I hoped was a reassuring smile, and Alice seemed pleased with my response. Mrs. Brackton nodded, and I saw her gathering her thoughts.

"It's rather difficult, you see," she said, looking down so she didn't meet our eyes. "That evening at the ball, I was preparing to take a drink of the Rutledge punch. We all know that when at the Rutledges', you're supposed to have at least one glass of that loathsome potion. Lynley had made a big show of having a glass as soon as we arrived, to much laughter. That's what he was like. Later we found ourselves by the punch bowl again, and Lynley teased me about not having had my glass yet, so he poured me a glass, but I held it for the longest time. I couldn't bear to sip it. So after a while, Lynley just said, 'Oh, all right, I'll have this one, too. Have a little bit for form's sake.' And he drank the rest."

Mrs. Brackton looked up, and now, I could see what she was feeling. Alice knew it, too. It was grief. It was fear and horror. The poisoned glass hadn't been meant for Lynley. It had been meant for her.

CHAPTER 13

Alice didn't say anything for a few moments. I realized that her comments about feeling awkward around the police had been an attempt to get Mrs. Brackton to talk about any enemies her husband may have had. She didn't expect this.

"You didn't get sick from your sip?" Alice finally asked.

"No. I barely touched it to my lips. As Lynley said, it was just for form."

"You are absolutely sure that Lynley didn't have another glass that was poisoned?" asked Alice.

"Yes. You see, I was there with Delilah Linde, who wasn't drinking anything—that is, no punch."

"Had she also had her glass earlier?"

"I don't think so. Lynley teased her about it, and she said she had been suffering a digestive ailment for several weeks and had been told to avoid all spirits. If I remember right, she had a glass of mineral water in her hand. She laughed and said we could check with her maid—she wasn't just trying to avoid the Rutledge punch. In fact, she said because she was of Dutch background herself, she actually liked the punch and was sorry she couldn't have a glass. Lynley said if she wanted, he'd drink a glass for her, too. Lynley was like that, very courtly."

Alice had to hold her temper at that but knew there was no

point in getting into an argument with a widow about her husband, whose body was still warm.

"So it was you, Mrs. Linde, and Lynley. Only you had a glass, right? And you fetched it yourself from the bowl?" Alice asked. Mrs. Brackton nodded. "What were you talking about?"

She shrugged. "What one always talks about at events like that—how pretty the debutantes looked, the quality of the band, and this year's fashions."

"It was a crowded room. People were coming around, waiters and maids. You know what it's like and how hard it is to see at the time, and how hard it is to see later," said Alice. "Could someone have poisoned the glass after you gave it to Lynley?"

"I don't see how. I took my little sip and gave it to Lynley, who drank it straight down. He started feeling sick just minutes later."

"But who would want to kill you?" asked Alice, more to herself than to Mrs. Brackton, but the poor woman looked like she was about to burst into tears.

"That's just it," she said, her voice trembling. "I have no idea. I don't know who I can trust. That's why I was asking you, Mr. St. Clair, if you had any connections in New York, with the police. I know, I've heard men talk about how the police can be owned by someone, but if you're not one of them, I can trust you, too."

"My father trusts Mr. St. Clair, so you may trust him, as well," said Alice, almost daring her not to. "You can trust both of us."

"I'm glad to hear that. Because I'm terrified." And she was. I could feel it coming off of her.

"Delilah Linde," said Alice. "She was the only one near you? I know others may have passed by, but she was the only one right there with you and Lynley?"

"Yes. From the time Lynley handed me the glass until I handed it back and he drank it. Of course, as I said, maids and waiters came by, and someone may have stopped to say hello, but one doesn't really pay attention."

"Tell me about Delilah. I was introduced earlier in the evening but don't really know her," said Alice.

"I didn't know her terribly well myself. Lynley knew her family, or really her husband's family. Marcus Linde is much older than Delilah, some thirty or thirty-five years older. He had been married before and only married Delilah a few years ago. He is a somewhat solitary man who dislikes events like these, and Delilah usually shows up with a cousin or family friend as an escort, I believe."

"Does she mind, do you think?" asked Alice.

"She doesn't seem to. She's a lively and beautiful woman who never lacks for attention, so it's not like she's alone. Marcus Linde is wealthy and gives her all she wants."

Alice frowned and thought for a moment. "I was with Mr. Rutledge and Philly Rutledge on the other side of the punch bowl table. We were laughing and talking. But at some point, I think I saw Mr. Rutledge looking across at the three of you. Was there anything happening, anything odd that you remember? It could be something one of you said, or a movement, anything out of the ordinary."

"I couldn't say . . ." said Mrs. Brackton, shaking her head. She seemed a little more with us now, and I think finding some people she could trust with the whole story made her feel a little better. Then she gave a shy smile. "Delilah is very attractive, as I said. She often catches men's eyes, and men look at her." She blushed a little. "Lynley did, but I didn't mind. I know I am somewhat plain, but gentlemen are like that." She seemed accepting of her lot in life.

"Why did she marry a man who was that much older?" asked Alice. Even I knew you didn't ask questions like that, but that didn't stop Alice.

"I don't know much about her. Her maiden name was Van

Dijk. They are an old family, but there were problems—reversals, bad luck, and a father who drank. Marcus Linde is extremely wealthy, and his first wife, I understand, was also younger, and well . . ." She coughed delicately. "Some men like having a young woman around as a companion." She shrugged.

"Victoria, I see now you were the intended victim and not your husband. There is a lot to figure out here. But men's business can spill over, and in ways we don't understand now, this may have had something to do with Lynley's businesses. He owned properties, I imagine."

"I don't know much," said Mrs. Brackton. "I know he had concerns by the docks, here in Manhattan and in Brooklyn, and he had to visit them every now and then."

"Did he have any business interests with Simon Rutledge?"

"Not that I know of. But maybe. He and Simon had been schoolmates, and so they always had a certain closeness with each other."

I could see Alice thinking about her next question, and I was curious to see if she had figured out a way to ask a widow if she knew her husband was one of the most hated men in New York Society. She was as brave as her father, but could she be as diplomatic?

Alice gave Victoria a warm, inviting smile. Almost conspiratorial. "Men take their businesses very seriously. Sometimes too seriously. They get into arguments, and arguments become fights and even threats. Did Lynley have any fights with anyone, perhaps recently?"

I had thought Mrs. Brackton looked beaten. But at Alice's question, I saw a spark there, and she favored us with a tight little smile. She wasn't as beaten down as I had thought. There was more self-awareness than I had given her credit for. And just because you've been knocked around by life, it doesn't mean you're stupid. Just unlucky.

"Oh, Alice, you are young and unmarried." Fresh tears fell

down her face. "I knew my husband. I knew what people said about him. He liked having his own way. He liked the house arranged the way he wanted it and the meals the way he wanted them. He could be difficult if things didn't work out the way he wanted them to."

"You are right that I am young, and there's a lot I don't know. But he doesn't sound that different from many other men I've met in this city," said Alice.

"Perhaps you're right. But with Lynley, it was taken to extremes. There was no discussing anything with him. He had a small group of friends, but they were bound together by history and background, from school and family connections. I don't think even his friends liked him. Is that an odd thing to say?" She gave a little laugh. "Still, we were husband and wife, and we had made a life together. We went to the right dinners and balls and invited the right people here, and there are worse ways to live your life. And now it's gone. There are no places for childless widows," she said.

"Did he have mistresses?" asked Alice. I had a mouthful of the excellent coffee all the better houses seemed to have, and I damn near choked on it. Talking of mistresses was bad enough, but talking about them with a recent widow was appalling.

I had hoped at least that the small part of Victoria Brackton that seemed to look clear-eyed at her marriage would address that particular betrayal, but it was gone now. She just turned red, and her hands fluttered around her head, as if she had lost control of her reactions.

"I . . . what a question . . . of course I . . ."

Alice wasn't having any of it. She leaned over and grabbed both of Mrs. Brackton's arms by the wrists and looked her in the eye. "No pretenses here. I need you to stay with me. Someone has committed murder. Someone may try again. After I'm gone, you can cry as much as you want, but I need to know this. Were there other women in his life?"

A flood of tears came out, but she nodded. "I never met them, but of course, one can't help but know . . . the talk . . . actresses, singers, artists' models."

There were women whom men married and women they didn't. It was the way of the world that sometimes a bad marriage was better than no marriage at all. Mariah would disagree and had walked away from her husband years ago. But my sister and I had learned to make our own way in the world, and that was something Victoria Brackton was not capable of doing. Sometimes it's harder to be rich than to be poor. "But that was the extent? He wasn't . . . he didn't lay his hands on you?" asked Alice.

"No. I gave him what he wanted, didn't make a fuss about what he did, and I don't think he cared enough about me to strike me."

I don't know why, but that sounded even sadder than if he had hit her. I thought it was odd that Mrs. Brackton didn't question the reason behind all of Alice's questions. She probably had no one to talk with and no one who knew the whole story. Just an endless stream of pity behind her back. I glanced at Alice and saw a little gleam in her eye.

"But your marriage, your life . . . it was a steady life? I mean, regardless of the other problems . . . Lynley was reliable?" Alice came down heavily on that last word. That's what they were saying about Lynley, that he was unreliable.

"What a funny question," Mrs. Brackton said, drying her eyes with a delicate handkerchief. "Reliable? I never really thought about that. I mean, one doesn't, do they? I got my allowance, he told me if he wasn't going to be home for dinner, but for the past few months . . . I didn't think of it that way. Yes, he was unreliable. Missing dinners without telling me or our butler. I handled our social calendar, of course, but messengers came, and they only spoke with Lynley. He wouldn't even tell me who sent them, and I thought it was something to do with business. I didn't put it all together. But I suppose that's one way to put it . . . he was becoming, in some respects, unreliable."

Alice nodded at that, and I think she was out of questions. But Mrs. Brackton had one. Again, I realized she was a little shrewder than I had thought. "You were asking about Delilah Linde. You don't think that she . . ." She couldn't bring herself to complete the accusation, but her eyes were wide.

"There's no reason to think that," said Alice, reassuring her, whatever she privately thought, and Mrs. Brackton seemed to accept that.

"So what happens now?" asked Mrs. Brackton, returning to her current problems. "Are there people you can trust? I'm terrified of leaving the house."

"You won't be leaving the house, anyway. You're in mourning. Have your servants been with you long?" asked Alice. Mrs. Brackton nodded. "Then I imagine you'll be safe for now while Mr. St. Clair and I look into this with people we know."

Oh Christ, I thought. *What are you planning now?*

"I guess people will be coming to call," I added. "Don't accept gifts of food from anyone. Only from your servants."

"I'll only be admitting people I know," said Mrs. Brackton.

I watched Alice closely to see how she'd react to that. She was often difficult, but when it was important, she knew what needed to be done. She leaned over to Mrs. Brackton and put a hand on her arm. "Victoria," she said softly but firmly. "There were no strangers at the party who could've put something in your drink. You need to understand that whoever is trying to kill you is someone you know. Accept nothing. Trust only me, Mr. St. Clair, and Captain O'Hara, our friend in the police. Anyone else is a suspect."

Mrs. Brackton hadn't thought that far, and I watched the look of horror come back to her face.

"But don't worry," said Alice, still firmly, and I heard her father's voice in her tone. "A few sensible precautions, and you'll be safe. Now, I still have one more question, more out of curiosity than anything. I saw your husband wore a ring, a signet ring, with XVII stamped on it. Mr. Rutledge also had one. Was that a club of some kind?"

Mrs. Brackton blinked, still thinking about how someone she may have known for years, someone she had sat down to dinner with, had tried to poison her.

"What? I'm sorry. The XVII? Lynley mentioned it once or twice. Some sort of club, as you said. Men from the best families. I don't really know the details." Now that wasn't fear; it was nervousness. She was lying—she knew more.

"When did he get that ring? Do you remember? It's very unusual."

"Yes, I do. He said a special delivery would be coming from a jeweler, and no one—not a servant, not I—was supposed to open it. He never did that. It was, oh, about three months ago."

I met Alice's eye and saw she knew we weren't getting the full story. Nor did Mrs. Brackton seem to connect the arrival of the ring with Lynley becoming unreliable. I wondered if Alice would press it, but she decided to let it go. She stood, and I did, too.

"We'll leave you now," said Alice. "I'm sure others will be calling. Take our advice, and you can always leave a message for me at the Caledonia."

"Thank you so much for coming—I think your visit has stopped me from falling apart completely." There was a pause, and then I saw for a moment that she wasn't just frightened. She was sad. "Every time I think about this, it comes to me, that it will be all right, Lynley will take care of it, and it starts all over again because that's the point, isn't it. . . . ? He always took care of everything, until recently . . ." She started to cry. Alice was surprisingly adept at handling this, however, putting her arms around Mrs. Brackton and soothing her with soft words until she calmed down.

After a minute or two, Mrs. Brackton gave Alice a kiss on her cheek, and then, not quite sure of my position, gave me a quick look. "And thank you, too, Mr. St. Clair," she said. She rang for

a servant, who showed us out, even as other callers were beginning to arrive: the cream of New York Society. They nodded
briefly at Alice, but she didn't stop to talk with them. We just
headed out the door and walked to the motorcar in silence. Alice
made sure we were alone before speaking.

"That was something," said Alice. "Here we were thinking
that with someone as disliked as Lynley Brackton, we'd have a
host of suspects, but with Victoria, we have to start from the
beginning—assuming she was correct, of course. It's so hard to
keep track of glasses." She seemed rather disappointed for a
moment but then brightened. "Although we found something
else out—his wife confirmed he was unreliable. At least as far as
the last three months, when the XVII got started. But I wonder
if, at some level, he was always unreliable—and that the XVII
simply brought out the worst in him."

"And speaking of the XVII, I have one question," I said.
"Why did she lie about them? I'm sure she knew more than she
was saying."

"Yes. I also felt she was hiding something. It seems to be
rather a secret. I don't know why because there are all kinds of
groups one knows about. Father is a Freemason."

"I'd heard that," I said. "Do the Freemasons have something
to do with the XVII?"

"I can't imagine what," said Alice. "But the men who attacked
us on Houston—they were working for Brackton, who was one
of the XVII, and so we must assume that it's the XVII who are
against us and Roth. I'm still working on what this may have to
do with Victoria and why anyone would want to kill her. I told
her that it may have to do with her husband, but I said that just to
talk. I can't imagine why someone who hated Lynley would kill
his quiet and inoffensive wife—if that's indeed what was planned.
Surely the XVII is not after one of its own."

I grinned at her. "You don't know much about husbands and
wives, do you?"

She folded her arms. "That's the second time you've said that to me. Very well, what deep insight does Special Agent St. Clair—who has never been married, by the way—have?"

"It means maybe she was targeted for reasons having nothing to do with her and everything to do with her husband. Maybe no one had anything against her, but some woman wanted Lynley Brackton for herself." Alice frowned, and I could see she was deep in thought.

"Miss Alice, let's think about that word—'unreliable.' We keep hearing it about Lynley Brackton. Your aunt seemed to think being unreliable was about the worst thing you could be, and as different as she and I are, I agree with her."

"What do *you* think it means—to be unreliable?" asked Alice.

"Lots of things. When I was growing up, unreliable meant you weren't doing your part on the ranch. Cattle wandered off and died. In war, unreliable meant men were killed. But I'm thinking about other things." I wondered if I should be starting this conversation with Alice. Even I forgot how young she was sometimes. "With men and women, reliability is what you want in a marriage. You can talk about love and romance, but what holds two people together at the end of the day is reliability. I haven't been married, but for what it's worth, I've seen some things." I'd rarely seen Alice looking so astonished, and I wondered if I had said too much.

"Mr. St. Clair, are you giving me lessons in marriage?"

"Don't be ridiculous. You're just a little girl—no, don't interrupt me. I'm not giving you marriage advice. I'm giving you detective advice. If you want to understand this, you're going to have to think about what the word 'unreliable' means in all situations. Especially to be an unreliable husband or wife."

She didn't come back with one of her usual smart remarks, and I thought I had really reached her.

"That's surprisingly insightful, Mr. St. Clair. I didn't think you had it in you. I wouldn't have thought that Mr. Brackton was desirable as a husband. He was a deeply unpleasant man—and unreliable, as you point out. I'm sure when she recovers from shock, she'll realize she's well rid of him. Perhaps he was more unreliable than we had thought, got another woman with child, and her only path to security and respectability was to marry him, so she tried to get rid of his current wife. Of course, it would have to be a woman currently single."

"Dear Lord, Miss Alice, what an appalling thought."

She laughed at what she decided was a compliment. "Surely even in Wyoming women have babies seven months after getting married, and everyone just shrugs and says that Junior arrived early. It happens in New York and even among the better families."

"But they don't kill over that. And even if this woman we're imagining really wanted to go to any length to ensure Brackton would marry her, he couldn't properly get married until a year after his wife died. I know that much."

"Perhaps," said Alice. "Of course, a woman in that position would not be thinking clearly. But this has given us something to work with. Might there be a woman in the picture who somehow deluded herself that if Lynley was available, he'd marry her? If she was one of his mistresses, he'd just throw some money at her and send her away."

"You're now an expert on mistresses?" I asked.

"I just keep my ears open. There are so many mistresses among the great families, I wouldn't be surprised if they started their own labor union. Anyway, she'd have to be optimistic to the point of stupidity to think that Lynley would marry her, even if he was available. For now, we have two people we need to talk with. One is that maid you spoke with—did you get her name?"

"Cathleen O'Neill. And I found out that she's off this afternoon, in case I thought of more to ask her. But I don't know what, and it doesn't seem like she wants to talk more."

"I want to find out why she was nervous enough to question

you about it. She may have known something or seen something and doesn't want to make any trouble. Maids are terrified of getting into trouble. The second person I want to speak with is Delilah Linde."

"Why her?"

"She was there. And she's beautiful, and beautiful women attract attention. Also, there's that marriage of hers with that much older man, who nevertheless doesn't want to show off his attractive young wife in public. I wonder what she saw or heard that evening. I think we can rule her out as a suspect—she had no apparent reason to kill Victoria. We just don't know enough yet to draw conclusions. Anyway, let's start with Cathleen O'Neill. Delilah Linde isn't going anywhere, but I want to reach that maid because she's off this afternoon, so you can get her out of the house. Also, we need to speak with her before she confides in a butler or someone who tells her to forget she saw anything."

"We can't just show up at the Rutledges' and remove a maid to question her, Miss Alice."

"But she already knows and likes you."

"Maybe. But what kind of excuse do I give for wanting to see her? Whoever answers the back door is going to ask."

Alice grinned. "Mr. St. Clair, you look just like the kind of man who might be calling on a lovely young maid to take her out on her afternoon off. Surely you can convince the butler that you're madly in love with a comely Irish lass. Now let's get ourselves some lunch downtown. I think you know where I want to go."

Chapter 14

There really wasn't much to say about Alice's plan, so I just cranked up the motorcar, and we drove to a funny little place downtown Alice had become fond of. The restaurant was owned by Jews who came from a country in Eastern Europe called Romania, and they had this clever way of curing beef, smoking and seasoning it. They called it pastrami and served it on rye bread with sharp mustard and a little pot of pickled cucumbers so sour that your lips puckered. With glasses of beer, it made a great lunch.

I wondered if the Roths ate like this in their home. Dulcie was a good cook, but for the most part, the English and Dutch families who ran the town had nothing to brag about when it came to cooking. With Mariah's Southern cooking, Chinatown, and this food from Romania, I didn't feel any need take up residence in one of the great mansions.

Alice delighted in our lunch and in looking around the restaurant at the other diners, who were mostly working folk. We stood out there, the cowboy and the Society girl, and Alice and I could tell when someone recognized her, which thrilled her. Her photograph appeared regularly in all the illustrated press, so when we were out walking, you could count on at least one person recognizing her.

As we were feeling good after the sandwiches and beer, I thought I'd bring up the plan to speak with the maid, Cathleen.

"So to get her out of there, I'm supposed to pretend I'm courting her, and then when she comes to the back door, I try to see if she can talk to me, as it's her afternoon off. Or if she can find another time. Is that it?"

"That's right. Reassure her we will be discreet."

I decided to tweak her, so I smirked and said, "A pleasant enough assignment."

Alice wiped away the last of the beer foam from her lip. "Why is the assignment pleasant?" she asked, suspecting I was having a joke at her expense.

"She's a lovely little thing. You know how adorable those Irish girls are. When I pick her up for our meeting on her next afternoon off, it'll be fun pretending to be her suitor."

"Are you trying to be funny, Mr. St. Clair? Because you aren't succeeding. This is work. Not a chance for you to enliven your workday by seducing an innocent girl who has to make her way in the world. Whatever amusement you gather during your workday should come from our partnership. You can meet maids for your entertainment on your own time."

"Don't fret, Miss Alice. I'm sure Stephen Lesseps will be having you over for dinner to meet his folks very soon, even if you did more or less abandon him at the party. It doesn't matter—a man likes a woman all the more if she's a little cool to him. Unless . . ." I took some beer and fixed her a look. "Unless you've got your eye on Mr. Roth. Not that I'd blame you. He's good-looking and seems pleasant enough, and your father may be broadminded enough to accept a Jewish son-in-law."

She looked as if she was about to get angry, then mastered herself and gave a toss of her head. "You're just trying to get a rise out of me, but I won't give you the satisfaction. You pretend to flirt with maids because you just can't admit how much you missed me when you were stuck in St. Louis. Don't deny it. And don't pretend there is anything more entertaining in your life than being with me. Now come—we want to get there before Cathleen leaves."

"How do you know she's going to leave?"

"Servants always leave. They're stuck inside all day. They never miss a chance to get outside."

We got back into the motorcar, and as I drove to the Rutledge mansion, I rehearsed what I was going to say to the butler and to Cathleen when she was summoned. Alice was reading my mind because as we parked, she said, "Keep it simple, Cowboy."

"I think I know how to romance a maid," I said. Alice just gave a cluck of annoyance.

"We may not even have to rely on your acting skills," she said. "Let's just wait for her to leave. She'll probably want to change into her street clothes, and we can catch her around the corner. I don't see any friends waiting for her—that is, a maid or two from another house—which might've been a problem, and it's not so crowded that we'll miss her."

We didn't have to wait long. A few minutes later, a maid walked up the stairs that led from the servants' hall downstairs to the street. Only a servant leaves from the basement entrance.

"That's Cathleen," I said. I started to get out of the motorcar, but Alice grabbed my arm.

"No. Something's wrong. Look at her dress. That's not a normal street dress. She's wearing her Sunday best. And it's not Sunday. Look how purposefully she's walking. She's determined to go somewhere."

I agreed. I don't know much about women's dress, but I could tell Cathleen was deeply committed to her path, and she might've seen us but was looking straight ahead as she turned and headed west.

"Can you follow her in the motorcar without losing her?" asked Alice. "She might see us if we walked behind her, but I don't think she'll noticed anyone in a motorcar. It won't occur to her."

I thought if there were no sudden turns we'd be all right, and in fact, she kept straight at a brisk pace. The neighborhood started getting a little rough as we headed into the area called Hell's Kitchen, where I'd never had a need to take Alice. Powerful gangs controlled the area, and even police only entered it in groups. I made sure my Colt was within easy reach.

"Do you think Cathleen is visiting family here?" I asked. Plenty of Irish lived there.

"Perhaps. But that doesn't explain her dress. No one would wear a good dress in a neighborhood like this except for Sunday mass."

She kept walking along Fifty-third Street with the same purposeful stride and then suddenly entered a small church in the middle of the block. We pulled up across the street, and there were a couple of local boys, no more than twelve or thirteen, hanging around and curious about the motorcar.

"It looks like a Protestant church," I said. It was fairly plain, like some of the German churches I knew on the East Side. "Why would an Irish girl be going to a Protestant church?"

"Because it's not a Protestant church," said Alice a little smugly. "See the sign? It's St. Benedict the Moor. It's a Catholic church."

"So maybe it's her old parish church. But St. Benedict the Moor doesn't sound like an Irish saint."

The boys had come closer to the motorcar to have a look, close enough to hear us, and they laughed.

"It ain't an Irish church, mister."

"So what is it? Italian?" I asked. Not that I could imagine an Irish girl among the Italians. "Portuguese?"

"I'll tell you for a quarter," said the boy.

"A dime," said Alice, producing one from her bag. "Now tell me about this church."

"It's a colored church," said the boy, examining the coin to make sure Alice hadn't given him a counterfeit.

"Liar. Most colored folks I know go to Baptist churches," I said.

"It's a colored church," the boy repeated. "Ask anyone. Mass on Sundays like any other Catholic church."

Alice looked at the church again and then gave a self-satisfied smile. "Of course. Mr. St. Clair, this young man has given us the unvarnished truth, even if it did cost me a dime. St. Benedict the *Moor*. Moors are from Africa. Young man, want another dime? We're going inside. Watch the motorcar for us."

"Fifty cents," he said.

"A quarter," countered Alice, and he shrugged. "And you don't get it until we get back." Alice jumped out and started crossing the street, even though she knew I hated it when she moved fast like that without waiting for me to accompany her. And then one of the boys, looking at Alice's retreating form, had to make a vulgar remark about her, not realizing that I have very good hearing. So I turned to the boys and made some vulgar remarks myself that would've earned a slap from my mother and let them see the revolver on my hip, which scared the hell out of them.

"And if I see one damn scratch on this motorcar, I'll knock both of you into the middle of next week." Then I chased after Alice, who was walking up the steps. "Miss Alice, you know you can't leave my side. Especially in a neighborhood like this."

"For heaven's sake, no one is going to start trouble in front of a church. Now let's see why our Irish maid has a sudden need to visit a church for colored people right after a murder in her house and a fearful appeal to a sympathetic Secret Service agent. I won't believe it's a coincidence." With that, Alice pulled the door open, and we entered the church.

We found ourselves alone in a dark entranceway. Alice looked both ways and then stepped through into the church itself. I took off my hat and looked around. It was pretty but fairly simple, nothing like St. Patrick's Cathedral, which was a real showplace of a church, as far as I could tell. Anyway, it was only dimly lit, and I didn't see anyone there, unless they were deliberately hiding.

"Cathleen is short. Maybe she's slumped down in one of the seats. Also, isn't there a vestry or office or something?" asked Alice. I didn't know. One thing Alice and I had in common was that neither of us had spent a lot of time in churches.

We walked down the aisle, our footsteps echoing in the empty building. We reached the end, and Alice looked around, down each row. We saw no one, and then at the end, Alice looked up to the front, where the priest stands, and there was a door there.

"I bet we can find someone on the other side."

"I don't think we can just step onto the altar and walk in on a priest, Miss Alice. Priests are big keepers of secrets, and you can't just interrupt. What would you say to him, anyway—that you were chasing an Irish maid?" With all of her antics, Alice had so far stopped short of desecrating holy ground.

"But where is Cathleen?" she asked, practically stamping her foot. "She must be with the priest, but why? Why come all the way to a church for Negroes to talk to a man of the cloth when you can't throw a stone in this city without hitting an Irish priest?"

Alice continued to look around, and I watched her think. Was Cathleen doing extra work here? Was she up in the bell tower sweeping out the cobwebs? But no—I remembered she was in her Sunday best.

"Peter Carlyle," Alice finally said and gave a self-satisfied smile.

"What are you talking about? What does this have to do with Peter?"

"It has everything to do with Mr. Carlyle. And a panicky maid in her Sunday best." With that, Alice bolted right up to the altar and to the door in the back. I had no choice but to follow her. I'd endangered my life alongside Miss Alice. Now I was getting a chance to put my immortal soul in peril. And I wasn't even Catholic.

Alice was standing inside a small office. On the left was a young, bespectacled priest behind a desk. And opposite him, also sitting in a chair, was Cathleen O'Neill. And Peter Carlyle. To say the three of them were startled would be a gross understatement. But Alice? I had never seen her look so proud of herself, and that's saying a lot.

The priest was the one who recovered first, and he stood. "Excuse me? Can I help you? We don't have many visitors this time of day." He peered more closely and then grinned. "Say, you're Miss Roosevelt, aren't you?" That made it even better for her.

"Yes, I am. And this is Mr. St. Clair, my bodyguard. And you are . . . ?"

"Oh, sorry. Father Lucas Bennett. At your service, Miss Roosevelt."

"Miss Roosevelt? Joey?" asked Peter, who had now found his voice. Cathleen was looking terrified, and now it was the priest's turn to be confused.

"You know each other?" he asked. I was beginning to feel like I had walked into a bad comic play.

"Mr. Carlyle is a friend of Mr. St. Clair's and is in charge of keeping the family motorcar in repair. Miss O'Neill, we haven't met, but you must be Mr. Carlyle's fiancée? Best wishes."

And it came together then and there. Peter didn't want us to know where he was that night because he was with his white fiancée. Cathleen was upset because she knew they had taken him away and might do it again. She was in her Sunday best because she was getting married today.

Good for you, Miss Alice.

"Don't worry, folks, we're not here to make trouble," I said. "It's just . . . well, it's a long story."

"Actually, you could help," said Father Bennett. "It seems the young couple here came without any witnesses."

"We hoped someone would be around," said Peter.

"We're not Catholic," said Alice.

"That's not strictly necessary," said Father Bennett. Alice seemed amused at that, and sensing something was going on, the priest continued. "I have, uh, one or two things to take care of before we start the ceremony. I'll be back in a moment." He stepped out of his office and left me and Alice alone with the happy—if somewhat confused—couple.

CHAPTER 15

We all had questions for each other, and it was hard to say who was more surprised. Alice spoke first.

"This explains a lot," she said. "I am happy for you, of course, but if you had been a little more forthcoming with us, Mr. Carlyle, we might've avoided this."

"Miss Alice," I said and gave her a look. "Don't upbraid a man on his wedding day." She sighed dramatically.

"So the two of you have found out what we're doing," said Peter, looking back and forth at us. "Do you mind telling me what both of you are doing here?"

"Helping you," said Alice. "At least, indirectly. This is part of our plan to find out who killed Lynley Brackton. Miss O'Neill here seemed very concerned about it, so we followed her. And apparently saved you from having to go into the street looking for a best man and maid of honor. There's something more here, I think . . . but Mr. St. Clair is right." Alice smiled brightly and suddenly looked a lot more girlish. "This is a wedding. And we are pleased to participate."

The bride seemed reassured at that and smiled at Peter and took his hand.

"So, Joey," he said. "You're surprised at my choice of wife?"

"I'm surprised that you're Catholic," I said.

"That's my mother's doing," said Peter. "She was of Creole background in Louisiana. Anyway, Cathleen and I met when I dropped off the Rutledge motorcar one day. And one thing led to another." He looked at her again, and I could see they really loved each other. I guess it finally grounded her enough to speak. A wedding is enough to rattle any girl, never mind finding out that the president's daughter is going to be your maid of honor.

"Mr. St. Clair. Miss Roosevelt. I can see what you're thinking," said Cathleen. "We are making a very hard life for ourselves. But I must say that my life, and certainly Peter's life, has already been hard. At least now, we will face a hard life together."

There was no possible response to that, but after about a minute, I said, "Congratulations, Miss O'Neill. You left Alice Roosevelt speechless. No one has ever done that before."

Peter thought that was funny. Alice just gave me a sour look, but before she could say anything, Father Bennett came back. "If you all are ready, we can begin." We followed him back into the church proper, where Alice and I witnessed the wedding. I don't know about Alice, but it was my first Catholic wedding, my first time at any Catholic service, and I even got to participate. It didn't take too long. The priest pronounced them man and wife, blessed us all, and then we were back on the street.

"Do you have any immediate plans?" asked Alice. "You require a wedding meal. And it will be my treat." The question was where. This wasn't the kind of wedding party you could take to just any restaurant. But Peter said he knew a place nearby that wasn't too fussy.

Alice and I left the couple across the street to pay the kids to keep watching the car. As we finished the negotiations, Alice whispered to me, "Mr. Carlyle knows something, and he won't discuss it with me because I'm a woman and the president's daughter. But draw him out. He has information or insights that could be of great help to us."

"What do you mean?"

"Don't be difficult," she said. "Cathleen was too nervous and Peter too cautious. This is about more than a wedding. Find out." And with that, we rejoined Mr. and Mrs. Carlyle. Alice did a nice job setting things up, neatly leading Cathleen a little ahead of us, talking about whatever young women talked about. I was close enough to keep an eye on her but still able to talk to Peter.

"Congratulations," I said. "I hope you'll be happy together."

"Thanks, Joey," he said, then he laughed. "Who'd have thought my wife would get Alice Roosevelt standing up for her and I'd get a war hero."

"War hero, nothing," I said. "If anyone is brave here, it's you." He looked at me to see if I was just teasing him, saw I wasn't, and just smiled and shrugged. "I should've realized what this was about," I continued. "When we sprung you from the Tombs, you said you weren't doing anything illegal, at least in New York. There are a lot of places where a marriage like yours is against the law, like most of the South, but it's legal in New York, if not all that common."

He laughed again. "Yeah, that was a hint."

"But there's something else, isn't there?" I asked. "I don't know how long you two have known each other, but if you didn't even bother to plan for attendants, I'm guessing this wedding was put together pretty quickly. Is this about what just happened?"

That sobered him up fast. "It's not just about my arrest, not just. We may want to get out of town fast. Something bad has happened. And it's been happening for a while."

"I'm not with the cops. I answer to the president and that's it. You can trust me."

"Yeah, I know. Things have been hard lately. Not just on Negroes, but the Irish, the Italians, the Chinese, the Jews. You hear things, about fear and anger, about how this city has changed and not for the better." It was true. I knew that the city had doubled in size in the last ten years, mostly due to immigrants. "Anyway, there's a gang out there, making trouble in some of the neighborhoods, among the Negroes and the immigrants.

Threats and violence. No one seems to know anything about them. If we were down South, I'd think it was the Klan. But it's been subtler, although no less bad. In the poor neighborhoods where the immigrants live, there has been trouble and more threats. And me and Cathleen—well, look at us. Mixed marriage, Catholic, immigrant, Negro. And now, I feel after my arrest I got a bull's-eye on my back."

"Let me guess," I said. "This new gang—I bet you've heard a name whispered in the dark. They're called the XVII."

Peter stopped. "How the hell did you know that?"

"We've come up against them already. We're looking into it. We've heard from other sources that there has been trouble, as well—you're not the first. Has this been going on for a while?"

"Things have gotten bad in the past few months. I don't know what happened."

"I do. I think that's when the XVII really got launched. We've run into them in Society."

"When you say 'we,' do you mean the Secret Service?"

"I mean Miss Roosevelt."

"The president's daughter has launched an investigation? God almighty," he said. "She's something."

"She's something else. We're made some progress. This goes up to some powerful men, and the attacks in the poor neighborhoods are almost certainly related to Brackton's murder."

"I'm glad you're finding something out because things have gotten worse for me. That cop, O'Hara, only let me go because he couldn't pin it on me. But if he knew I was married to a maid who could've killed Brackton at my bidding, we'd both be in the Tombs. Well, I owe both of you. Let me know if I can help." I said I would.

Alice bought some wine on the way, and the restaurant wasn't that bad. It was mostly filled with dockworkers, but people minded their own business there. The couple had a stew, and we all had wine, and Alice and I joined them at the end for some pie and coffee.

"What do you have planned for your married life?" asked Alice. "Please tell me you're not setting your bride up in a room over a garage."

Peter laughed, and Cathleen smiled. "No," he said. "That's not the long-term plan. We were going to wait a bit"—he looked at me quickly—"but thought to get started now. I have an older brother, Ben, who's been working as a Pullman porter. We have some money saved up and are going to buy a building and set it up as a guest house. We'll live there, Cathleen will be the house-keeper, and Ben knows how to run things. I'll keep working at the garage. We just need three hundred dollars more. 'Til then, I'm still at the garage, and Cathleen's at the Rutledges', so we need to be quiet about this."

"I wish you luck. Mr. St. Clair and I will send as much busi-ness as we can to the garage, so your boss will have to give you a raise."

The party broke up soon after.

"I have tomorrow off. Miss Rutledge worked it out for me," said Cathleen. That got Alice's attention.

"Philly Rutledge? She knew about your secret engagement and this marriage?" asked Alice.

"Yes. I care for her, helping with her hair and dressing, and she's been covering for me with her mother, and in return I helped her—"

Cathleen suddenly figured out who she was talking to and stopped.

"You helped her . . ." prompted Alice.

"Just helped her when she needed some extra assistance," added Cathleen.

At that point, Peter jumped in to say he had the key to Ben's room, as he was on a run out West somewhere. We all thanked Alice, and Peter told me again, quietly, that he'd do anything to help. We said our goodbyes and went back to the motorcar, where we gave the boys their final fee and drove off.

"The Rutledge household is full of secrets, it seems," said Alice when we were alone. "Mr. Rutledge is hiding his argument with Brackton. Cathleen O'Neill hid her engagement and marriage. And she was clearly hiding something on behalf of Philly. You heard that—'in return, I helped her . . .' I wonder why Philly hasn't told me? It must be something big."

"It could be something awkward, something she might be embarrassed to have a friend know."

"Would she be afraid I'd judge her?"

"That idea came to mind," I said.

"I don't see why. I'm very accepting. We'll come to that later. For now, that was an entertaining afternoon. Something for my memoirs, anyway. But I hope it had some practical use, as well. Did Mr. Carlyle have anything to tell you?"

"Yes, he did. It seems our friends at the XVII have been active." I summarized our conversation, and Alice listened thoughtfully.

"All kinds of connections there," she said. "The XVII doesn't seem to like anyone except native-born, white Protestants, and if what Mr. Carlyle said is true, this is bigger than we thought. One of their number is murdered. Someone they don't like is accused. And then they're after us. We need to know more about them. I suppose it's too late to call on Delilah Linde."

"Do you think she killed Lynley? Or rather, tried to kill Victoria and then killed Lynley? But why? And we can't forget it was a last-minute decision."

"I don't know how she was involved, but she was. Maybe she was the killer—she was certainly in the right place. We're going to call on her tomorrow. I want another view of that conversation. Someone went to a lot of risk and trouble to kill Brackton that night. Perhaps there was a reason he had to die that night, before he did or said something else, as I said, but I think there may be another possibility. Someone hated him so much they'd take any risk to kill him that night."

CHAPTER 16

I saw Alice into the apartment, as usual, and Mrs. Cowles was there to greet us. We hadn't told her what happened the previous day on Houston Street. Not that it was anyone's fault, but there was no need to upset her or to have a conversation about what Alice was doing in a barbershop.

"I understand you called on Victoria Brackton," said Mrs. Cowles. Alice and I both saw what was happening. We were both still on probation, and Mrs. Cowles wanted to let us know she was keeping an eye on us.

"Yes, I thought it would be a kindness."

"Yes, it was. But you were hardly a close friend of the Bracktons'. Wasn't she surprised to see you?"

Now, a lesser woman would've made an excuse at that point, which might've made Mrs. Cowles even more suspicious, but Alice just stuck out her chin and said, "I am Alice Roosevelt. Everyone is always pleased to see me, in good times and bad."

"Oh, are they now? I'm delighted to hear that," said Mrs. Cowles. "I'm sure you were a great solace to her. I'm assuming that your motivation was only to comfort the afflicted and not to indulge your fascination with crime."

"Of course," said Alice, wide-eyed and full of innocence. I put on my best poker face. "And I expect to visit her again, once the initial mourning period is over and she finds herself alone. She doesn't even have any children, I believe." And then Alice made a very good impression of being casual. "Of course, it would help if I knew a little bit more about her late husband and her marriage. As you said, he was a difficult and unreliable man, but she seemed to mourn him. I wonder why."

Mrs. Cowles gave Alice a speculative look. "Very well. If you're going to pursue a friendship with Mrs. Brackton during her mourning period, I suppose it's fair to say that despite her late husband's difficult nature, he had a superficial charm. It would do you well to know that many men of poor character hide their deep deficiencies with a casual charm."

"It must've been more than superficial if Mrs. Brackton genuinely loved him."

Mrs. Cowles smiled wryly. "That's a wise observation, Alice. You are old enough to know that women and men always don't form attachments for logical reasons. You should think about that when choosing a husband. I have some letters to write now but will see you at dinner." With that, she swept out of the entranceway.

"That was interesting," said Alice. "Mr. St. Clair, I would like your opinion. Is that true? Do women really love unsatisfactory men?"

"All the time. And men love unsatisfactory women."

"Well, that much I knew. You only have to look at which women are surrounded by men at a debutante ball to see the foolishness of men. But I had hoped most women had more sense. It will bear thinking about in this case. For all her unhappiness, I think Victoria is genuinely mourning her husband. We'll consider that further. Anyway, it was a productive and entertaining day. I'll see you at breakfast tomorrow, when we'll discuss how to approach Delilah Linde. I think she's keeping a secret."

"Your aunt will find out. Sooner or later, it's going to be pretty clear what you're up to, Miss Alice."

She just smiled. "I'm just making social calls. And half of

Society was at that party, anyway. I shall sleep the peaceful sleep of the pure of heart, Mr. St. Clair. Meanwhile, you still roll a cigarette so much better than I can. Could I impose upon you to roll me one now?"

After a companionable smoke, I went down to my room. I wasn't as at ease as Alice was. We had landed in the middle of something, and I couldn't see the connections yet. But like Alice, I didn't have any trouble falling asleep. Working men rarely do.

★   ★   ★

I felt refreshed the next morning and joined Alice in the breakfast room. There was a pile of bacon, and then the maid came in with plates of French toast, well soaked with egg and fried a perfect golden brown. The usual excellent hot coffee completed the morning.

"My aunt already had her breakfast," Alice said. "She has morning meetings of one sort or another and is just gathering a few items in her room." That was fine with me. I didn't dislike Mrs. Cowles. Indeed, I admired her. But she made me nervous over breakfast, as if she'd catch every little mistake in manners.

We heard a ring at the front door, which was surprising because usually the doorman downstairs called up. It must have been someone the doorman recognized. Or someone who slipped by. Either way, it was odd, and I quickly intercepted the maid heading to the door and looked through the peephole myself. It was Captain O'Hara, and I opened the door.

"What brings you here? In the better families, no one makes social calls this early. You should know that."

"Very funny, St. Clair. It's not a social call, as you damn well know. You did me a good turn with Simon Rutledge, who was very grateful for my discretion." He grinned. "And actually, you did me a second good turn . . . but we'll come to that. Anyway, I know you and Miss Alice have a lot of interest in the Brackton murder, as you were there, so since I was in the neighborhood, I thought I'd call in person."

And then I heard Alice's quick footsteps. It hadn't taken her long to figure out something interesting was going on at the front door.

"Captain O'Hara. What brings you here at this early hour?"

He looked at Alice, took off his hat out of respect, then looked at me a little uncomfortably. "Oh, go ahead and out with it," I said. "Miss Alice will only get it out of me, anyway."

"It seems one of our witnesses was just killed. Delilah Linde, who was with Brackton when he was poisoned. She was poisoned herself. Found dead this morning."

Alice looked like she had been slapped. She had been counting on getting some information out of Mrs. Linde, who was the closest witness to the poisoning and a possible suspect.

"I felt I owed you the information before it became public," O'Hara said. *And before Alice tracked you down to your office in the Tombs where you couldn't easily get rid of her,* I thought. "We're still trying to untangle this, and I'll let you know if we find out any more. Miss Roosevelt, St. Clair, have a good morning." He turned but wasn't nearly fast enough for Alice.

"Oh, no you don't, Captain. I have a lot of questions. Come with me right now." She actually grabbed him by the arm and dragged him inside. "We have bacon and French toast. Our cook always makes more than enough. And hot coffee."

Dulcie stuck her head out of the kitchen to see what the fuss was about and was struck dumb at the sight of Alice propelling a New York City police captain into the family breakfast room.

"Some more coffee," I said to Dulcie. "That's a good girl." She scowled at me. It was bad enough she had to serve Secret Service agents, but now cops, as well?

Captain O'Hara looked very nervous. City cops weren't welcome in good houses in any situation, certainly not as guests. But like Alice said, there was plenty of French toast and bacon, and soon the maid came out with more coffee, and O'Hara relaxed enough to help himself.

"So you said she was poisoned?" prompted Alice.

"Right. The doc said it was probably late last night, but she wasn't found until this morning. It seems she and her husband sleep in separate rooms." He grinned. "Damned if I know why. I had met her at the Rutledges'. If I had a wife who looked like that, there would be no separate bedrooms."

I guess in telling the story he forgot where he was, so I gave him a quick smack on the side of his head. "For God's sake, O'Hara, watch your mouth. Miss Alice is only eighteen."

He had the grace to blush, which is more than Alice did.

"I'm very sorry," he said.

"Both of you just stop it," said Alice. "It's going to take a lot more than that to shock me. Now tell me step by step what happened."

"Right, yes. Mr. Linde had already turned in for the night in his room. A maid found Mrs. Linde in her bed and a bottle next to her. Looked like a small wine bottle with a cork. The maid said it had been delivered after dinner."

"For Mrs. Linde?" asked Alice.

"That's right. It was addressed to her. The maid was very sure of that. The doorman said some street kid delivered it. Even if we could find him, I'm guessing he'd have no idea who gave it to him."

"But there must've been a note. Who would drink wine that came from an anonymous messenger?"

"You're right," said O'Hara. "And it wasn't wine. There was a note supposedly from Simon Rutledge saying he had heard Mrs. Linde hadn't had any punch because she had been feeling unwell, but she could have some now."

"That's grotesque," said Alice. "Men do silly, mock-chivalrous things like that, so she wouldn't question it. I'm assuming you've already checked with Simon Rutledge and found he didn't send it."

"Of course. We wondered if maybe she meant to share it with her husband, but Marcus Linde says he always hated Rutledge punch. Apparently almost everyone does. I guess you have to be rich to do something so bad with liquor no one wants to drink it." He shook his head at that. "He said he thought Simon was being 'a bit much' sending the bottle to his wife but put it down to shock."

"We know that Delilah Linde liked the punch but was not having any because of digestive issues," said Alice. "It was discussed at the party, so it was probably widely known there. But probably not known to anyone else."

"Was Delilah Linde the intended victim at the party all along and not Mr. Brackton?" O'Hara wondered.

I felt bad that we were keeping Victoria Brackton's secret from O'Hara, but we had made a promise.

Mrs. Cowles walked into the breakfast room. She raised an eyebrow with perfect elegance. It had been a modest surprise when Alice had invited me as a breakfast regular, using the excuse that it was efficient to go over the day's plans over coffee. But a New York City police captain?

O'Hara quickly stood, looking like he'd rather be anywhere else in the world. Alice was equal to the task.

"Aunt Anna, this is Captain Michael O'Hara of the police department, who worked with Father when he was commissioner. Captain O'Hara, my aunt, Mrs. Cowles."

It looked to me like O'Hara considered giving an explanation and then decided that was a nonstarter. But Alice rolled with it.

"It's about security issues, Aunt Anna. Now that I'm back in New York, I expect to be much more visible, and I thought it would be prudent to coordinate my protection with both the police department and the Secret Service."

"I see. How practical of you, Alice," Mrs. Cowles said with just a hint of sarcasm. "Captain O'Hara, members of the police are always welcome at the Roosevelt table. And Alice, if you decide to augment your breakfast meetings with naval officers, firemen, or the cast of the Folies Bergère, just remember to let Dulcie know in advance so she can buy enough bacon. Good day, all. Gentlemen, please try to discourage Alice's interest in crime. Alice, people are coming for dinner tonight, so don't be late."

With that, she was gone. I was used to it by now, but O'Hara seemed a little overwhelmed.

"Miss Alice, your aunt knew you were lying. This will come back to us," I said.

"I know. But in politics, everyone lies. The important thing is to make sure the lie is plausible." She waved her hand to indicate that discussion of this particular topic was over. "Captain, what are your plans?"

"I don't really know. I'm wondering if it's just random, someone killing rich people. Maybe anarchists." That was like a bucket of cold water in my face. Not anarchists. Not again.

"Hardly," said Alice. "This is too subtle and complex for anarchists. Although it might be a lunatic."

"Well, I'll have to talk to the detectives and see if they've turned up anything. Miss Roosevelt, thanks for your hospitality. St. Clair—"

"Did you say you owed me something again?"

"Oh, yeah. That mechanic we arrested—Carlyle. I owed you for getting him out because if you hadn't done it then, I'd have to do it now. He couldn't have mixed up a batch of that Rutledge punch and slipped it to the Lindes. And the Lindes patronize another garage for their motorcar, so there's no connection. I guess we start from the beginning. But if we get stuck, this gets passed over my head. I'm going to have to arrest someone. But I don't know why."

"That's an odd phrase," I said. "What do you mean you don't know *why* you have to arrest someone?"

"Mr. Rutledge said it to me that night. It was kind of offhand, like he didn't know what he was saying because he was tired and upset. He said, just to me, 'The thing is that he was a widely hated man. I don't blame whoever did it. But we have to find him, anyway.'" O'Hara shrugged, as if he couldn't understand the ways of the rich. "What I'm saying is, if a poor man was killed, a poor man no one liked, anyway, we wouldn't spend five minutes looking for the killer. But here we have a rich man no one liked, even the other rich people, and we have to find who did it."

I thought of what Alice had said earlier. It didn't matter if you didn't like the man; you were all part of the same group, the same clubs, and that meant everything. I thought of the XVII, and I knew Alice did, too.

"They take care of their own," I said.

O'Hara nodded at that and seemed to understand. "Anyway, thanks again," he said after some thought. I saw him out, and when I got back, Alice was musing over her coffee.

"It wasn't an outsider. We're sure of that now," said Alice. "This is inside. The use of the punch. Someone who knows details of how these people live." Then she frowned in thought. "We keep talking about one person. But what if it's not? I suppose it's possible that Delilah is the original killer, and she was killed in turn for revenge, although we don't know any reason."

"Possible. But as you say, we don't have any motives for anyone yet."

"No. But let's keep an open mind on possibilities. Anyway, I don't care if his wife just died. We're going to question Marcus Linde today."

"Miss Alice, you hardly knew his wife. You don't know him at all. What kind of excuse are you going to make?"

"It'll take you about fifteen minutes to drive there. I'll have something by then."

CHAPTER 17

Marcus Linde may have been mourning his wife, but if he had to mourn, he had a comfortable place to do it. His house was really grand, much like the Rutledges'. I liked how shiny the floor was in the entranceway, and I think it was real marble. You could practically see your face in it.

"I'm afraid there was a tragedy today, and Mr. Linde isn't receiving anyone," said the butler.

"I have heard. I'm Alice Roosevelt, and I'm here in an official capacity, sent by my father, the president, to speak with Mr. Linde in this difficult time."

We were apparently just going to have to hope that Mr. Linde never sent a thank-you note to the president about this.

The butler wavered for a moment. He knew exactly where Alice stood within Society and was just wondering if her appearance and position trumped the usual rules.

"One moment. Please follow me," he finally said. He led us to a parlor off the entranceway before leaving to see if we were to be admitted.

It wasn't one of those dark and heavy rooms. There was just one bookshelf against the brightly papered wall, a few comfortable chairs, and some tables with some delicate-looking knickknacks.

"Mrs. Linde decorated this room. This shows a woman's touch," said Alice. "No man would set a room up like this."

"And what does that tell you?" I asked.

"That Mr. Linde let her have her way. Not all men do that. Mr. Brackton probably didn't. Did you look around the foyer? The same spare, clean look. He let her have her way, the new, young wife married to an older man. I suppose he really loved her."

The butler came back and said, "Mr. Linde will see you now." His eyes flickered to me, but Alice rolled right over him. "Thank you. My bodyguard will come with me."

We followed him upstairs, and again, it seemed like a much more cheerful place than most of the other grand houses I had visited with Alice. We were shown into what seemed to be a sort of study. Here was one room Delilah had not been allowed to decorate, with its solid wood furniture and shelves containing the fine leather-bound books that every gentleman's study in New York had to have. It was a comfortable but dark room, with none of the light Delilah had given to the other rooms we had seen.

Marcus Linde was sitting in a tall, leather-backed chair, wearing a suit even I could tell was a little old-fashioned. I guessed he was in his sixties, and Delilah Linde had been not quite thirty, so that was quite a difference.

He had probably been handsome as a young man and even now still looked distinguished. He had strong bones in his face and deep blue eyes that were still full of life, even if I could see the sadness there now. His hair was that silvery white that had probably once been the same pale yellow as mine. Although getting on in years, he didn't seem in poor health. Maybe he had just reached that stage where he was tired of people.

"Miss Roosevelt. I was on the board that helped choose your father as commissioner some years ago. I wouldn't have thought he'd have remembered, or heard about my bereavement so quickly that he sent his daughter to me to extend his commiserations."

He knew she was lying. But Alice was more than equal to it. "One of the advantages of being a close confidante of my father's is that I know what he wants without our even having to discuss it. And I know that he shares my deep sadness at the tragic and untimely death of Mrs. Linde. And that he wants to let you know the full might of the New York Police Department is being brought to bear."

"Thank you, Miss Roosevelt," he said. He gave us a sad smile to match his eyes. "I'm still a bit in shock. I was so much older than my wife, and yet she dies first. The police have already questioned me, and I gather this has something to do with the recent death of Lynley Brackton, although I can't see the connection. Unless someone is trying to kill leading members of New York Society."

"I was at Philly Rutledge's party when it happened," said Alice. "And I think there's more to it than just a lunatic."

Linde raised an eyebrow. "You're not only your father's confidante; you're also his successor in the police department?"

Alice smiled brilliantly. "Come now, Mr. Linde. We both know there are things one just doesn't want to discuss with the police. Even in your sorrow, I am sure you can realize that the best chance you have for catching your wife's killer is being frank with me. I know people. I'm the president's daughter. You can trust me."

Linde gave that some thought, and then he turned to me. "You're Secret Service, aren't you? Are you here in an investigative capacity, or as Miss Roosevelt's bodyguard?"

"Joseph St. Clair, sir. I'm just along for the ride. And to offer my own condolences."

"I see. I believe I know what you're thinking. I am going to trust you—the president's daughter and the Secret Service—in the hope that you will use whatever influence you have to keep the police from poking around my business." He took a moment to gather his thoughts. "You're thinking I don't seem like a man mourning his wife because I haven't fallen apart. I know there is Society gossip. But I want you to know we had a real marriage, even if it wasn't conventional. We built a life together. As I did with my first wife, even if it was different. I loved Delilah and shall miss her deeply, whatever people say. I always knew I'd have to say goodbye to her sooner rather than later, as marriages go. I just didn't know she'd be the one leaving first."

"Mr. St. Clair and I accept that, Mr. Linde," said Alice. She looked very serious. "He and I have been privy to some aspects of these murders that the police don't know about. I would like you to trust me and answer a few questions."

Linde nodded. "I can't imagine sitting here discussing this with a little girl. But considering the sheer bravado with which you got into this house and into my room, I'm actually thinking of trusting you. St. Clair, I know you're just along for the ride, as you say. But is she genuine?"

"Oh, yes, sir. That's the frightening part."

Alice took a moment to flash me a dirty look, but I think she owed me thanks. I could've easily ended everything right there.

He gave a dry chuckle. "Oh, very well. What do you want to know, Miss Roosevelt?"

"Thank you, Mr. Linde. I assure you that your confidence is not misplaced. Now, I understand that Simon Rutledge supposedly sent your wife a bottle of Rutledge punch. Did that surprise you?"

"Yes. I thought the murder at his home must've rattled him. It seemed a rather vulgar gesture and very out of character for him. I just wished it had occurred to me, as the police later told me, that it was a hoax. Once I learned that, it made perfect sense."

"But you didn't drink it? Mrs. Linde liked Rutledge punch, but not you, and presumably someone knew she wouldn't think of sharing it with you?"

"I'm afraid that's the correct conclusion. She's of Dutch background, and I'm not. It's in the blood."

"Your wife was heard at the party saying she had a digestive ailment and was told to avoid spirits in the coming weeks."

"That's true," said Linde. "She had been complaining about digestive issues in recent weeks. The doctor wasn't concerned. He thought it was too much rich food—we have a very fine cook here—and told her to eat more simply and avoid strong drink and see if that helped. But why would anyone want to kill Delilah? She was married to me. We had dinner together most nights. She shopped, went to lunch with friends, and attended parties with a cousin or family friend, since I don't particularly enjoy events like that. It was a very ordinary life."

This house, this life, was ordinary? I thought. But I guess when you're used to it, anything is ordinary. At any rate, Linde looked sad now, and I was guessing he was right; we all mourn in different ways.

"Maybe this was about you?" Alice asked. "Maybe it was a threat about something you've done. What connections do you have with Lynley Brackton?"

"Excuse me, Miss Roosevelt? What do you mean by connections?" He shifted and seemed unhappy with the question. He'd spoken freely about his wife, but now Alice was seemingly getting close to something sensitive.

"I'm thinking of Lynley Brackton, who was killed with punch as well. They must be related. Did you have a business relationship with him?" Alice persisted.

"He was not a well-liked man. I'm not sorry he's gone." That was blunt, and Alice clearly thought so, too. It was similar to what Rutledge had told O'Hara about Brackton.

"Let me guess, Mr. Linde—Mr. Brackton was not a reliable man. Is that correct?"

"What an interesting observation, Miss Roosevelt," said Linde, and I could tell she had rattled him. He had yet to answer either of Alice's recent questions. She just kept looking at him, however, with great patience, but she had that certain look, and I knew that her patience was going to come to an end very soon.

"But getting back to connections, as in business ventures, investments. In business, as in politics, I'm sure sometimes deals are made with people we don't like." She raised an eyebrow and smiled faintly.

"I can't possibly see what relevance that has. I do have extensive business connections, but my business is settled over negotiations. When necessary, lawyers are involved. But not poisoned drinks."

"Lunacy is not confined to the social sphere," said Alice, and I could hear the steel in her voice. She was not intimidated. "You and Lynley Brackton are connected by a poisoned drink. Simon Rutledge—his house was used as a murder site, and someone knew him well enough to set him up as author of the second poisoning. I also happen to know that Abraham Roth was threatened."

Now that got his attention. He leaned forward. "Young Roth? How does he come into this?"

Alice smirked. "Come now, Mr. Linde. You can't expect me to share if you won't."

Linde had been indulging her, but now he was angry. "Are you insinuating something, Miss Roosevelt?"

"I'm only trying to figure out why someone is passing around poisoned drinks. And I frankly can't understand your objection to my question. It's simple enough. I'm going to be discreet, which is more than the police will be." Then her eyes slid to me. "The Secret Service has a primary responsibility for financial crimes. Maybe they'd be interested."

Linde leaned back, and the color in his face disappeared. "I don't think I have any more to tell you." There was a button within easy reach, and he pressed it. A few moments later, the butler showed up and just stood there. "I am expecting some visitors soon and will see them downstairs. Please show Miss Roosevelt and her companion out." Linde quickly left without saying goodbye.

The butler was a little politer. "May I get you anything? Or may I show you out?"

Alice looked fit to be tied. She had wanted to get more out of Linde, and now he was out of reach. I could see her mind working.

"Very well," she said, stood up quickly, and promptly fell down.

"Damn it! My ankle. My God, it hurts." She sat on the floor clutching her leg and rocking back and forth. I sighed. I guess I was going to be pressed into service as a doc, and in fact, I had seen more than my share of twisted ankles and other injuries while working on a ranch. I knelt down close to her.

"Where exactly does it hurt, Miss Alice?" I asked. She brought her face close to mine, then smiled and winked. It may have been the scariest moment of my entire life, and for a moment, I actually considered just throwing her over my shoulder and walking right out the front door.

I turned to the butler, who seemed concerned. He clearly wasn't an emotional type, so it was hard to tell.

"Could you give us a few moments?" I asked. "It's going to take a little while until she's ready to walk again."

"We'll ring when we're ready," said Alice.

"Very good, miss," he said, and with a bit of reluctance, left the room into the hallway. We heard him walk down the stairs, and then Alice jumped up.

"For God's sake, what are you up to now?" I asked.

"I'll tell you when I find it." She headed though a far door opposite the exit into what was apparently Mr. Linde's dressing room and made a beeline for the man's dresser. "Fortunately, men are very predictable. This shouldn't take long."

"If we're caught—"

"Stop complaining, and make yourself useful. Stand guard outside, and warn me if anyone comes."

"Oh, hell," I said.

"And there's no need for vulgar language."

I stepped outside and kept watch while Alice pulled open one drawer after another. I figured I'd just tell anyone who came by that the princess was resting.

"Aha!" she finally said. "Come see, Mr. St. Clair." I headed back inside, and Alice was triumphantly holding a ring—a signet ring stamped with XVII. "Another member. Very interesting. No wonder he didn't want us asking about business—not if it had to do with the XVII. Do you think he wasn't wearing it because of us? Has word gotten around that we're looking into the XVII? Does he know?"

"Maybe. But you've proven your point. Let's go."

"I'm going to keep it and wear it on a chain around my neck."

"Miss Alice, be reasonable. He's going to miss it. You don't need a trophy."

"Oh, very well. I suppose you're right." She put it back and closed the drawer, then rang for the butler. "Give me your arm, Mr. St. Clair. I'm going to have to give a good impersonation of someone with a limp." The butler arrived, and Alice leaned heavily on me as we followed him downstairs and out the door. When we were on the sidewalk, Alice skipped to celebrate her victory, and I thought she might even do a cartwheel.

"Miss Alice, you can't pull stunts like that. We came damn close to getting caught."

"But we didn't. If you thought it was so dangerous, why did you go along?"

"God only knows," I said.

"It's because you care for me a great deal. I know you do." She said it with just a hint of uncertainty, which was very unusual for Alice.

"That must be it," I said. She looked at me closely to make sure I wasn't making fun of her, then decided to take me at face value.

"We have a number of avenues to explore now. We need to know more about the XVII and what they want. Why was it so important for the XVII to warn me off on Houston Street? What were they afraid I was going to find out? Were they really so afraid of what I may have heard at the Rutledge ball? Edwin Chester seemed to have a definite antipathy toward anyone who isn't a white Protestant. As he's an agent of the XVII, can we assume it's one of their guiding principles? It makes sense, seeing as the XVII are apparently behind intimidation in the poor neighborhoods. Meanwhile, what does all this have to do with women? One was almost murdered. One was actually murdered. Let's walk. I need to stretch my legs after that little farce, and I want to talk."

It was a pleasant day, and so we strolled along Fifth Avenue, along with the other well-dressed people. More than a few recognized Alice with small smiles and slight bows of the head. Alice acknowledged everyone with a nod and smile in return. Some probably realized that I was her bodyguard, while others were thinking, "My God, it's Alice Roosevelt keeping company with a cowboy."

I normally don't like trying to take care of Alice in crowds, but it was a mild group of people on the avenue, and unlike on Houston Street, trouble wasn't likely.

"Marriages, Mr. St. Clair. We've seen two unusual marriages so far. At least, I think they're unusual. Mr. and Mrs. Lynley Brackton. I can't find anyone to say a good word for him, and yet I think his wife genuinely misses him. Yes, she was frightened she would be killed next, but she is genuinely sorry he's gone. Odd, but there you have it. And Marcus Linde. An old man and a young wife—I think he was telling us the truth, that he cared for her in his own way. I heard it in his voice when he said how he mourned her. But he didn't go out with her, and they had separate bedrooms. Of course, I understand many couples in Society have separate bedrooms, but I don't think the Lindes were married long, and the captain was right—she was young and pretty. Anyway, I think he's upset at her death."

"What does that tell you?"

"We keep coming back to marriages. I don't know. I don't know about marriage, not much, and as we've established already, neither do you."

I laughed. "No, Miss Alice, I don't know much. But I know something from what I've seen. I've seen husbands and wives who bickered constantly, and yet when one died, the other practically fell to pieces. And some seem perfectly content and don't even seem to care when they're apart. Every marriage is different, and only the two in it really know what it's like."

Alice stopped and looked at me with surprise. "Mr. St. Clair, how philosophical. I didn't know you had it in you. Aunt Anna is right about you. She says you're really quite smart, but you pretend to be slow so no one expects too much from you."

Again, I laughed. "If I think about that enough, I'm sure I'll find a compliment there somewhere."

"I'm sure, as well. You no doubt noticed that Mr. Rutledge and Mr. Linde weren't shy about saying how much they disliked Brackton. It's unusual. Not that they disliked him, but that, under pressure, they admitted it openly. And yet they were all members of the XVII. That's worth thinking about. For now, I think we're going to have to find out more about those women, about those marriages. That's the heart of the matter here, I'm certain. Whom can we ask about these people?"

"You've always said that everyone in Society knows everyone else. Can't you just call on your rich friends and ask them for the dirt?"

"I wish. But they will all close ranks with tragedies like these. Everyone is too respectable. Picking up gossip is one thing.

If I just wanted to know about affairs and who's drinking too much and who's gambling too much, I could pick up a lot. But when it comes to murder, no one is going to talk to the president's daughter. We need to speak with someone unrespectable, someone positively disreputable."

We walked for a while in silence, and then suddenly, Alice stopped and grinned. "I know who can help. Who is more disreputable than a journalist? Mr. St. Clair, take me to Herald Square."

CHAPTER 18

New York has lots of newspapers but none more famous than the *Herald*. I'd never been concerned with keeping up with the news, but I had to admit it was a lively read, and there were thousands of New Yorkers who agreed with me. It wasn't quite to Mrs. Cowles's taste; she said it was more entertaining than informative, but occasionally on a quiet evening, I'd find a back issue in the lobby, and it would keep me amused for a while.

Mrs. Cowles had warned Alice about talking to newspapermen. My understanding was that Alice could talk about parties and things like that but couldn't insult anyone or venture into politics beyond supporting her father. But I wasn't too worried, as any misbehavior regarding the press was more objectionable than dangerous, so I wouldn't be held accountable.

Unless she did something really ghastly.

As we drove, it was as if Alice could read my mind. "Don't worry. We're here more to ask questions than answer them. Newspapermen always know what's going on, and perhaps they can be persuaded to share some of their insights with us. We're talking about the lowest kinds of rumor, and newspapers excel at that sort of thing, none better than the *Herald*."

The *Herald* occupied its own building in a busy square named for the paper. It was one of my favorite buildings in New York, although I had never been inside. It was a funny, foreign-looking building, long and low. Alice told me it was supposed to look like Italian mansions and was designed by someone called Stanford White, who she said was the most famous architect in the world.

I parked the car outside and looked up at the statues.

"That's Minerva, the Roman goddess of wisdom," Alice explained. "And all of those owls are also symbols of wisdom." That made sense. Newspapermen needed all the help they could get.

You could watch the big presses from the street through windows on the main floor, and it had become quite a popular site. We had a quick look at the pressman running an afternoon edition. We entered the building, and Alice was instantly recognized. Indeed, I doubt if there was a newspaperman in New York, probably in the country, who wouldn't recognize Alice on sight.

"Miss Roosevelt!" said a shiny-faced office boy shuffling papers at the front desk. He stood at attention. "How may I assist you?"

"We'd like to see Miss Felicia Meadows," said Alice.

"Oh . . . yes, of course." He seemed surprised but not unhappy. "I will take you there personally, if you will follow me." He set off at a brisk pace down busy hallways. Everyone was in a rush: men in shirtsleeves barking orders, phones ringing, and the clacking of the new typewriting machines. They had one down at the Secret Service headquarters, but the clerk there treated it like something sacred and wouldn't let any of the agents near it.

"So who's this Miss Meadows?" I asked.

"Of course, you wouldn't know," Alice replied. "She covers Society. That's what women reporters do, and for the most part, only women read their articles. Lots of people dislike her."

"Why?"

"The rule is that you're supposed to be in the newspaper only three times in your life—when you're born, when you're married, and when you die. Miss Meadows, and others like her, disagree.

They know all kinds of things and publish everything they hear. She's written reams about me." She sounded proud about that. "But I've never met her, and so I'm very curious."

"It's none of my business, Miss Alice, but this Miss Meadows doesn't sound like the kind of person your aunt wants you to talk to."

"Oh, no. She'd have all kinds of fits," said Alice cheerfully.

We stopped at a small office, where a woman of about thirty was sitting behind a desk and looking intently at some pages through a pair of spectacles. She had a pleasant, round face and brown hair rather carelessly done up. She was much more simply dressed than Alice and could've passed for any of hundreds of young women who worked in offices throughout the city.

The boy rapped on the open door, and the woman took her spectacles off and looked up. Those eyes—that's what made her different. They were as green and hard as emeralds, and her pretty mouth pursed in amused surprise.

"Miss Meadows, this is—"

"Oh, I know who this is, Jackie. Thank you." The boy excused himself and left, and Miss Meadows motioned for us to take two seats jammed between the wall and the front of her desk.

"So it's Miss Roosevelt and . . ." She smiled wryly at me. "Wyatt Earp."

"No need for silliness," said Alice. "This is Joseph St. Clair of the Secret Service, my bodyguard."

"What did you do to merit an assignment like this, Mr. St. Clair?" asked Miss Meadows. I couldn't tell if she had decided my assignment was an honor or a punishment.

"Secret Service agents aren't allowed to talk to the press," I said. Alice gave another one of her dramatic sighs.

"If you must know, Mr. St. Clair was a deputy sheriff in Laramie and a sergeant with the Rough Riders before my father assigned him to my detail. Now to the matter at hand. I've come for some assistance."

"Really? I assumed when the president's daughter shows up in my office with an armed cowboy, it's to make a complaint."

"Why should I complain? You have a job to do, and you do it well. I find your articles amusing."

That surprised Miss Meadows. "You read me regularly? For pleasure?"

"When I get a copy of the *Herald*. My aunt finds your column, indeed your entire newspaper, disgraceful and won't have it in the house."

Miss Meadows laughed. "I can believe that. I'm glad there are no hard feelings. Now tell me what I can do for you."

"I need some information about certain people in Society, and I think you might have the details."

"Really? Who is more central to New York Society than a Roosevelt?"

"I have information. But not the information you probably have. Deeper things than are usually discussed in Polite Society."

"Who are we talking about?"

"The late Delilah Linde and her husband Marcus, and the late Lynley Brackton and his wife Victoria."

That lovely mouth curved into a knowing smile, and she watched Alice with great interest. "Yes, two deaths so close together. The police are saying a sudden illness in both cases, but no one believes them. Everyone here assumes it's murder, even if nothing has been officially stated." O'Hara was apparently still maintaining the fiction that it was just death by natural causes. But he probably couldn't do that forever.

"I am glad to hear you say that. I cannot speak on behalf of the police, but I can tell you—and you may not quote me—that you are absolutely right. But as for what I need from you. You're probably aware I was at the Rutledge party when Mr. Brackton was murdered, but just because my father was police commissioner doesn't mean the police keep me in their confidence. I'm not here for the legal implications. There are events, social connections, decisions about invitations. Sudden deaths like this, even natural, bring certain things to light. If I can get information today, it will save embarrassment tomorrow."

"What makes you think I have information beyond what I put into my column?" she asked.

"I think your job is not that different from politics. You don't make use of it all, not right away. You use it strategically. And if you cause a major scandal, if you couldn't show some discretion, you would put yourself out of business. Also, I know a little something of the law. There are things you know and things you can prove. If you publish things you cannot prove, there are libel laws in this country, and powerful and wealthy people spend a lot of money on attorneys. But I didn't ask you for what you can prove. I asked for what you know."

Miss Meadows looked impressed. I was, too. "Very shrewd, Miss Roosevelt. Very well. I have information. But it's worth a lot. What can you give me?"

"How about this? The Gadsden ball later this spring. You and you alone get a look at what I'll be wearing. And the name of my escort, in advance."

"People misbehave there when it gets late. I want three anecdotes I can print."

"I can give you that. But you have to be discreet with what I tell you. I can't see my name posted anywhere. It won't do me any good if people think I know too much. I'll get you two anecdotes, and I will have to remain anonymous."

Miss Meadows thought that over for a moment, then said "done" and leaned over the table to shake Alice's hand. I was impressed once more. I thought you had to be a senator to pull together a deal as neatly as Alice had. Someone was keeping her eyes and ears open in Washington and learning her lessons.

"Now I'll tell you what I know. I don't even have to check

my notes because I've been poring over them after the two deaths. Lynley Brackton was an unapologetic womanizer with a doormat for a wife, the kind who accepted everything he did and is probably mourning him right now." *Good instincts*, I thought.

"Why? Why did Victoria accept that?" asked Alice, genuinely puzzled. Miss Meadows shook her head, then looked at me.

"You—Mr. St. Clair. You look like you've kicked around. Have you told Miss Roosevelt that sometimes with marriages things aren't that straightforward?"

I just smiled. "I told you, I can't talk to the press."

"Oh, let's call this off the record. That means I don't quote anything either of you say, even anonymously. All off the record today."

"That's acceptable," said Alice. "'Off the record' happens all the time in Washington."

"Fine then," I said. "I told Miss Alice that marriages are complicated and don't work the way you think."

"You got that right. We're all born to be something. Victoria Brackton was born to be a victim. As long as he eventually came home and behaved among their friends, she turned a blind eye to every actress or shopgirl he picked up. Apparently, there was no one serious or long-term. I don't know much about her, but if you're curious, I might be able to get more from the arts desk."

"How do you get all this information?" asked Alice.

"Oh, my dear, you have no idea. I talk to many, many people. My job is 10 percent writing and 90 percent listening."

Alice considered that for a moment before saying, "And the Lindes. What can you tell me about them?"

"Ah, yes. That's a rather more complicated situation. Marcus Linde is fantastically wealthy and has always lived a quiet life. Delilah Linde was born Delilah van Dijk. It was a good family and an old one, but money management wasn't their strong suit, and after a succession of wastrels and drunks, almost nothing is left. She has a brother in New York, but he's not spoken about— doesn't mix with Society anymore now that he's come down in the world. Named Miles. A good marriage was her only option. I think Marcus Linde is older than her father. Still, they each got what they wanted." She smirked.

"Older men like young women. I've seen that myself," said Alice, who didn't want to look unsophisticated in front of Miss Meadows.

"If that were the half of it, my dear. You know he was married before?"

"Yes. His wife died some twenty years ago when they were in Europe. That's the story that goes around in Society, at any rate. Of course, it was before my time."

"A story. That's for sure. She didn't die, Miss Roosevelt. They got divorced. He gave her a very nice settlement, and she made a new life for herself in Paris. She wasn't of any particular family, so no one really missed her."

Alice frowned. Divorce in Society happened, but people were quiet about it, and if Linde didn't want to make it the official story, I could understand.

"Do we know why?" asked Alice.

"I don't think Mr. Linde was the marrying kind. He's what's often known as a confirmed bachelor."

"But he did marry. He married twice," said Alice, looking confused.

"Well, yes," said Miss Meadows. "But these were not conventional marriages. That is, marriage as it's usually thought of." We saw a glimmer of understanding in Alice's eyes. Alice knew a lot, and she was smart as a whip, but there were still things she had to learn.

"Mr. St. Clair, do you want to explain to Alice what we're talking about?" asked Miss Meadows.

"No, not really," I said.

"Fine. Miss Roosevelt, I don't know where Society girls get their information from, or when, but Mr. Linde was not interested in normal relations with his wives. Is that clear?"

"I see now," said Alice, full enlightenment coming to her. "So why get married at all, then?"

"Who can be sure? Maybe he just liked the company— somebody to organize the intimate dinner parties he liked, to decorate his house, to have someone to talk to in the evenings. I'm not married, either, Miss Roosevelt. I can tell you his first wife was only nineteen when they wed, and I don't think she realized what the deal was when they got married. Maybe even he didn't realize what he was getting into. Anyway, they got a divorce, he gave her lots of money, and she made a nice life for herself in Paris."

"And the second Mrs. Linde?"

"She was a little older, and so was he. I bet his situation was made a lot more explicit to her. I've never been in their home, but I hear she made it very nice."

"I was there, and you're right. Didn't I say that, Mr. St. Clair? I said the house showed a woman's touch."

"There you go," said Miss Meadows. "And Mrs. Linde didn't do too badly out of it, especially as she had no money of her own. She got jewels and servants and fancy dresses. I bet that she planned on someday patiently nursing him in his final days before becoming the wealthiest widow in New York."

"I like the way you think, Miss Meadows," I said. She gave me a mock bow.

"All right. I see what is going on here," said Alice. "Mr. Linde got everything he wanted, and Mrs. Linde got to live like a queen. But what if she wanted more? Other men were probably attracted to her."

"I'm sure. Is this leading to whether Mrs. Linde took lovers? If she did, she was very discreet. I haven't heard anything."

"Also, if she did and was reasonably discreet, would Mr. Linde even mind?"

"A very shrewd observation, Miss Roosevelt. Although I don't have any more information on Mrs. Linde, I like the way you think." Now, Alice gave Miss Meadows a mock bow. "Anyway, you now know more than you did when you came in and can take some comfort in that."

"I do, indeed," said Alice. "Thank you. This has been very helpful, and I'll keep my end of the bargain."

"Then we'll drink to that," said Miss Meadows, and I was surprised and amused to see her pull a bottle of whiskey out of her desk drawer.

"You like whiskey, Cowboy?" she asked.

"Not while I'm on duty," I said, and Alice snickered.

"We're done with business here. All off the record, both our words and our actions," said Miss Meadows. I wanted to be hospitable, so I took out my flask.

"Bourbon," I said. Miss Meadows produced three shot glasses.

"Miss Alice will take your whiskey but not my bourbon," I said.

"You don't like bourbon, Miss Roosevelt?" asked Miss Meadows.

"She's a kid. Bourbon is for grown-ups," I said, and Alice glared at me. The whiskey was good, and since we were off the record, I told Miss Meadows some stories about growing up in Wyoming, working as a deputy sheriff, and charging up San Juan Hill. She seemed entertained, and I liked making her laugh. As I said, she had a really lovely mouth.

Alice wasn't happy. She didn't like being out of the limelight, and she didn't like it when I paid attention to any other woman. So there she was, getting into a sulk as Miss Meadows talked about growing up a brewer's daughter in New Jersey and crossing the Hudson to seek her fortune.

Finally, Alice stood. "Miss Meadows, I thank you and will give you the particulars on the Gadsden ball as we get closer."

"Perhaps this can be the start of an ongoing relationship," said Miss Meadows.

"Perhaps," said Alice a little coolly. And then Miss Meadows looked at me. "You, too, Joey."

I winked at her. "As Miss Alice said, perhaps. Thanks for the whiskey, Felicia." With that, we were off. I'm a good deal taller than Alice, but even so, I almost had to run to keep up with her.

"We have things to do," she said. "At least, I do. You apparently have nothing to do other than flirt with lady journalists."

"Oh, come, Miss Alice. I was just being friendly."

"I didn't think she was all that attractive," she said.

"Maybe I was a little tickled to talk with a woman my own age. Maybe I liked talking with someone a little more like me."

Alice stopped at that, right in the hallway, and busy office boys pushed past us, as they spared a glance for the famous president's daughter. She looked at me as if she were seeing me for the first time.

"That is a very introspective remark, Mr. St. Clair. You repeatedly remind me of your hidden depths." We started walking again, and she gave me a sidelong glance. "I still don't think she was that attractive."

"She has a lovely mouth."

"If you say so," she said, indicating that I was entitled to my opinion no matter how stupid it was. We headed out of the building and found some hot dogs and Coca-Colas in a hole-in-the-wall restaurant.

"What do we have?" asked Alice. "Remember, we're the only ones who know that Victoria was the intended victim. So someone is out to kill two women in New York Society. And someone is out to warn us off. Here's the question I keep coming back to: what is the connection between the XVII and the murders? The Bracktons and Lindes were members. Why should they be victims?

"Is there another group fighting back against them? Is it all some kind of insane coincidence? And why are they called the XVII? There is a business connection here," said Alice slowly between bites of hot dog. "I'm sure about that. Whoever sent those men after us on Houston—that was about business, not just personal. Marcus Linde was upset over the business connections, not his wife. Rutledge, Linde, and Brackton are all men of business in this city with a lot of control, and they seem to be deeply worried about changing demographics. They are worried and threatened about the growth and power of immigrants—and that includes the Roths, who are definitely outsiders."

"A good summary. So what's next?"

"We have two paths, and we're going down both of them. We need to find out more about both the Lindes and the Bracktons, and that means Mrs. Linde's brother. It's getting late, and we're having people for dinner, so we'll start fresh in the morning. What are you doing tonight?"

"There will probably be a game in the basement with the building porters." And then, because I couldn't resist, I said, "Maybe Felicia would like to join us."

"Mr. St. Clair, shut up. Just shut up."

CHAPTER 19

The next morning turned out to be a lot busier than we expected. I was up in the breakfast room at the usual time, and Alice was already digging into her eggs and bacon. A maid was clearing a coffee cup.

"You just missed my aunt. She'll be off to a political breakfast in a moment. I managed to wriggle out of it. Anyway, she said she wanted to speak to you."

"To me?" That was startling.

"Don't worry. If she were angry, I would've heard already. Anyway, I want to talk to Mrs. Linde's brother. I'll have to think about where to find him."

The doorbell rang, and I went with the maid to get it. It was Captain O'Hara once again.

"It's the coffee, isn't it?" I asked. "You come back for the coffee. I don't blame you. They have the best coffee here."

"Never mind the coffee. I'm doing you another favor. I have the medical report on Mrs. Linde. Nothing too surprising. It seems it really was that punch that killed her; there's wolfsbane in her system." He handed me some papers. "I can't let you keep this, but you can look at it over here."

"Thanks, Captain. It's not that we don't appreciate this, but there must be a reason you're being so nice. This is more than you owed me."

He rubbed his chin with his thumb as he thought about it and looked a little embarrassed. "I'm in a tight place, St. Clair. We're supposed to figure this out, but you know what we're up against. I can't ask them anything, people at that level. And the politicians owe everything to those people, and they're all over me. I'm going to have to arrest someone, anyone, as long as I don't touch the wrong people. But you're federal. You're outside it all."

I held up my hands. "Wait a minute. There is no Secret Service role here. I'm just Miss Roosevelt's bodyguard. It's just that Miss Roosevelt—"

Now O'Hara raised his hands. "I don't want to know what Miss Roosevelt is up to. I don't want to know anything. Look, St. Clair, I know Peter Carlyle is a friend of yours, and I don't want to set him up for this. I'm trying to do the right thing here. I'm—"

Alice entered at that moment. "Captain O'Hara. Another breakfast visit? It's silly to stand there on the threshold in the hope that I won't notice."

"The captain brought Mrs. Linde's case file. We can have a look."

"Splendid. Captain O'Hara, come inside. Let me see those papers." But I tucked them into my jacket pocket

"After Mrs. Cowles has left. You don't want to have to explain what this is."

"I suppose you're right. But I will have questions, most likely, so come on through." O'Hara and I followed Alice, who stuck her head into the kitchen and asked for more bacon and eggs. I didn't hear Dulcie's reply, which was probably just as well.

We had barely made ourselves comfortable, with O'Hara savoring some of that great coffee, when the doorbell rang again. Once more, there was nothing from the doorman, which likely meant more police.

"One of your boys?" I asked O'Hara, but he shook his head.

"I'm coming with you," said Alice.

"You're staying here," I said and followed the maid. I was greeted by a surprise—Mr. Harris, head of the Secret Service's

New York office, and my immediate superior. He was his usual dapper self with his well-oiled hair, perfectly trimmed mustache, and a suit that was both more expensive and better pressed than mine.

"St. Clair. Glad I caught you. Can you explain to me what the hell this is?" He wasn't happy as he pushed a copy of that morning's *Herald* at me, and I had a bad feeling.

"Mr. Harris? Welcome," said Alice, who joined us in the entranceway. "You've played host to me enough times in your offices. Let me now be your hostess." She saw the *Herald* and raised an eyebrow as she briefly met my eye. "Do come through and have some coffee."

That disarmed him for a moment. "Thank you, Miss Roosevelt, but I really need to speak to Mr. St. Clair."

"There's nothing you can tell Mr. St. Clair that you can't tell me. We have plenty of coffee, and more bacon and eggs will be coming in a moment."

"Well . . . if it's all right with you, Miss Roosevelt," he said, and we walked into the breakfast room together.

"Mr. Harris, this is Captain O'Hara of the police department. Captain O'Hara, Mr. Harris is head of the New York office of the Secret Service and Mr. St. Clair's superior. Have a seat, and pour yourself some coffee"

"Well, thank you," said Mr. Harris, who was looking more and more like a man who had had the rug pulled out from under him and couldn't figure out how it had happened. "This shouldn't take long." He poured himself some coffee and opened the paper. "Mr. St. Clair, you are aware that agents are not allowed to give interviews to the press."

Alice had seemed so sure that we could trust Miss Meadows, and I was a little hurt to think she had betrayed us.

"I wasn't aware I had, sir."

"It's in one of those women's columns, written by a certain Felicia Meadows."

"I can't believe that. She promised everything was off the record," Alice said.

"So you know about this, Miss Roosevelt?" asked Mr. Harris.

"We went to visit her at the *Herald* offices, and as you know, Mr. St. Clair had to stay with me. Those are your rules. Anyway, what's this all about?" She snatched the paper from Mr. Harris and read aloud:

"Dear Readers, have any of you seen who has been squiring Alice Roosevelt around town? The president's lovely daughter is always in the company of her Secret Service bodyguard, and how lucky she is! Agent Joseph St. Clair, a veteran of the Rough Riders, is an actual cowboy, born and raised in Wyoming with a delicious Western drawl, broad shoulders, a handsome weather-beaten face barely shaded by his corn-colored hair, and a charming smile. Don't all my lady readers wish they had such an escort!"

Alice got more and more worked up as she read, which Mr. Harris and Captain O'Hara were pretending not to notice. At any rate, Miss Meadows didn't lie to us, not really. She didn't quote me or reveal anything she had promised to keep private. Alice knew that, too.

By the end, Alice was both angry and embarrassed, and Mr. Harris broke the awkward silence. "Mr. St. Clair, do you have anything to say about this?"

"I think 'weather-beaten' is a slight exaggeration, sir."

"Oh, this is ridiculous," said Alice. "It's clearly not an interview, just a silly list of attributes. Any further discussion is a waste of time. I'm surprised to see you give credence to this—"

At that point, Mrs. Cowles walked in looking more than a little surprised. After eighteen years of supervising Alice, it took a lot to surprise her. The other two men and I all stood.

"My goodness, Alice. Your breakfast meetings continue to grow in popularity. You might want to tell Enid to set the dining room table if it grows any larger."

"I will," said Alice. "You met Captain O'Hara yesterday, and of course you know Mr. Harris, who is Mr. St. Clair's superior in the Secret Service office."

"Ah. You no doubt came to see Mr. St. Clair about this," she said, showing her own copy of the *Herald*. Mrs. Cowles always seemed to know what was going on before anyone else did. I don't know how she did it, but it wasn't much of a surprise that she had found out about that particular column.

"Well, actually, ma'am . . ." said Mr. Harris.

"I don't see the harm, except that it seems to embarrass Mr. St. Clair. Alice, were you really visiting Miss Meadows? I had hoped you would find better ways to occupy your day, but if this is all she got, you clearly showed some restraint, and one must be grateful for small favors. Alice, gentlemen, good day." And with that, she strode rapidly out the door.

Captain O'Hara and Mr. Harris had something quick to eat. I could tell my boss was relieved Mrs. Cowles wasn't upset about the *Herald* article but still wasn't happy that I was the subject of one of the women's columns. He was trying to find a way to blame me. Alice, meanwhile, fetched some paper and a pen and was making notes as she flipped through the report.

O'Hara mentioned he had seen Christy Mathewson pitch for the Giants at the Polo Grounds recently, and I said I hoped to see him later in the season. Mr. Harris pretended he was above baseball and didn't participate in the conversation. He finished his coffee and then said, "That cowboy hat of yours. Do you really need to wear it?" I was attached to my Stetson, so I didn't answer, and he didn't seem to expect me to.

"Miss Roosevelt, thank you. Captain, a pleasure. I'll see myself out." Mr. Harris stood and took his *Herald* with him.

"Have a pleasant day, and thank you for visiting," said Alice to Mr. Harris, who tipped his hat as he left. When he was gone, she continued, "I think I have what we need. Thank you very much, Captain O'Hara. This is very helpful."

"But you didn't get it from me. Still, I'd appreciate it if you could let me know if you hear anything." He took the report back, thanked us, and left, as well.

"Get anything interesting there?" I asked.

"Yes. I didn't understand all the medical details any more than I believe Captain O'Hara did. But like he said, she died of poisoned punch, too. It's what we expected. But I did get something else of interest. Clipped to the report was a card from a certain Amelia Rushcroft with an East Side address. That is interesting."

"Why? It was probably just a friend."

"No, it wasn't," said Alice a little smugly. "First, Society is rather small. If we don't know each other, we at least know each other's names. I've never heard of a Rushcroft. Which means Mrs. Linde would have to be friends with someone outside of New York Society. But even more important—and I bet Captain O'Hara didn't realize this—that wasn't a calling card. Ladies' cards look a certain way. That looked like a business card." She gave that some thought. "If Mrs. Linde had business with someone, we will go and say we have business there, too." I saw the address, and it was on a side street on an elegant East Side block, so although I'd be careful, I wasn't too worried. But I was surprised.

"Miss Alice, there aren't any businesses in that part of town."

"I wondered about that myself. And there's no business name on what seems to be a business card. We shall see. Meanwhile, thanks to our efficient police force, we have a list of other relations nearby—including her brother, Miles. He doesn't seem to live in an upscale neighborhood. Like we heard, the Van Dijks have come down in the world, so it makes sense he now lives off the beaten path. But it's early for social calls, as I'm frequently reminded, so we'll visit Amelia Rushcroft first, whoever she is."

CHAPTER 20

I knew we'd be coming back to Miss Meadows and the newspaper article, and Alice wasted no time.

"I am sorry about Miss Meadows's article," she said as we walked across the lobby to the Caledonia garage. "But it's really your fault."

I laughed. "How is that?"

"You were flirting with her. No wonder she was tempted to write about you, violating the spirit—if not the letter—of our agreement."

"Oh, I was? I didn't realize it."

"See, this is what my aunt was talking about, your pretending to be stupid. You turn on that Western charm and then pretend to be surprised at the results."

"You sound just like my sister," I said.

"I like and admire Mariah, so I take that as a compliment. Just try to make your behavior a little more appropriate to the occasion."

"I guess it's just my misfortune that my Western charm doesn't work on you," I said.

That stopped her, and she gave me a hard look. She hated to think someone was making fun of her. I knew what she was thinking, so there was no need to say it out loud: I was Alice's personal property, and no one else could have me.

"Watch yourself, Cowboy," she said.

"Yes, Princess."

We got into the car and drove to the address we had for Amelia Rushcroft. I'm sure Alice was right, that the police assumed Rushcroft was just a friend of Mrs. Linde's. They wouldn't bother a Society lady unless they had a strong reason to, and just the possession of what they thought was a calling card wasn't enough.

I was right—the address was a townhouse, and it didn't look like a place of business. There was no sign or brass plaque outside like you might find at a doctor's office. It was a small house and didn't look fancy, but it seemed well tended, and we were admitted by a uniformed maid. It didn't look dangerous, not on this sleepy street.

"We have some business to discuss with Amelia Rushcroft," Alice said.

"Do you have an appointment, madam?" asked the maid when we were inside. Alice looked a little startled. Not only was she annoyed at not being recognized, but she was too young to be called "madam."

"No. But I was recommended by the late Mrs. Delilah Linde."

"One moment, please," said the maid. She walked down the hallway to a closed door and entered, closing it behind her and leaving us alone in the hallway. There was a stairway heading up, but it was dark, and the place was quiet. It was odd, not being shown into a parlor. I didn't like things being odd, and I made sure my Colt was clear of my jacket while keeping an eye on the other hallway doors.

Alice started to say something, but I put my finger to my lips, and she stopped. She knew when silence was important, and I wanted to hear if anyone was coming. The hallway was dimly lit, and a good carpet muffled any sounds, so I wanted to keep all my senses focused.

The far door opened, and the maid came back. "Miss Rushcroft will see you now," she said to Alice and turned to me. "I can show you into the parlor," she said.

"He stays with me," said Alice. The maid looked like she was going to argue the point but then thought better of it and led us both to the room. I slipped ahead of Alice to look first. It was a pleasant office. Mrs. Cowles had a room like that at the Caledonia where they kept the telephone. The furniture was feminine, but you could tell it was an office, a place of business, with its filing cabinets and a typewriter machine on its own table.

Behind the desk was a woman I'm guessing was in her mid-forties. She looked welcoming, like someone's mother, with dark brown hair pulled neatly back, and I could see a few streaks of grey. Her clothes were neat and simple like Miss Meadows's or any other woman with an office job.

Everything looked safe, so I brought Alice in. Miss Rushcroft dismissed the maid with a flick of her hand and then motioned to us to sit down.

"Are you sure you don't want to wait outside, Mister . . ."

"St. Clair. Joseph St. Clair. And no, thank you, I'll stay here."

Miss Rushcroft gently shrugged and turned to Alice. I could see Alice was thinking furiously, trying to figure out who Miss Rushcroft was and what she was doing.

"What can I do for you, Miss Roosevelt? No, you won't be surprised I recognized you. You are quite well known. You say Mrs. Linde recommended me?" She gave Alice a shrewd look.

"Yes. And I'm interested in whatever services Mrs. Linde obtained from you."

"I think that's rather unlikely," said Miss Rushcroft. "You don't know who I am or what I do. That much is clear. But I admire you for bluffing your way in here."

She didn't seem upset. In fact, she was amused, and her smile was welcoming. Nevertheless, Alice wasn't backing down. She didn't look embarrassed or guilty. "Oh, very well. You caught me. But I have a very good reason for being here. Since we're sitting here comfortably, won't you enlighten me?"

Miss Rushcroft smiled warmly. "I'm discreet but not secretive. I'm a midwife, Miss Roosevelt."

I knew Alice had just warned me about my behavior, but I thought it was funny that the president's unmarried eighteen-year-old daughter had gone in to seek the services of a midwife. So I laughed. And watching me, Miss Rushcroft laughed, too. Alice just glared at me, but then she yielded, too, and allowed a smile.

"I can imagine your being surprised now," said Alice. "But I had to get in to see you. My connection with Mrs. Linde was not a lie."

"I heard about her death. It was very sad, but I don't know any details. You seem to believe she was a patient of mine, but I can't confirm that, of course."

"But you're interested, concerned, that her death is related to the diagnosis of pregnancy you gave her, aren't you?" Alice looked triumphant at that and practically kicked up her heels. It took Miss Rushcroft aback for a moment. I meanwhile wondered why the doctor who examined the late Mrs. Linde didn't catch that. I could see him being given a discreet bribe to keep it out of his report.

"I've never met the president, but I hear he's a sharp one, and you're your father's daughter, that much is clear," she said, and I don't think Alice could've had a nicer compliment. She turned a little pink.

"Thank you," she said. "But I'll lay my cards on the table. You said you're discreet, and I know I can't get something without giving something. Mrs. Linde was murdered—poisoned. I'm trying to figure out why or how. She had your card with her, so I'm guessing she was pregnant. And one more thing . . ." Alice stuck out her chin. "I don't believe her husband was the father of her child."

That stopped the conversation for a while. Miss Rushcroft broke the silence.

"That's a rather . . . extraordinary statement, Miss Roosevelt. Even if I had any information regarding parentage, I couldn't possibly comment on that. But I think we've gotten ahead of ourselves. Can I ask the full story of why you're here? And who's the cowboy?"

I took out my badge. "I'm Miss Roosevelt's Secret Service bodyguard."

"And I thought I had a hard job," said Miss Rushcroft and rolled right along to keep Alice from reacting. "So what did I do to merit a Secret Service investigation?"

"It's not about the Secret Service. It's about friends of mine," said Alice. "You may have heard that a man named Lynley Brackton died at the recent Rutledge ball. Again, I'm trusting your discretion. We just found out Mrs. Linde was killed the same way, and she was standing right next to Brackton when he was poisoned. I am trying to make sure the right person is arrested, or more immediately, that the wrong person is not charged. You as good as admitted to me that Mrs. Linde was having a baby. From what I observe about their marriage, I don't think Mr. Linde was the father of her child."

"That's an astonishing thing to say. Unless you were intimate with Mrs. Linde, I don't see where you're getting that."

"I can't give you my sources, but I will tell you what Marcus Linde said to me. 'Whatever people say.' Those were his exact words. He would truly mourn her, whatever people say. I thought that was so strange. They might say that because it wasn't a marriage in a traditional sense. He let her be lady of the manor, decorate and run his house, amuse him over dinner, and she got to dress up and go to parties as the wealthy Mrs. Linde. I'm sure it worked well. He may have even known already she was with child but didn't much care. Not that he'll ever tell me or anyone else. But it made a difference to someone else, I'm sure. It made a difference to the man who did father her child, don't you think?" She raised an eyebrow.

That was a hell of a speech—I'd give her that. I guess that's what comes with being from a political family. It made sense, but there was no way she could've known it for sure, and all we had to go on were Linde's vague comments and the information our reporter friend Miss Meadows provided. Miss Rushcroft might've laughed or even thrown us out of her house, but I could see in a minute that Alice had gambled and won. Miss Rushcroft looked very uncomfortable.

"And one more thing," Alice continued. "She came to you. Why hide the fact that you're a midwife? It's a good, even noble, profession, one every woman needs, and yet you don't even have a simple brass plaque outside. Because they come to you for discretion even beyond what is usual. It's one thing to bear another man's child, but it could be ruinous if anything leaked out."

Miss Rushcroft smiled thinly. "You're an interesting one, Miss Roosevelt. You're right that I serve the best of Society, and I am known for my discretion. You need someone who will convince mother, father and the rest of Society that a child born seven months after a wedding is merely premature. Yes, you've clever. But you didn't come here just to show off. You say there's murder involved? I don't see the connection, and I'm sure I don't want to know. But what do you want from me?"

"I want to know the father of Mrs. Linde's child. And in return, I promise discretion, too. If I can find out what I need, it ends here. I will not discuss your name or this meeting with the police, but if they keep up their investigations, they will eventually make their way here. And that won't be good for business."

I could see Miss Rushcroft thinking that over, trying to weigh the consequences of cooperating or not, and then finally reaching a decision.

"I appreciate your offer. As I said, I have never met your father, but he's respected as a man of honor, and I will assume his daughter is to be trusted, as well." Whether Miss Rushcroft knew it or not, few compliments could've pleased Alice more. "If Mrs. Linde were still alive, I wouldn't betray her confidence, but as she is gone, I will confirm that yes, she was with child, and she was frank with me about the paternity. Or perhaps I should say halfway frank: she told me that her husband was not the father but not who the actual father was. I think she was afraid there would be talk if the child ended up not looking like his father, and she wanted to make sure she had my full cooperation in advance. But I assure you, Miss Roosevelt, I never asked for a name, and Mrs. Linde never offered it. It was more than I needed or wanted to know."

Alice leaned back in her chair and studied Miss Rushcroft for a few moments. No one said anything until Miss Rushcroft resumed speaking.

"But I can tell you who would certainly be able to give you more information. Her brother, Miles. She mentioned him in her initial talk with me, and I gathered they were close, or at least had been before her marriage." She smiled wryly. "I've gotten rather good at reading women's emotions."

"We were going to meet with him in any event. Of course, as I promised, I'll keep your name out of it. We have never met." Alice stood and extended her hand. "Thank you very much, Miss Rushcroft."

"It has been . . . interesting, Miss Roosevelt. I wish you luck. I genuinely liked Mrs. Linde, and if you can find out who killed her, that would please me greatly. Just one more thing. I don't know who, if anyone, Mrs. Linde told about her condition, but they might've known she was unwell. Like many women in such a state, she suffered from stomach upsets. I told her to eat bland foods and avoid alcohol and that it would pass in a matter of weeks."

"That's helpful. Thank you."

She handed Alice her card. "Someday, my dear, you will get married, and as the president's daughter, you will need and want a discreet midwife."

Alice gave Miss Rushcroft a cheeky smile as the sophisticated young lady fell away and I saw again the young girl Alice was. "I'm sure, Miss Rushcroft, but if my aunt finds that card and figures out who you are, even I would be hard-pressed to explain how I came to have it."

We said our goodbyes with expressions of goodwill all around, and the maid showed us out the door.

"You heard what Miss Rushcroft said about diet and alcohol," said Alice. "That was the excuse Mrs. Linde gave at the party for not having any punch. Only it didn't come from a doctor but a midwife. Did anyone else realize that, either at the party or beforehand? Does it have anything to do with her death, which must be connected to Brackton's? Did Mr. Linde know? Would he care?"

"I couldn't say, Miss Alice, but I can tell you that was quite a trick you pulled in there, getting her to part with all that information."

"I thought I was rather good," she replied, half with pride, half with uncertainty.

"You got what you came for. I think your father would've been proud."

"Really?" she asked, and again, she looked like a little girl.

"Yes, having served under him, I can say I think he would've." I grinned right back at her. "On the other hand, your aunt would've handed you your head."

Chapter 21

Miles van Dijk lived in Queens, which is basically a collection of villages next to Brooklyn on the far side of the East River. It was a bit of a drive. They kept talking about building a bridge to Queens, but at the time, the only way to drive there was indirectly over the Brooklyn Bridge. That was fine with me because that bridge was just about my favorite thing in New York. It was more impressive than any building I'd seen, and I never got tired of driving on it and seeing the great view of New York's harbor.

Of course, my feelings were a little tainted by the memories of the last time Alice and I had crossed it—during the little adventure that led to some scandalous court cases and my temporary exile to St. Louis. Alice remembered, too, as I could tell from her smirk.

"That was something, the last time we were here, wasn't it?"

"As I recall, you were rather upset by the end," I said.

"Well, at the time," she said grudgingly. "But we did accomplish something. We really did." She turned to me for confirmation.

"We sure did, Miss Alice."

It was still a little quieter on the far side of the river, so I liked getting out of Manhattan every now and then. We drove through different neighborhoods on our way, some nicer than others, and Alice looked around curiously. One of the things about being really rich, especially as a woman, was that you didn't get to see a lot of different kinds of places. Whether it was Manhattan or the summer places in Newport, rich people tended to stay in rich people places.

We found Miles van Dijk's home on a street of modest houses with a bit of green between them, and although it seemed nice enough, it was pretty simple for the son of one of the city's great families. If they had really lost their money like we were told, it must've been a big shock. We parked out front and walked along the stone walkway that cut through a badly tended lawn.

"He's not living as nicely as his sister did," I said. "We knew the family had problems, but this is pretty far from Fifth Avenue."

"They each made a decision," said Alice.

"But who made the right one?" I said.

"Once again, I see that you've developed quite a philosophical bent," said Alice approvingly, and she rang the bell.

There was no maid or any servant to open the door; Van Dijk let us in himself. He looked surprised, but he must've heard the motorcar out front. So he was expecting someone, just not us, and I decided to keep my eyes and ears open while we were there.

"Mr. van Dijk? I'm Alice Roosevelt. I'm a friend of your late sister, and I've come to give you my condolences."

I hadn't met Delilah Linde, but everyone said she was a beauty, and I bet Van Dijk looked like her when he was better fixed up. Presently, Van Dijk peered at us through bloodshot eyes. He hadn't shaved in a day or two or put a comb through his hair. But I didn't smell any drink, and I was assuming his disheveled state was due to mourning. It was interesting because he had fallen apart, and Mr. Linde hadn't. I remembered what Miss Rushcroft said about brother and sister being close, and that bond could be a stronger one than marriage.

"Alice Roosevelt. I recognize you, but have we ever met?" He sounded more confused than upset.

"No, I don't believe so. But I knew your sister. I've already called on her husband, Marcus Linde, and I thought it would be appropriate to call on you." She paused, and Van Dijk continued to peer at us. He was in his shirtsleeves, and I think he had been sleeping in his clothes. "Do you think we could come in?"

He didn't say anything, just stepped aside and let us in. The absence of any servants was obvious. The place was dusty—there was no maid here, at least not more than once a week, and men like Van Dijk weren't raised to do housework. Alice gave the place a critical look, as Van Dijk led us to a small parlor with faded furniture that had probably come with the place.

We all took seats. "I am deeply sorry for your loss," said Alice. "I had just seen your sister at Philadelphia Rutledge's debutante party, and she had looked well and happy. It was a great shock to all of us."

He nodded absently.

"Will you excuse me for a moment?" he asked and then left the room. We heard him somewhere else in the house. He came back with rolling papers and tobacco. Alice turned to me as if to say, "Let's join him." So I reached into my pocket and rolled one for me and one for her. She'd gotten better at it in the months we'd been together, but I was still faster and neater. I lit up my cigarette and then Alice's, and soon the three of us were puffing away.

"Sorry about that. I needed that to start the day," Van Dijk said. For the first time, he seemed to notice Alice was smoking, too. He smiled. "Miss Roosevelt, excuse my lack of hospitality. It didn't occur to me the president's young daughter smoked." I guess I didn't count, just being the help. "I may not be in full possession of all my faculties, but I'm still aware enough to know that the first daughter didn't get a motorcar and chauffer and drive across the river to pay a condolence call on a man you haven't met." His smile was almost a smirk, as if he had a joke on us.

"This isn't my chauffer. This is Agent St. Clair of the Secret Service."

"The Secret Service. My goodness. What have I done to merit a visit from such distinguished visitors as President Roosevelt's daughter and the United States Secret Service?"

I realized then that it doesn't matter how far you fall; if you're born into one of the great families, you hold on to the same arrogant attitude forever. A small part of me admired him for it, but mostly I thought he was ridiculous. I was well on my way to actively disliking him.

"Very well, Mr. van Dijk. I don't know how your family ended up like this, and I don't care. But your sister is dead. And there are some questions about the manner in which she died." Then, maybe feeling she had been a little harsh, Alice calmed herself a bit and said, "Although I really am sorry for your sister's death. I understand you were close."

"We were. At least at one time. She thought I ought to sell myself to a nouveau riche wife, and I thought she shouldn't marry a man who wasn't going to be a proper husband. Yes, I know that much about Linde. But Delilah, despite her name, was a good girl. She was supposed to find a rich husband, and by God she did. Anyway, as you probably heard, we've come down in the world, and I was stuck having to get some sort of job, even though I was prepared for nothing. You'd normally find me pushing papers around a desk, but they let me stay home out of respect for my sister. Anyway, I have some better prospects and will be moving out of here soon." He blinked. "Did you say something about the way she died?"

"Yes. I don't know what they told you. But her death is being treated as suspicious. It's becoming clear she was murdered."

"Murdered? Who told you she was murdered? They said it was a 'sudden attack,' whatever that means. Who'd want to kill her? What are you getting at?" He was upset and angry but a little worried, too.

"I know things," she said with a tone like a schoolgirl taunting a classmate. If it was designed to irritate Van Dijk, it worked because he got up quickly. Too quickly, and I didn't like that, so I got up, too, and pushed him down into his chair again.

"What the hell—"

"Let's keep it civil," I said. Alice was looking smug.

"Don't you touch me again," he said, trying to sound menacing—and failing.

"Then don't move too suddenly."

He shook his head. "Tell me what makes you think my sister was murdered," he demanded of Alice.

"In a minute," said Alice, still in that superior tone of hers. "First, tell me why you're so upset. This isn't just about your sister dying. You'd be grief-stricken. But you're angry. Tell me why, and I'll tell you what I know."

He sighed. "It's about everything. It's about how we found ourselves, bad luck, failed investments, a father who drank. It wasn't supposed to be like this." He puffed on his cigarette. "Families like yours and mine, we used to run things. Now half the city seems to come from Ireland, from Italy, from God knows where. Coloreds coming up from the South. It's all different now. The city isn't what it was." He took another puff and fixed a look on Alice. "Your father made a big mistake inviting Booker T. Washington to dinner. He made a lot of people angry."

Right now, though, Van Dijk's problem was Alice's anger because she tolerated no disrespect toward the president.

"I didn't drive out to Queens to hear you criticize my father," she said, and her tone was ice cold. "He's a great man. And why do you care, anyway?"

"I'm a New Yorker, Miss Roosevelt, but my mother's people came from Georgia." I thought of the sergeant from Georgia I had flattened, and I'm sure Van Dijk's Southern relations had no better view of Sherman's march through Georgia than he had.

Alice was looking at him curiously now, as if seeing him for the first time. "Mr. St. Clair and I were accosted by some men who had a similar disregard for certain city residents." That took him by surprise, and I watched him try and fail to think of something to say several times.

"That leads me to wonder something else," said Alice. "Have you heard of a group called the XVII?"

His face turned red at that, and once again, he forgot himself. "Where the hell did you hear that name?" he shouted and made for Alice. I thought he was going to try to shake an answer out of her, but I was ready this time and grabbed him by his shirt.

"Don't make me do this again," I said, and I shoved him back down.

"Or what? Just what are you going to do next, Special Agent St. Clair? Shoot me?"

"Don't tempt me," I said. I glanced at Alice, who seemed astonished. Then she smiled.

"We got a little off the subject," she said. "You wanted to know about your sister. All I can tell you now is that the police believe she may have been murdered. And we also found out she was expecting a child. I don't think it was her husband's."

"For God's sake. Christ almighty."

"I'm not particularly religious, but I was hoping you'd have more to offer me than blasphemy," said Alice.

"I'm not even going to ask what makes you think her child wasn't her husband's. But I will say from what I know about my brother-in-law that you're probably right. And to answer your next question, I have no idea who the father is. That would've been a surprise for Linde. Everyone would know it wasn't his, but as her husband, he'd have to accept paternity."

"And as she was married, the real father couldn't possible claim the child as his own."

Van Dijk gave her a cool look. "Pretty sharp, Miss Roosevelt."

"Please. Take a guess about who it might be. It's important. It's about more than your sister." But he just shook his head.

"Very well. Let's get back to the other thing that made you angry. To the XVII."

He mastered himself but with a lot of effort. "Miss Roosevelt, I wouldn't throw that name around if I were you."

"And I wouldn't threaten me, if I were you," said Alice.

"What in God's name do you want from me?" he shouted, and he was angry, but again, I also saw fear, and I wondered why. He looked from one of us to the other, and he finally seemed to get some perspective. What started as gossip had become something a lot more. "What is this about? Why do you want to know all this?"

"You've heard of Lynley Brackton's death, even all the way out here, haven't you?" asked Alice.

"Of course. The rumor was that he was killed by a servant he had had an argument with, and the police were just poking around for proof."

"Do you believe those rumors?" asked Alice.

Van Dijk gave us a sour smile. "Brackton had a talent for making enemies wherever he went."

"So we've observed. But there may be more to it than that. First of all, your sister died from drinking Rutledge punch, just as Lynley Brackton did. She was speaking with Lynley Brackton and his wife Victoria right before he was killed. Mr. Linde, Mr. Brackton, and Simon Rutledge, the host, are members of a club called the XVII, which has been up to some unsavory activities, including—and especially—tracking me. This is looking worse and worse."

Van Dijk looked a little skeptical, but I saw a trembling in the fingers that held his cigarette.

"You know these people. You were certainly close with your sister, so you must've known Marcus Linde. I would find it hard to believe you don't know Brackton or Rutledge. You've been dancing around this, Mr. van Dijk. Let's have some answers."

But he didn't give her any. What he did was look quickly over our shoulders at the door. I hadn't heard anything, and it was a quiet street. He was definitely expecting someone, and I guessed he was trying to find an easy way to get rid of us before someone knocked on the door. That was the great thing about having a big house with servants. They could turn people away for you. Maybe he thought being quiet was his best strategy, but I could've told him that wouldn't work with Alice.

"What about any business relationships? Do you have any financial ties to your brother-in-law? Or to Brackton or Rutledge?"

That got his attention. He eyed her sharply and thought of the answer for a while before saying, "What an odd question. No. Would I be living here if I had ties to Brackton or if Linde were helping me out? Marcus never saw any reason to help his wife's brother." We heard the bitterness in his voice.

"But you said you were moving?"

"No thanks to any of them. A business deal came through—but never mind. What in God's name are you getting at? Who sent you here, and why do you even care? This is something the police should be handling." Yes, he was nervous. The why of it all was less important to him than the fact that we were there asking about things he didn't want to talk about.

Alice didn't respond to him. She was busy noticing things. "You're missing a ring on your right hand," she said. I looked, and there was a pale white band of skin on his ring finger. He seemed surprised but only for a moment.

"It was a family signet ring. I had to hock it to keep myself in this luxury." But he was shifty, and I saw him look at the door yet again.

"I think it may have been the ring of the XVII," she said.

"And I think he was expecting someone else from the way he keeps looking at the door," I added, looking at Alice.

"That makes perfect sense, Mr. St. Clair. He thought someone else was coming and had his ring on. He removed it quickly
when he saw was us. I bet he has it in his pocket. You're one of
the XVII, aren't you? Did you know about those men sent to
bother me when I was going about my business on Houston
Street? Show me that ring. Now."

CHAPTER 22

Van Dijk just put his head in his hands like someone who had run out of options. But like some card players I've known, he was planning to take it to the end.

"Mr. St. Clair, search him," said Alice. Normally, I would've stopped it there, but this guy was acting like a threat. Also, I definitely didn't like him. I stood.

"Come on, pal. Stand up and put your hands up. Work with me, and this won't take long."

"I'm still a Van Dijk. I'll see you in hell before I let some cowboy search me. You have no legal authority here. I'll call the police on both of you."

"Yeah, police," I said. "You really want to bet your word with a bunch of cops against the president's daughter and a Secret Service agent?"

He thought that one over, then sulkily reached into his pocket and pulled out a heavy ring just like the one we saw in Marcus Linde's bedroom dresser. He slammed it on the low table in front of us, and Alice picked it up.

"What is the XVII?" she asked. "And what does it have to do with me?"

"You will never tie me to anyone who may have accosted you, and there's no law against carrying a ring. I still don't know what the hell you want or what you're talking about. If you're done, I'd like you to leave my house."

But he was too late. I heard a motorcar engine on the quiet street. Van Dijk looked nervous again, and I knew we'd have company.

"Miss Alice, stand by the fireplace over there. I need you out of the way for a moment." She didn't like being ordered around, but she could see some excitement was coming, so she obeyed without comment. At least I wasn't asking her to leave the room.

I stood and took out my Colt. "Mr. van Dijk, get facedown on the floor behind this couch."

"You can't be serious."

"I'm really starting to hate asking you everything twice. The next time I have to ask you something twice, I'm going to shoot you."

"He'll do it," said Alice. "I think you should listen to him." With bad grace, he lay down flat on the floor, and before he knew what had happened, I had cuffed his hands behind his back. I could see he was about to protest again but then thought better of it.

"Don't say anything, and we'll be fine," I ordered. The motorcar stopped in front of the house. I peeked through a curtain and saw two men, much like the ones who had stalked us on Houston Street. Again, they weren't professionals. If these were the people Brackton had recruited from his warehouses to serve as the muscle of the XVII, they needed better training. They should've noted another car parked in front of the house and been more cautious. But they rang the doorbell, and I opened the door fast. Their eyes got big when they found themselves looking at the Colt.

"Hands up," I said, and with my free hand, I pulled them one by one into the house and pushed them face-first again the wall.

"You're not police," said the older of the pair, half startled, half angry. He was dressed in a suit that was in even worse shape than mine. The other didn't look much older than Alice and was dressed more like a workman. He seemed too surprised to talk.

"Secret Service. I'm federal. Now lean." When you really made someone lean with their hands up against a wall, you had them good because it would take them too long to regain their balance to come at you. I reached in their pockets and removed both their guns, then told both of them to lay down next to Van Dijk. He looked up, and it was clear from the way their eyes flashed at each other that they were all friends.

"Just shut up," said Van Dijk, and that told me everything. As bad as things were for him, he was the manager, and these guys were the help.

"My goodness!" said Alice. She stepped forward, and there was excitement and delight all over her face.

"You had a girl here?" asked Cheap Suit of Van Dijk. He seemed astonished.

"She's Alice Roosevelt, the president's daughter, you idiot. She was visiting. Now don't say anything."

"Mr. St. Clair, if you give me one of their revolvers, we can march them to the police together," offered Alice.

"For God's sake, don't give her a gun," said Cheap Suit, his voice full of panic. He was no doubt wondering what the president's daughter might do with one. I thought that was funny.

"Don't worry. She's such a bad shot she'll probably miss all of you and shoot me," I said.

"That's a disloyal remark," said Alice, and I realized I had to take charge before things got any stranger. Fortunately, Alice got back on track.

"But never mind all that. You're no doubt agents of the XVII, comrades of the men who assaulted me on Houston Street. There's a lot I don't know. But let's start with who you are, what your goals are, and most importantly, why are you interested in me? All I did was involve myself in the death of one of your members,

Lynley Brackton, and the death of the wife of another, Delilah Linde."

"Miss Roosevelt," said Van Dijk with great patience. "Understand this. I haven't the vaguest idea of why anyone attacked you. These two men are associates of mine who have done nothing illegal. I have done nothing illegal. And yet I'm being held cuffed, at gunpoint, by a crazy cowboy. I have nothing more to say, except to ask how long you're planning to hold us here."

"Oh, we have a lot to discuss, Mr. van Dijk. I'm assuming these idiots don't have anything useful to say. Mr. St. Clair, could you get rid of them?"

"You have a coal cellar here?" I asked

"In the back," said Van Dijk.

"All right, guys, get up slowly and head out the front door." I marched them around the back and had them open the metal doors that led to the cellar.

"How long are you going to keep us here?" grumbled one.

"That depends on your boss. Will he tell us what we need to know in half an hour, or will it take half the night?" They walked down the stairs, and I slammed the door shut, turning the latch to keep them there. When I was back inside, I found Alice was living up to the Roosevelt policy of never being idle. She had sat down at a small desk and was going through various papers.

"Mr. St. Clair," complained Van Dijk, still cuffed on the floor. "If you are a Secret Service agent, you know full well she can't go through my papers without a warrant. In fact, this whole thing is illegal. Forcible detention, kidnapping—"

"Stop fussing. All I see here are bills from your tailor and wine merchant. No wonder you're stuck here in Queens if you spend so much on cases of Bordeaux. I don't see anything here about the XVII, however."

"That's because there's nothing to see," said Van Dijk, clenching his teeth. "It's a club. We get together and drink too much and complain about the government. That's it."

"The government? You complain about my father?" He wasn't making a good case for himself.

"No, the city government."

"I don't like that, either. Mayor Low and Manhattan District Attorney Jerome are both Republicans," said Alice. I thought Van Dijk was going to cry.

"How about this? I'll uncuff you and let you sit on the couch," I said. "No reason we can't be comfortable while we talk. You have any beer here? We'll see how fast we can get through this. I told your friends that their residency in the cellar is based on how quickly you tell us what we need to know, so if this takes us into the night, it'll be your fault."

"That sounds good," said Alice. She marched into the kitchen and found some beer and glasses. I uncuffed Van Dijk. He gave me a wounded look and rubbed his wrists while making himself comfortable on the couch. We each had something to drink.

"The XVII," said Alice. "There have been two murders connected to them, and a good friend of ours is going to be arrested and hanged if we don't figure it out. And if you don't satisfy my curiosity, I will truly have your men in the cellar marched to a police station where they will implicate you and the other men who were harassing me in about an hour, and then you'll follow them to jail. So please tell us who you are and what you're up to. First of all, where does that name come from? The number of members?"

He thought that over, weighed his options, and then began to talk.

"No. It's a reference to the seventeenth century. To belong, your family has to have been here at least that long."

My grandmother was a Cheyenne Indian, so maybe I'd qualify, but I don't think that's what they had in mind.

"What is your goal? We've heard you were harassing residents in some of the poorer neighborhoods—immigrants and Negroes. Why?"

"Miss Roosevelt, we're just about the public good. Even though you're young, it can't have escaped your notice how the city has changed in recent years, with immigrants pouring in from a score of countries. They bring their food, their languages, their religion. New York has been the largest and most powerful city in this country since the revolution. It is one of the most important cities in the world. We don't want to see it destroyed, diluted until it is not recognizable, until it is no longer powerful. That's all."

"And you think you're going to fix this problem by harassing the impoverished families who live in those neighborhoods?"

"Not harass—merely provide a level of discipline and security the police and city government are not in a position to impose."

Alice leaned back and considered that. I don't think she believed what he said. Heck, I don't think *he* believed what he said, and he finished his beer and looked down at his feet.

"I notice that you don't mind when those same immigrants work cheaply in the manufacturing business. Dear God, I come from as wealthy and privileged position as any man in the XVII, but at least I'm not a hypocrite."

"Miss Roosevelt—"

"Never mind," she said, waving her hand. "If we get into a political discussion, we'll be here into the night, and I have other things to do. So you sent thugs into poor neighborhoods to frighten poor people—"

"It wasn't my idea. That's not what we were supposed to be about. Our goal was to be more of a private police force to augment what city authorities offered. It was Brackton who started taking it in new and violent directions. The others thought he had gone too far, as well. There was talk of trying to rein him in."

"It sounds to me that he had become . . . unreliable."

Van Dijk nodded sadly and bent his head. "That's well put."

Alice gave me a quick look and a smile, and I winked at her.

"You mentioned others. Who else is in the XVII? I know Marcus Linde and Simon Rutledge are. Is there a list?"

"I'm not in a leadership position. I don't know if there is a list or who would have it. Brackton recruited me to help him with the 'ward work,' as we called it."

"And that's your new job, isn't it? You're taking over from Brackton as the director of this 'ward work,' aren't you? You're getting money from the leadership of the XVII, which is why you can afford to leave here. Those two men now locked in your coal cellar are from Brackton's businesses but will now be under your authority."

"Miss Roosevelt, I am not Brackton. We are going to be returning to our original mission. We will be curbing Mr. Brackton's excesses. You misunderstand me."

"I doubt it," she said coldly. "But I am going to offer you some advice, which you badly need, because I don't believe you're much smarter than the two apes locked in your cellar. There is a whole city police force that doesn't want your help. A police force full of immigrants and the sons of immigrants. But that's not your worst problem. Soon, you'll be getting in the way of the gangs— the Irish, the Italians, the Chinese, the Jews, the Negroes. The first time your men cross any of them, they'll be found floating in the Hudson."

Van Dijk was looking worse and worse. Alice had made it clear that not only was he completely lacking any sense of Christian morality, he was incompetent, as well. It was a bad combination.

"So we've established the reign of terror the XVII was visiting on the slum neighborhoods. Now let's look at some other people. What about the Roth family? What threat did they pose to the XVII?"

"That was different. The Roth family threatened us in other ways. You may not be aware of this, Miss Roosevelt, but Jews are becoming increasingly influential in the finances of this city, upending the old Dutch and English families. Young Abraham, it was said, was expanding internationally, involving foreigners."

He took on a new tone, less embarrassed and more lecturing, explaining to this little girl how business was done in the city. It was the wrong idea. Alice hated been lectured by anyone, and especially by Miles van Dijk.

"And you were going to fix this by sending a few men to threaten him? The Roths aren't poor immigrants who can be bullied. What is wrong with you?"

Van Dijk shook his head. "Miss Roosevelt, it's not just a couple of men. The XVII is larger than that, made up of powerful men from the best families. I don't think you realize who you're dealing with here."

"Yes, she does," I added. "That's your problem, sir. She knows exactly who she's dealing with."

Alice giggled. "Nicely said, Mr. St. Clair." She turned to Mr. van Dijk. "People keep underestimating both of us. As I said, we'll discuss economics and politics another time. For now, let's talk about the death of Mr. Brackton."

"Why would we want to kill him? He was one of us. But plenty of other people wanted to."

"I'm sure." She paused as I watched her think. "Would you be surprised to learn that it wasn't Mr. Brackton's glass that was poisoned, but Mrs. Brackton's? She handed it to him at the last moment. She was supposed to be killed, not him. There were just three of them there. I thought the murderer might be your sister until she was killed herself. One woman was murdered, and another was supposed to be murdered. Both of them were married to men of the XVII. Now, tell me what that was about."

Van Dijk was reaching his end. He was in an especially unfortunate position, stupid enough to get himself involved in something he couldn't understand and couldn't control, and yet smart enough to realize it.

Alice could read him. She was only eighteen, but Roosevelts were politicians, and she could see what was going through his mind.

"Mr. van Dijk," she said, and she was quieter now, almost gentle. "The only way this ends well is if you trust us. Two people are dead."

"The police will find someone," he offered lamely.

"No, they won't. Because I won't let them. Why did someone want Mrs. Brackton dead? Why did someone want your sister dead? I know you cared for Delilah."

He pushed his hand through his hair. "Delilah was a sweet girl, and she was a good girl. She did what she felt was right to live her life. If she was with child because her marriage was less than . . . complete, I don't know anything about that. She was no longer the girl who I once knew. Our lives have been somewhat separate for some years now, and apparently, I didn't realize how separate. We do what we feel we must, Miss Roosevelt, and per-haps I misunderstood her. Or her husband."

I almost felt sorry for him.

"I accept that," said Alice. "But what about Mrs. Brackton? If you knew Lynley, you must've known Victoria."

"Somewhat," he said with a little hesitancy. "Not very bright, from my limited discussions with her. She tended to fade into the background. Absolutely devoted to Lynley, willing to do any-thing to make his life comfortable. One almost felt at times that she was more like his dog than his wife."

"What a delightful metaphor," said Alice, her voice full of chill.

"You asked me about her, so I told you honestly. If you don't like it, don't ask."

"Fair enough. But see if you can express yourself with a little less vulgarity." That was rich, coming from Alice. "But you can think of no reason why the wives of two prominent members of the XVII were targeted, the same way, so close together?"

"You're sure it wasn't a mistake?"

"Yes. Someone knew your sister would drink the punch. And no one could've known that at the last minute, Victoria would give her glass to her husband. Fortunately, she's been warned to be careful now."

"It must be a lunatic then. I don't see anything here that connects the XVII with those deaths. Many prominent men belong to this group. That certain people—like you and the Roth family—were harassed is unfortunate. I am sorry Lynley saw that as an appropriate response to what is just a political disagreement. I realize you are upset and have me at a certain disadvantage—both of you—and so I have answered your questions. But I will remind you again that you are keeping me against my will and have locked up two men in my cellar."

Unfortunately, he had a point, and Alice saw it, too. But she did have a parting shot. "Very well. But this isn't the end. You are wrong—there is a connection between those deaths and the XVII. Mr. St. Clair, it's time to leave."

"We have a little housekeeping first," I said. I emptied the revolvers and pocketed the cartridges while Alice looked on.

"Can I have one of them?" asked Alice.

"That's theft!" said Van Dijk.

"Oh, do be quiet. Mr. St. Clair?"

"No. But you can toss them out back where the men can find them," I said. She seemed a little huffy I wouldn't give her a loaded gun but did as she was told and came back a few moments later.

"Very well," Alice said to Van Dijk. "We're leaving now. You can let the men out of your cellar when we're gone, and they can find their revolvers in the grass. Just stay out of my way as we continue our investigations, and we will keep your cooperation in mind later."

It should've been funny, this girl giving a grown man a

dressing down like she was a tough old city cop, but watching the look on Alice's face, it wasn't funny at all. Mr. van Dijk certainly wasn't laughing.

I said a good day, and Alice and I left the house. I paused by the thugs' motorcar, then took out my jackknife and slashed one of their tires.

"Why, Mr. St. Clair, what a clever idea!"

I cranked up our motorcar, and we headed back to Manhattan.

"That was entertaining," said Alice.

"Glad I could oblige," I said. "Of course, you do know I have to report this to Mr. Harris at Secret Service headquarters."

"Report what? Nothing happened. Nothing important, anyway."

"Miss Alice, there's a secret group of armed men out for us. Now the first two—well, they could've just been a couple of average toughs. But we seem to have a conspiracy here, and it's more than one man can handle."

"You can't do that, Mr. St. Clair. If they think something serious is up, we'll get sent back to Washington and miss all the fun."

"I'm paid to protect you, not amuse you."

"But we're the only ones who can solve this! What if they decide to arrest Peter again? Or someone else who's innocent?"

I sighed. "Miss Alice, I have my orders—"

"Ha! Don't forget that I know that you disobeyed orders in Cuba to save the life of your captain. My father didn't get the Medal of Honor, which he richly deserved, because he complained about the War Office's incompetence in sending back sick and wounded men. So don't talk to me about orders and responsibilities. We have higher responsibilities."

We drove in silence for a while. "Oh, hell," I finally said.

Alice giggled. "I knew you'd see it my way," she said. "You still have responsibilities. They're just new responsibilities."

"What about my orders?" I asked. Alice grabbed my free arm and gave it a squeeze.

"You still have orders. And I'm giving them." She giggled again. "Here's my first order. We're going to pay another visit to Miss Meadows."

CHAPTER 23

"Now you're really playing with fire, Miss Alice," I said as I drove back to the *Herald* building. "You're a smart girl, I'll give you that—"

"Thank you," she said, looking carefully at me to see what was coming next.

"But Miss Meadows is a pretty sharp girl, too. She's lived by her wits, and just look at what she did to me. You've won't be able to pull a fast one on her like you've done with others. Her loyalty is to the *Herald*, and she wants to use you to get the story of her life. You need to be careful."

I saw a bunch of emotions roll over Alice's face. "First of all, she didn't embarrass me. She embarrassed you, and that's why you're being silly about this. And nothing she said indicated she's smarter than I am. We're simply trading favors and information, not 'using' each other. You're being silly because you're infatuated with her, that's all. Personally, I think you could do better."

"You do, Miss Alice? I'm going to try to consider whether or not that's a compliment."

"Forget your romantic life for a moment. Let's talk some more about Delilah Linde. Who was she? If she had an affair, could it have been with Lynley Brackton?"

"That's a possibility. It would explain why she was near him at the punch table. Also, you heard what your aunt said. He was charming on the surface. For her, that may have been enough. That's all she wanted. She may have not been the smartest girl in the world, and whatever his other good points, Marcus Linde wasn't the kind of man who could make a young woman like Delilah happy. She got what she was missing from Brackton. And—just maybe—she wanted a child, even if the child wasn't her husband's."

"Mr. St. Clair, you are now the expert in what keeps young women happy?"

"Yes, Miss Alice," I said, dead serious. "Yes, I am."

She crossed her arms and sulked until we reached Herald Square.

There was a different office boy on duty when we walked in, but Alice just said, "Miss Roosevelt and escort to see Miss Meadows" and strode right by him before he could even respond.

The advantage was to Alice, as she really did catch Felicia Meadows by surprise as she was scribbling away at her desk.

"It's Miss Roosevelt . . . and the sheriff. If you're here about complaints, I can point you in the direction of my editor, but he isn't going to care."

"I'm not here to complain," said Alice and took a seat.

"What about you, Cowboy, are you here to complain?"

"His name, again, is Mr. St. Clair, and he doesn't like being called 'Cowboy,'" said Alice. Miss Meadows raised an eyebrow. "Anyway, we're rather busy, and I imagine you are, too. So I'll get down to business. The information you gave me was accurate and useful. Thank you."

"You're welcome," said Miss Meadows, looking a little surprised. "You came down here just to say thanks?"

"No. Not just. I want even more. I realize I need a lot more information, and you seem to have it. It occurred to me that you probably know even more, and I'm willing to pay for it in coin I know you will appreciate."

Miss Meadows tapped her pen on her desk for a few moments before speaking. "You may have overestimated me. I have bits and pieces here, gossip. I don't keep dossiers on everyone in Society. Not formally. Anyway, I'd have thought for the most part you had your own sources. Who's more connected in New York Society than the president's daughter?"

Alice looked a little unsure of herself for a moment, which didn't happen often. She took a deep breath. "In Society, murder shuts all doors. If this were just about cheating spouses or fortunes lost to gambling, I might be able to get what I need. But this is murder, and Society isn't going to gossip. Also . . ." She hesitated. "I'm still considered very young. Because of my age and my position as the president's daughter, I'm not well placed to hear a lot. I will be over time but not yet."

Miss Meadows leaned back and grinned. "I bet you will. Hell, I bet you'll get your own column here someday."

Alice hadn't liked admitting there was something she couldn't do and was pleased Miss Meadows responded well.

"Thank you. There are some people whose relationships are unclear to me. Maybe you have heard things about what they've been doing recently, something one of your sources heard. There's some overlap here with what I asked you already. First, I want to know about Abraham Roth—"

"Oh, he's talked about enough," said Miss Meadows. "Son of Reuben Roth, who practically runs Wall Street. The son is sharp, too, and handsome in a sort of . . . foreign way. Jewish, you know, or he'd be marrying into one of the best families. But they never marry outside their faith."

"Do the Roths have any financial dealings with the other great families? I'm thinking of other families at the Rutledge party, such as the Rutledges themselves, the Lindes, or Delilah's family, the Van Dijks?"

Miss Meadows pursed those lovely lips. She wrote down the names and then traced her pen along her jawline as she considered.

"Miss Roosevelt, I don't know if you realize what you're asking. I cover Society news. Business is another department, and no women work there." She sounded a little bitter about that, and I didn't blame her. I knew enough about newspapers to understand that even though there were women here and there, it really was a man's business. "I hardly know anything about Wall Street, anyway."

"But what about Nellie Bly? She was a woman journalist."

"Oh, Nellie Bly!" said Miss Meadows. Even I had heard about her, a woman journalist who wrote all kinds of stories and set a record traveling around the world. "She was something, but Miss Roosevelt, that's not the kind of thing I do. Although I suppose . . ." She wandered off for a moment, then those eyes became shrewd. "You said you'd pay me in coin that I could use. What would that be?"

Alice suddenly looked proud of herself, which made me nervous. She got that look when she was about to pull off something big.

"You wanted to know what was going on at the Gadsden ball. What if I could do something better? What if I could get you in?"

"Miss Roosevelt, even you couldn't convince a Society hostess to let a reporter wander around at a big event with her guests."

"But we wouldn't tell anyone. Have you been to Boston? You'll be a distant cousin from Boston. No one knows who you are by sight, so you can just use an assumed name."

My first thought was the potential downside for me if Mrs. Cowles found out about this and it blew up in our faces. Could I pretend I hadn't known anything about it?

"I'll need an escort," said Miss Meadows. Her eyes slid over to me. "Why not Mr. St. Clair here, since he's in on it, anyway?"

"Mr. St. Clair is far too busy with his security responsibilities," Alice shot back before I could even think of a good response. "You need someone from Society, of course. I'll set you up with

Stephen Lesseps, who took me to the Rutledge ball. I can't go with him again, or people will start talking. He's a good dancer and not very bright, so he won't question you, and he'll be glad to do a favor for me."

"I could get a lot of information from that, if they thought I was one of their own. This could be very big for me." She checked her watch. "I'll need to get started now because I imagine you need this information quickly. I'm going to have to pay back some of the men I'll be getting any information out of . . ."

"Excellent. It's a deal," said Alice, and the two women shook on it.

"Assuming you can get what you need tonight, you can join me at breakfast at eight tomorrow at the Caledonia. I'm starting a new tradition of breakfast meetings."

"Breakfast at the Caledonia? That sounds inviting. I'll gather what I can and meet you tomorrow."

"Very good. We have a talented cook and serve the best coffee. Come, Mr. St. Clair, let's give Miss Meadows time to do her work and gather her team. Meanwhile, we can start making notes for our next tasks." She was out of the office in the blink of an eye, before anyone could make any objections.

With considerably less enthusiasm, I stood and prepared to follow her. My mind was still trying to take in the deal Alice had made, smuggling a reporter into one of the biggest Society events of the year in exchange for secrets about some of those same people. To say nothing of inviting that same reporter to the household of the president's sister. What could this mean for Alice if it worked, and what could it mean for me if it failed?

It was clear what it could do for Miss Meadows. She'd be playing with the big boys.

"You seem a bit disturbed by this, Mr. St. Clair," said Miss Meadows, and a smile played across those lips. "Still annoyed about my write-up about you?"

"Nah. That was kind of flattering. I think the other Secret

Service agents were jealous they didn't get a write-up in the *Herald*. No, I'm thinking of how this might play out," I said.

"For you? What about for me? I have my honor with the rest of my newsroom on the line. I could lose my job."

"Heck, miss. You'd get a new job. If this thing falls apart on my watch, Alice's aunt, Mrs. Cowles, will have me shot."

"Have some faith. I'll buy you a drink when it's all done."

Alice was waiting for me and tapping her foot in the hallway.

"Come on," she said. "You can flirt with Miss Meadows on your own time. I want to get back in time to call Stephen Lesseps and let him know who he'll be taking to the Gadsden ball."

"I hope you know what you're doing, Miss Alice," I said.

"Your faith in me and my abilities is underwhelming," she said.

★ ★ ★

There wasn't much else on for the rest of the day, but it had been busy enough. Some local politicians were coming around, and Mrs. Cowles was expecting Alice to be a good girl and talk nicely to them and their wives.

"What are you up to this evening?" asked Alice.

"There should be a card game in the basement," I said. "Beer and tobacco."

"William T. Jerome, the Manhattan district attorney, will be coming to dinner." Alice sighed. "I don't suppose Aunt Anna will allow me to drink and smoke in front of him."

We drove back to the Caledonia, and Mrs. Cowles greeted us at the door. "Good, right on time. I want to go over the guest list with you tonight, to discuss topics you might want to bring up with our guests and"—her voice came down heavy—"topics you might want to avoid."

"Of course. I know the Brackton–Linde murders are off the table, and I'll be a good girl. Speaking of that, I did, of course, pay a call on Marcus Linde."

My first reaction was that Mrs. Cowles wasn't buying that, but Alice didn't look furtive. She met her aunt's gaze right back. "Naturally, as I am a member of a leading family, it would've been very rude if I did not call on such a prominent citizen as Mr. Linde. Did you know that he was on the committee that appointed Father police commissioner? Indeed, my visit was more than a social kindness; it was an official duty."

I thought I deserved some kind of prize for not laughing.

"Is this newfound devotion to duty and comforting the bereaved applicable only in cases of murder?" asked Mrs. Cowles. "I recall having to bully you into attending the funeral of the mother of a congressman in Washington last month."

"She was ninety-two. It was hardly as tragic or unexpected as in these cases. Anyway, the point is that I am doing what I'm supposed to do and meeting with the leading families of New York." She paused, and I could see she was planning the next sentence carefully. "Unfortunately, I don't know the family very well. Can you tell me anything about them?" She did her best to sound casual. Mrs. Cowles looked at her.

"I suppose that's a reasonable question. I don't know Marcus Linde very well. He doesn't like to socialize, so one doesn't see him at the major events. He's very wealthy, cultivates rare books, or maybe it was rare coins. Some sort of expensive, solitary hobby, I believe. His first wife died abroad." I bet Mrs. Cowles knew that marriage had really ended in divorce but didn't want to discuss that with Alice, and I hoped Alice would go on pretending she didn't know, or it would lead to uncomfortable questions.

"Yes, I heard that, too. What about Mrs. Linde, that is, the second wife, who just died? She was a Van Dijk."

"Yes. A rather sad family, plenty of trouble, mostly brought on themselves via bad decisions, drunkenness, and gambling. Your father was very upset and offered help, but you can't help people who refuse to see they have a problem." Mrs. Cowles shook her head. "I knew Mrs. van Dijk, Delilah and Miles's mother. The children took after their parents. Miles was not strong, not morally strong. Your father said some men rise to adversity, and some are diminished. Miles was the latter, I'm afraid. Like his father. I don't know what he's doing now." We did, of course, and Mrs. Cowles was right—he hadn't risen to it.

"What about Delilah Linde, née van Dijk?" Alice was pushing it too far.

"I believe we're moving beyond family background and wandering into more idle curiosity—but I think I will indulge you," said Mrs. Cowles. "There is a lesson there for you. If Miles was like his father, Delilah was like her mother. Beautiful and sweet, but . . . she wanted more. This is what I want you to know, Alice. She got a certain life by marrying Marcus Linde, a life of financial comfort and position, which she had lost. But to marry a man like Marcus Linde who is . . . older and perhaps not an ideal choice for a young bride—that requires sacrifice. And I'm not sure, from what I have heard, that Delilah realized that."

Little went on in Society that Mrs. Cowles didn't know, and I wondered if she knew about Delilah's condition. Or at the very least, had anticipated it.

Alice nodded. "I suppose Miles could've married a social-climbing nouveau riche heiress, with all that would entail."

"That's a very cynical observation for an eighteen-year-old girl," said Mrs. Cowles. "But apparently, he didn't want to go that route."

And from what I saw, he wasn't willing to accept the sacrifices required of his choice, either, throwing in his lot with Brackton and his crew.

"So what lesson is there for me?" asked Alice, a little challengingly.

"That no matter what advantages you are born with, you have to make choices and accept the sacrifices that come with those choices. You can't have everything, and by trying, you end up with nothing."

Alice glanced at me, and I know she was thinking about both Delilah and Miles. Was Delilah's death related to her pregnancy, to choices she didn't want to make? Miles's refusal to accept choices led him to the XVII, and now he was one step away from prison.

Alice gave me a mischievous smile and turned back to her aunt. "Your point is well taken. Do you think Mr. St. Clair has learned it, as well?"

Mrs. Cowles looked at me and then laughed. "Oh, dear me, Alice. Mr. St. Clair has had a hard life. I imagine he learned about trade-offs and sacrifices by the time he was ten. Considering that most men in our set wait until their thirties to learn that—if they ever do—that's impressive." Alice looked at me curiously and smiled.

"Thank you, ma'am," I said.

"But that's enough for now. It's time for you to get dressed. Mr. St. Clair, we'll be staying in, so you'll have the rest of the day off. Right now, I have a few arrangements to check," she said and swept out of the room.

"Well," said Alice when we were alone. "That was interesting. And we got more than I thought we would. Delilah Linde wouldn't accept the limits of her life. Neither would Miles. I wonder . . ."

"You wonder what, Miss Alice?"

She grinned at me. "I wonder exactly what other men haven't learned at thirty that you learned at ten. We shall see. Good night, and I'll see you at breakfast."

I wished her a good evening and headed downstairs. Often, I'd be able to wheedle a dinner out of Dulcie, but with important people coming, she'd be even more bad-tempered than usual, and I had had enough for one day. I picked up a meat pie from a little place under the El and stopped by the doorman on my way back in.

That talk about the Lindes was interesting, but I had other

things I wanted to mull over. The doorman read the *Herald*, and I knew he kept a pile of back issues in the package room to give to any porters or servants who had to wrap something up. I took a few copies and headed back to my half basement room.

While I ate, I read some of Felicia Meadows's columns. I'm not a good judge of journalism, but there was no denying she had a way with words, and I could see why the *Herald* valued her. When I finished, I gave her some further thought. Then I checked my wallet to make sure I had plenty of money, filled up my flask with bourbon, and headed to my card game.

CHAPTER 24

The next morning, I joined Alice at the usual time for a breakfast of pancakes and bacon.

"Did you have a good evening?" I asked.

"Yes, thank you. I think I'm properly coming along as a political hostess. Many of the guests seem to appreciate my humor. I'm not sure Aunt Anna does, but I think the general consensus was that I was amusing. How'd the card game go?"

"Not much amusing conversation, as you'd say, but I came out ahead, so nothing to complain about. Mrs. Cowles still here?"

"Yes, she has some sort of breakfast meeting, which I managed to wriggle out of. You're worried that Miss Meadows will come before Aunt Anna leaves. It may be a little tricky, but I have the matter well in hand, Mr. St. Clair. There's a pretty good chance my aunt will walk right by. Meanwhile, I left word with the doorman that Miss Meadows was expected and could be sent straight up."

"And if Mrs. Cowles does come around and see us?"

"If, if, if . . . you have an unpleasant habit of always looking at the worst possible outcome of any event."

Before I had a chance to think of a suitable reply to that, the doorbell rang.

"That'll be Miss Meadows." I just shook my head and went with the maid to answer the door.

"Miss Meadows, you're looking well this morning," I said. Indeed, she was looking pleased with herself, and maybe it was my imagination, but her hair was done up nicer than usual. Her eyes were especially bright, and there was a liveliness to her step as she entered the apartment. She looked around with curiosity at the spacious entranceway and expensive decorations. I showed her into the breakfast room.

Alice stood to greet her. "You look like a woman bearing a lot of information."

"Yes, Miss Roosevelt, I am. I think you'll be very impressed."

"Tell me all! But first, please, have a seat, and help yourself to coffee and breakfast. Our cook Dulcie excels at breakfast." Miss Meadows appeared delighted with the bounty. She struck me as the kind of girl who just took something on the run on her way to the office.

After helping herself to eggs and bacon, Miss Meadows pulled a notebook out of her bag. "Miss Roosevelt, my colleagues and I have found out quite a bit. Understand, these are things we know but can't necessarily prove, quiet words in our ears, background talk. So we can't publish anything yet because of libel laws, like we discussed earlier. But we can at least hold the information and maybe use it."

Miss Meadows had a generous-sized bag with her and pulled out a notebook. "First, I'm going to talk about Wall Street," started Miss Meadows, consulting her notebook. "As our finance editor says, the business of New York has always been business, and Reuben Roth, that is, the father of your friend Abraham Roth, has been very busy with some big deal in recent months, but no one knows exactly what." Alice looked disappointed at that, but Miss Meadows raised a hand to forestall any protests. "But there's more of interest here. Working with the finance editor, I found out something that normally would not be that remarkable, except for the context. I think Reuben Roth has something going on with Simon Rutledge. And to hide it, instead of visiting each other or using their usual subordinates, they've been using their children."

"Philadelphia? Philly Rutledge has been a business courier for her father?"

"It would seem so," said Miss Meadows.

Alice glanced at me, and I knew what she was thinking: this was the secret that Cathleen O'Neill was keeping for Philly, even as Philly was keeping the secret of Cathleen's engagement.

"I can understand Abraham," said Alice. "He's not formally in the family business but rather has his own related business. He was saying how after college his father sent him to wander around Europe for a few months, and when he returned, his father set him up importing antiques and other fine goods from the Continent. Maybe his father is involving him in the family business quietly. But Philly?"

"You don't think she's sharp enough?" asked Miss Meadows. "I don't believe it's usual to involve a young woman like that in something like this. So this must be very big."

"Philly is a bright girl. And I know as her father's only child, he wants her to know the leading officers of the family firm — and vice versa. But I wouldn't have thought Simon Rutledge would involve his daughter in such details. Or that she would be bold enough. What makes you think this? How can you be sure?"

"Think about that, Miss Roosevelt. She's a young lady of Society. People are interested in the other ladies she meets, the merchants she patronizes. And that's what connects her to her father's business. It seems that every Thursday, Simon Rutledge is driven to the Wall Street offices of the family firm, and he reviews the books and chairs meetings. As you said, Philadelphia typically goes with him but then is sent home in the family car after lunch, although she's been seen shopping in the better stores before going home. But on two occasions at least, she was seen leaving the family motorcar—and entering Abraham's offices."

"Very good," said Alice, spearing some bacon in delight. "You've hit a rich vein there. Presumably, Simon Rutledge meets with other members of his firm, reaches some sort of decision, and passes information through Philly to the Roths. And Abraham Roth was at her debutante ball. The Roths have been threatened, as have I. I'm seeing the connections."

"Then you'll love this next bit," said Miss Meadows, turning a page in the notebook. "Another one of my colleagues had some insights into the darker parts of Society life."

"Ooh, this is going to be good," said Alice with more enthusiasm than a young lady should have for a topic like that.

"I can offer you something courtesy of an easily bribed bank teller—and we shouldn't delve too deeply into the details there. A colleague was following the fall of the Van Dijks and any connections to Marcus Linde, who saved Delilah. It seems that Miles van Dijk suddenly had some money again."

"We gathered," said Alice. "We went to visit him, and he said he had a new job. A job with a certain . . . organization."

"Indeed? You may know some things even the *Herald* staff doesn't know about. Anyway, you may be right, but that's not where the money came from. At least not all of it."

"Really? His brother-in-law was helping him out after all?" Alice asked.

"No. A check was sent to him by Simon Rutledge. The day after the death of Lynley Brackton."

"That sounds like a bribe," said Alice.

"That's what we thought. And the timing is very suspicious. It must relate to the murder."

"I agree," said Alice. "This is fascinating. It means that there is some kind of connection, so close after the murder. Everything is tying together."

"And we have one more thing for you," said Miss Meadows, flipping another page in her notebook. "There's still some Society secrets we have to reveal. One young reporter knows some clerks, and from time to time, I get some information from them. And I don't know if it relates to anything else, or if it's just men being men." At that, Miss Meadows gave her a thin smile. "But it seems Abraham Roth has a girl. You can't hide everything—all you need is one loose-lipped clerk bragging one night after one drink too many with his friends. It seems that money coming out of Abraham Roth's import-export business has been used to purchase a townhouse. The perfect hideaway for a mistress."

Miss Meadows looked closely at Alice as she helped herself to more coffee. I think she was wondering if that would upset or embarrass Alice, but if it did, neither of us saw any sign of it. "I don't know who it is, but that's what men do when they have a lot of money and want to quietly set up a lady friend. Anyway, I wrote out the address for you." She pulled a slip of paper out of the notebook and handed it to Alice. I looked over her shoulder—it was an address on a quiet West Side street.

"Really? I thought better of him," said Alice. "How do you know it's Abraham and not his father?"

"It could be," said Miss Meadows. "You never can tell. But why run payments for a mistress through a clerk who works for the son's end of the business? Why risk your son finding out? He could've done it through his own accounts. It must be Abraham, not Reuben."

Alice looked at me as if this were my doing.

"It's not my fault. I can't afford to keep a girl like that," I said.

"Otherwise, you would?" asked Miss Meadows.

"Mr. St. Clair is constant. Mostly," said Alice, and she eyed me again. "Anyway, that does bring us to another topic, and now that I've gotten your information, I'd like your insights on information I already have. Again, you have to sit on this until the whole story is out."

"Of course," said Miss Meadows, and her eyes were shining. I could tell she was thinking that this arrangement was going to be even better than she thought.

"It seems the late Mrs. Linde was carrying a child. And I'm betting Lynley Brackton was the father." She watched me and Miss Meadows for our reaction. "Mrs. Brackton has clearly always been obedient. And I'm betting Delilah Linde was, too, the young wife married to the much older man who was used to having his way."

"That is . . . something," said Miss Meadows. Alice was pleased she had surprised the older woman. "But can you prove it?"

"Well, no. Not yet. But it makes sense from what we know about all of them. Mr. St. Clair, will you give me odds that he was the father of her child?"

I tried to think of why that could be wrong, but it made a lot of sense. "I won't take your bet, Miss Alice. It explains why Mrs. Linde was sticking with Brackton at the party."

"Yes. Now both of you think on this: let's assume that Marcus Linde knows for an absolute fact he can't be the father. He knows there will be talk, and he's a proud man. Let's say he knew his wife was having another man's child. He loved her—in his way. But she betrayed him. So I could see he'd want to kill Brackton and his wife, but why Victoria? And he wasn't even at the Rutledge party. It would've been impossible for him to make an arrangement like that."

"He could've hired someone," I said. When you had Linde money, you could hire anyone to do anything.

"But it's too bizarre," said Miss Meadows, who seemed just as excited as Alice at this new line of inquiry. "Even if he did that, he'd open himself up to blackmail from whomever he hired.

And why hire someone to do it at a party with so many possible witnesses?"

"But it's possible he just didn't care if his wife was with child," I said. "It's possible he might've wanted a child, even if it wasn't his in the full sense. Maybe he didn't care about Society talk. He apparently didn't get out much, anyway."

Alice gave that some thought. "You may be right, Mr. St. Clair. It's so hard, people with their odd motives and passions."

The thing of it was, we couldn't get away from Victoria's story. She was very clear that she was the target. The shadow of the XVII was over all of this, too.

"I don't know how all this fits in, but it may. There are a lot of pieces here, a lot of secrets, and a lot of things we can follow up on. We have to think about how to best approach Simon Rutledge and Miles van Dijk about the money changing hands right after the murder . . ." She forgot about us for a moment as she thought.

"Follow up on what, exactly?" asked Miss Meadows. "You told me about Mrs. Linde and Brackton, but there's even more here? You've trusted me thus far. I can really move ahead if I can bring a big story in. What's this all about?"

She looked so hopeful; that sharp look fell away for a few moments, and she seemed very young.

"Of course," said Alice. "That seems fair. Mr. St. Clair and I have come to the conclusion that Mr. Brackton's death, and then Mrs. Linde's death, were murders somehow involved with a group called the XVII. There will be a big story; I can promise you that. I will give you the full details. But—" Alice leaned over the table. "If I see one thing in the paper about this before we're ready . . ." She didn't finish the threat. Her look said it all. Miss Meadows recovered herself and gave Alice a cool look back. She extended her hand. "Once again, Miss Roosevelt, on behalf of myself and the colleagues, I'm going to have to work with on this, we have a deal."

The breakfast meeting was winding down. I thought we might actually get Miss Meadows out of the apartment before Mrs. Cowles came by, but I congratulated myself too soon. We heard her brisk steps in the hall, and then she entered the dining room.

CHAPTER 25

Miss Meadows and I stood. I wasn't sure that Miss Meadows knew who this was, but Mrs. Cowles had that look about her that made you take her seriously.

As usual, Alice was up to the task. I think she had learned at a young age that when you looked surprised, it only made you seem guilty of something. Business as usual was your best bet.

"Good morning, Aunt Anna. We thought you had left. May I introduce you to a member of the press? This is Felicia Meadows, who wrote that embarrassing profile of Mr. St. Clair, but he has decided to overlook it with a great generosity of spirit, and we're all friends now. This is Anna Roosevelt Cowles, my father's sister. We were having a most interesting discussion, and I am learning a great deal about how the press works."

We had a couple of moments of silence before Mrs. Cowles spoke.

"Miss Meadows, I am familiar with your work, although I am not a regular reader. Alice, I am glad you are learning, but I trust you are not giving unauthorized interviews."

"Of course not. This is what is called an 'off the record' discussion. I thought it would be a good idea to learn how to cultivate the press, and why not start with a woman?" Alice said smoothly.

"So you get information. What does the *Herald* get in return?" Mrs. Cowles asked. No one said anything, and I was curious to see how Alice would respond.

"A very nice breakfast. Also, the promise of an exclusive interview at such time as I am in a position to talk more openly with the press."

"With all due respect to the reporters from the *Herald*, you don't think it's unfair that you are excluding, for example, reporters from the *Times*? From the *Tribune*?" asked Mrs. Cowles.

"This is just the beginning," said Alice. "I expect to get to know reporters from all the major papers."

"What a noble goal," said Mrs. Cowles. But her eyes said something else. "I must be going. Miss Meadows, Mr. St. Clair, good day to you all." She had one final look for Alice that said, "If I find out you're up to something you shouldn't be, I'll make you regret it for the rest of your life, young lady." Then she strode out the door.

The doorbell rang again.

I left Alice with a somewhat overwhelmed Miss Meadows and followed Mrs. Cowles into the foyer. I stepped ahead of her and the maid who came to answer the bell, and after checking the peep hole, opened the door to a very unhappy-looking Captain O'Hara. After the recent meeting in the dining room, I wished O'Hara had arrived a minute later.

"Damn it, St. Clair. Something's happened, and I need—" I put my finger to my lips, but Mrs. Cowles was standing right behind me.

"Oh, good morning, ma'am," said the captain.

"Captain O'Hara was just meeting with us to coordinate security for the Gadsden ball," I explained to Mrs. Cowles. I turned to O'Hara. "Don't worry about problems at your end. We'll work it out later."

"Oh, ah, yes," he said, trying to change gears quickly.

The maid was still standing by. "Enid, please show Captain O'Hara into the dining room," said Mrs. Cowles. He gratefully followed Enid, leaving me alone with Alice's aunt.

"Mr. St. Clair. It's become abundantly clear that Alice has taken an unhealthy interest in the recent deaths related to the Rutledge party."

"Ma'am—"

"Don't say anything, Mr. St. Clair. It will be easier for you later to deny any knowledge if you don't lie to me now. That is a kindness on my part. I will find out what Alice is doing, anyway. You know I will. Good day." And with that, she was out the door.

I shook my head and headed back to the dining room.

Alice introduced the captain to Miss Meadows from the *Herald*, with each party wondering what the other was doing there.

"Captain O'Hara is here to coordinate security for the Gadsden ball," said Alice with so much sincerity I think she almost believed it herself. Just as well because there was no point in sending a still-curious reporter out the door, wondering why a city police captain was calling on the president's daughter.

"I think we're done here," said Miss Meadows. There were thank-yous all around, and I offered to show Miss Meadows out, even as Alice was encouraging Captain O'Hara to have some breakfast.

I opened the door for her, and she turned before leaving to give me a look with just a hint of mischief. "Your Miss Roosevelt has involved herself in a lot more than I realized."

"She's not *my* Miss Roosevelt. But yes, she has."

"She's going to be a piece of work when she grows up."

"You don't know the half of it," I said.

"And yet, I sense behind it all, you're keeping her safe, which is pretty impressive considering what she's up to. I think you pretend to be a lot dumber than you are. You're not fooling me."

That's just what Mrs. Cowles told me. I may have to work on

my act. At any rate, I didn't much think about what I said next, showing that I might not be faking my stupidity. "Maybe, Felicia, but I was watching you in there, and you're not hiding anything. You're smart as a whip, and anyone can see that."

It was worth saying something that dumb just to see that lovely smile. "Joey, you Western boys sure know how to turn a girl's head." And with that, she left.

Just a little dizzy, I made my way back to the dining room.

"How long does it take to see someone out?" asked Alice, a little annoyed. But she didn't seem to expect an answer. The captain had grabbed the last two pieces of bacon and the last waffle and emptied the coffee pot into a clean cup. He was lost in his own thoughts and looked moody.

Alice turned her attentions to him. "What, besides our coffee, brings you to the Caledonia?"

O'Hara sighed. "I don't like to do this, but we have more problems with the Brackton killing. His widow was sent a package with a bottle. Inside was apparently that punch they had at the ball. She called me, and I went over, but she wouldn't talk to me. She's just hysterical. Her maid is taking care of her, and I have a couple of men over there. Anyway, if you wouldn't mind, Miss Roosevelt, maybe you could come along and talk with her, as you know her."

"Ooh, a development," said Alice with just a little too much joy.

"I think she means that we'd like to know if you have any more details," I said.

"Not much. A maid found it left at the kitchen door in a box. The area is hardly secured. Anyone could've left it. There was no note. The maid brought it to Mrs. Brackton, who saw it was the punch. She had the police summoned. We took the bottle, and we'll have some chemists look at it, but you could actually see little pieces of the wolfsbane floating on top."

Alice considered that. "It seems ridiculous. Even if she hadn't already been frightened by her husband's murder, she still wouldn't drink something left by the door. And with the poison visible. No one could possibly think she'd end up drinking it."

"It was a warning," I said.

"Yes. Designed to frighten her," said Alice.

"I thought so, too," said O'Hara. "If that was the purpose, it worked. It worked very well. But they killed her husband, so why is this continuing with her? There was just one more clue— and I think you'll see that there's something that may show I was right all along." He looked a little pleased with himself. "There was a label on the box, meaning someone didn't just deliver it directly. They wanted to hide themselves. So they wrote the Brackton address on a label, put the label on the package, and then gave it to a street kid to deliver. I peeled the label off." He pulled an envelope out of his jacket pocket and produced the label. It was cheap, available at stationers throughout the city. We could see the penmanship was awkward, like it had been written by someone who didn't have much experience with a pen.

"I don't see how far this gets us," I said.

O'Hara looked a little smug. "Because you didn't see the label on the box Delilah Linde got." He produced that one from a pocket, as well, and put them down side by side. It was obvious the same person had written both.

"So now we know that one person is out to get both of them," said O'Hara. "Also, these labels look like a servant's writing— probably a woman. It looks like a feminine hand. I knew it. I bet in the end we connect it to someone who worked in the Rutledge house."

"That the labels match is very interesting, but we can't assume that a Rutledge servant was in on it," said Alice.

"I don't know what else to think," O'Hara said. "Do you have any ideas?"

"A question. Was the note for Mrs. Linde also in the same hand as the labels?" asked Alice.

"That's a good question. No, it wasn't. At least, not obviously. Maybe they disguised that hand so it would look like a man wrote it—perhaps to frame Mr. Rutledge. Or there are two people in on it. We just don't know yet. Anyway, Mrs. Brackton isn't saying much. Maybe you can get more out of her."

"We'll follow you there shortly," said Alice.

"I'd appreciate it. I have to get back there, and I'll wait for you. Thanks again for the coffee." I showed him out, and when I got back to the dining room, Alice was standing and ready to go.

"I hope the motorcar is gassed up because it's going to be a busy day," she said, and her eyes were glittering. I grabbed my Stetson, Alice went back to her room to get her hat, and we were out the door.

★ ★ ★

"You know what impresses me most of all, Miss Alice? Not that you can lie so well. I mean, I know you're a great liar. It's that you can keep track of them all. Telling Mrs. Cowles why you're meeting with all these people over breakfast, not telling Miss Meadows all the details of the XVII, not telling Captain O'Hara that Mrs. Brackton was really the target. I'm full of admiration."

"You can keep the sarcasm out of your voice," she said. "It is very difficult keeping all my prevarications consistent, but the more time I spend in Washington, the easier it gets."

I laughed. "I'm sure it does. Anyway, I agree with you about this latest poisoning attempt. I don't think someone necessarily wanted to kill Mrs. Brackton. They missed their chance, at least for now, and they want to scare her into keeping quiet."

"But about what?" asked Alice.

It was a short drive to the Bracktons', and the cop outside waved us in. "The captain is upstairs," he said.

A maid saw us into the parlor, and we saw O'Hara sitting in a chair and still looking unhappy. Opposite him was Mrs. Brackton in an elaborate black dress, quietly crying and being comforted by an older, motherly-looking maid, who was addressing the captain.

"... and I am sorry, Captain, but madam's doctor says she needs rest and you'll have to leave. You can come back later." I had learned a bit about the way the rich in New York had things set up with servants. Wealthy ladies had personal maids. You had to be somewhat older to get a job like that, and it was considered a pretty good deal. You didn't cross women like that.

They saw we had arrived. The maid recognized Alice, and the president's daughter was a lot more welcome than an Irish cop. She got her mistress's attention.

"Oh, Alice. I am so glad you're here." Mrs. Brackton smiled through her tears, and the maid slid over to make room for Alice next to her.

"Captain O'Hara told us the story. It must've been a terrible shock," said Alice.

"I did what you said," said Victoria Brackton. "I was on the lookout for anything suspicious and called the police as soon as it arrived. And then I told them to get you. What is this all about?" That led to a fresh wave of tears, and I was pleasantly surprised to see Alice, for whom patience was not a major virtue, quietly soothe her while the maid fetched some water.

Eventually, she pulled herself together, and then Alice said, "Victoria, this officer is Captain O'Hara. He was a close associate of my father's when he was commissioner. You can trust him. We have to tell him the whole story. It's become too dangerous not to. I think you know that, and that's why you asked for me." Reluctantly, Mrs. Brackton nodded.

"The full story?" asked O'Hara.

"Yes," said Alice. "We've concluded that Lynley Brackton was not the intended target. It was Mrs. Brackton all along. Victoria, tell Captain O'Hara the story."

Haltingly, Mrs. Brackton told the captain the story, just as she had to Alice and me, about how she had taken the glass and passed it to her husband at the last minute. O'Hara listened carefully. He asked a few questions to confirm the details.

"Victoria, I know you want to lie down. Just a minute more of your time," asked Alice. She leaned in close to Mrs. Brackton and laid a comforting hand on her shoulder. "I think someone thinks you know something, something that could threaten them. Did you know anything embarrassing about anyone in Society? Anything about Lynley's business?"

She just shook her head and sniffled. "Lynley never discussed business with me. And what would I know about gossip? Just what everyone else knows. I don't . . . I mean . . ."

It did seem odd, and Alice realized it, too. It was hard to believe that someone—that anyone—saw this vague, simple woman as a threat. But someone was trying to kill her—even frighten her to death.

Alice had nothing else to ask and so remained silent.

"If that is all, sir, I'd like to see madam to bed. This has been most distressing," said the maid. O'Hara absently nodded, and the two women left. The captain then turned to us

"If you two knew this, you should've told me. We've wasted valuable time and put Mrs. Brackton at risk."

"She was terrified and didn't feel she could trust anyone in the police," said Alice. "I knew she'd come around eventually, and meanwhile, I told her to be careful." She wasn't going to admit to any wrongdoing, so he turned to me.

"St. Clair, you carry a badge. You should've known better."

But Alice's small store of patience had been exhausted. "Oh God, do stop fussing. No harm done, and you know now. The question is why someone wants to kill this rather nice, not terribly bright woman. Mr. Brackton was an unrepentant womanizer, exceedingly unpleasant by all accounts. But why her?"

"I think it'll come down to an angry servant . . . or your friend Carlyle," said O'Hara.

"You're just saying that because you can't easily question the members of Society," said Alice.

"You're right about that. If I had a hard lead, I could lean on someone, but as it stands, I start bothering too many important people, and the next thing you know, I'll be getting calls from the mayor. Listen, Miss Roosevelt, I don't know what you're doing. I don't want to know what you're doing. If you're with St. Clair here, I'll assume you're staying safe. But if you don't find out something soon, I'm going to have to arrest someone. They'll insist on it."

"We're making progress," said Alice loftily.

"Very good then, but don't keep any more secrets from me."

Alice rolled her eyes and then stood. "I will keep you fully informed, Captain. Anyway, there's nothing more we can do here. Mr. St. Clair, we have people to visit. But first, I want to talk to Victoria's maid about how she's caring for her mistress." That maid seemed competent and hardly in need of Alice's advice. I think O'Hara knew, as well, that Alice had something up her sleeve, but there was nothing to be done, and I followed Alice out of the room. Apparently, servants in these houses always lived in small rooms at the top, and that's where we found the maid, who had already gotten her mistress to bed.

Alice knocked, and we heard "come in." The room was no bigger than mine in the Caledonia. It was the neatest room I had ever seen, nothing out of place and not a speck of dust on the few pieces of furniture. The maid was sitting on her chair reading a Bible. There was nothing on the wall except a cross. She stood when we entered.

"May I help you, Miss Roosevelt?" she asked. She seemed a little wary. I doubted if anyone had ever visited her except another servant. I had seen her be motherly with Mrs. Brackton, but alone now, she seemed younger than I had thought, probably under forty, with a pleasing face and a nicely round figure. I imagined what it did to her, being a maid to a lady whose husband had been murdered, a lady who had almost been murdered herself. Heck—being a maid for the Bracktons in the best of times. In another time and place, I'd have called her pretty.

"I wanted to talk about your mistress—not gossip," Alice said, reassuring her. "You and I have her best interests at heart, and I don't think there are many of us who do." That softened the maid, who would be inclined to trust the president's daughter. "First, may I have your name?"

"Elspeth Whatley, miss," she said.

"Very good. This is Mr. St. Clair. He is not a cop." Alice said that with a lot of meaning: "It's all right, he's not one of those heavy-footed Irishmen walking all over the good rugs."

"He's my protector and an important friend and advisor to my father." That was pushing it. The only thing I had ever advised the president on was choosing a horse.

Miss Whatley sat down as Alice took a seat on the bed. Since there wasn't another chair, I remained standing. "I see you're reading the Good Book. May I ask which church you attend?" asked Alice.

That surprised Miss Whatley, but she saw no reason not to answer. "The Dutch Reformed Church. I believe the Roosevelts are also members." However, the president was just as likely to show up with his wife at her Episcopal church, when he bothered going at all. From what I knew, the Dutch Reformed Church was for people who took their religion seriously.

"Yes, we are," said Alice. "I bring this up because when something like this happens, the police ask all kinds of impertinent questions, and as I see you are a good churchgoing woman, I can trust you to talk with me." She lowered her voice to show what was coming was a secret. "If you talk to me now, I can help you and your mistress avoid unpleasant police questions later." Alice knew just what to say—Miss Whatley sat up straight, with shoulders back, proud as anything to be entering into a conspiracy with the president's daughter.

"Whatever I can do to help, Miss Roosevelt," she said.

"Very good. Has Mrs. Brackton been out of the house since the death of Mr. Brackton?"

"No, miss." She raised the Bible in her hand to indicate she was making a holy oath.

"Which other servants does she talk with?"

"When he was alive, Mr. Brackton handled all matters with the servants. Now I do, on madam's behalf, and will continue to do so until matters are more settled."

"I don't like asking this, but again, to keep the police from bothering you, would it be possible for Mrs. Brackton to have slipped out without your knowing?"

"Impossible, miss. I am her constant companion and give her a sleeping draft at night, which I personally make up according to the doctor's instructions."

Alice nodded. "Has your mistress sent any packages recently? Perhaps to a friend?"

"She is not accustomed to making up her own packages," she said.

"Of course not," said Alice patiently. "But if she did, would she leave it for you to send out?"

Miss Whatley, still holding her Bible, said, "Mrs. Brackton puts all personal mail to go out on the table in the front hall. The butler sees they are given to the postman. She has not put any packages on the table in weeks. I would have noticed."

"I see. Thank you." Alice thought for a few more moments while Miss Whatley looked at her expectantly. "Just one more thing. Are you sorry about the master's death?"

It was like a mask came down. It was only for a few moments, but I saw in those eyes something I didn't see often—pure and total hatred. Then it was gone.

"Of course," Miss Whatley said.

"That's all the questions I have. Thank you for being so honest and for taking such good care of my friend."

Miss Whatley stood as we left. I found myself glad that Mrs. Brackton had someone in her life who cared for her.

"Nicely done, Miss Alice," I said as we headed back downstairs. "She sure hated Mr. Brackton. Why didn't you ask more about him?"

Alice just shook her head. "A lot you know about maids like Elspeth Whatley. You're right that she hated Lynley, but we still weren't going to get any more. Your loyalty to my father as a sergeant in his regiment was nothing compared with the loyalty of someone like her to her employer. We managed to get some descriptions of behavior, but nothing would get us any shared confidences. I was hoping to find a way for Victoria to have poisoned Mrs. Linde, which might've meant she also poisoned her own husband. But I just don't see how that could've happened. Miss Whatley may be loyal, but a religious woman like that wouldn't lie to me with her hand on the Bible. Oh well, it was worth a shot—although." She smiled. "I'd like to think Miss Whatley killed Mr. Brackton for making Mrs. Brackton so unhappy. Could she have slipped into the Rutledge house . . ."

"But she'd have plenty of opportunity to kill him right here," I said.

"I suppose you're right. The problem is that everyone had a reason to kill Lynley Brackton, including his wife, although if she was going to do it, you'd think she'd have done it years ago." Then she shook her head. "But I'm dealing with some ruthless, powerful men here, and all I can do is try to pin this on a beaten-down widow and a religious-fanatic maid. Let's not get derailed."

O'Hara was still downstairs, talking with some other cops, but came over when he saw us.

"Anything else you need to tell me?" he asked.

"No, and do stop your silliness. Now, Captain, you must know about the gangs in this town. Did you ever hear of one called the XVII?"

"That doesn't sound like a gang name. Where did you hear that?"

"Idle conversation. Good day." She turned on her heels and left the room before a suspicious O'Hara could question us further.

CHAPTER 26

"Once again, this has been profitable," said Alice. "Things are beginning to fall into place. Mrs. Brackton knows something, even if she isn't aware of it. I'm sure of it."

"Unless she's lying," I said. Alice considered that.

"About what? The package? The glass? You could be right. She may know something and is afraid to tell. Or maybe she's just happy, in some way, that her husband is dead, even if she is mourning him. I'd wanted to think she killed Delilah, but I can't see how, thanks to Miss Whatley. Again, we can't assume there is just one murderer." She stopped for a minute. "We can't even be sure we're getting the full story from Victoria. She said there was one glass, which she gave to her husband to drink. But she could be muddled, or lying again, because she's still afraid and doesn't want to admit what she knows. Maybe they each had a glass and only Lynley's was poisoned. It sounds like a stretch, her having a glass and her husband drinking it for her while she had nothing. I would like to believe that only Lynley was the target—who would want to kill Victoria? It's so frustrating. The more I think about it, the more complicated it gets. Also, even though the two labels are the same, that doesn't mean Lynley Brackton's death was related to either one. But right now, it seems someone is intent on threatening Victoria. When we know a little more, we can come back to her. Roth is tied in with Rutledge. The XVII is sharing funds—supporting Van Dijk. There's a conspiracy here. Remember our last adventure, when we had to corner a mistress? We found out a great deal. Thank goodness men have such little self-control."

I laughed. "Yeah, I remember her."

"Stop smirking. She was cheap and vulgar. Let's hope Mr. Roth's mistress is a little more . . . elegant."

"Why should she talk to you?"

She looked surprised. "I'm Alice Roosevelt. Everyone wants to talk with me." I laughed once more. "But again, I thought better of him. I thought he was . . ." She seemed at a loss of words to describe how disappointed she was in Abraham.

★ ★ ★

We drove to the quiet, leafy street on the West Side where the Roth mistress supposedly lived, similar to but even nicer than where the midwife Miss Rushcroft lived. Like many Manhattan streets, this one was lined with handsome brownstone buildings, which I thought were actually more welcoming than the marble you found in the really elegant neighborhoods. Alice was looking at the street numbers.

"There it is, on the left," she said. I saw it as well . . . and just kept going.

"Where are you going? There were plenty of places to park." She was annoyed and confused, but I continued on for another block before pulling over.

"Didn't you see the men hanging around out front? Two men in derbies?" I asked.

"More agents of the XVII?" asked Alice. "You can handle them."

"I appreciate the show of confidence. But I'll bet those two men are not with the XVII. I could see from the way they were looking, the way they held themselves, that they're professionals. I'm a professional, and I know one when I see one. They know what they're doing."

"So you can still handle them, professional or not."

"Miss Alice, there are three of them. With two outside, there is always one inside."

"And you have six bullets in your gun. I don't understand."

"Oh, for heaven's sake, Miss Alice, I can't just go in there shooting. What would I tell Mr. Harris about dead bodies falling down the front steps? We're going to have to be a little more strategic. But I'll tell you something. I don't think Roth is hiring bodyguards just for a mistress. There's a lot more to it than that."

"I agree. The mistress was an assumption but probably a false one." She paused. "Those guards—are they to keep someone in? Or someone out?"

"Now that, Miss Alice, is a very good question. I'd say that last one. If they were keeping someone prisoner, there would be no need for guards outside. It's someone who wants to be protected. We have no cause to go bursting in there."

"So what next? We have to get in. And since you don't want to start shooting, what are our next steps? You're the soldier."

"We're going to have to try something else. We can't break into that house."

She gave that a moment's thought. "I have an idea. I don't think you've been giving me enough credit. I did a splendid job on Houston Street, and I improvised marvelously at the Linde house."

"We had no other option on Houston, and you surprised me at the Lindes'. At least there was no danger there. I'm not going out of my way to put you in danger."

"But I won't be in danger. You said they were professionals. They wouldn't hurt a woman, not the president's daughter."

"Miss Alice—"

"Oh, for God's sake, we've done worse than this. Just listen." She outlined her plan briefly. "And I'm sure Peter Carlyle will help. He said he wanted to."

"Miss Alice—" I said again.

"Look at it this way, Mr. St. Clair. We are already involved. We're already in danger. Men are already after us. A simple operation like this will help end it. We're worse off *not* doing it. And you'll be right there."

I sighed. "One thing I've learned: politicians always have a sneaky way of turning the argument around, even when you know they're wrong. You'll do just fine in Washington." She laughed fully at that.

It wasn't far uptown to the garage, and Peter was glad to see us. His eyes got wide when we started explaining what we would do. I needed those two men where we could grab them, and then I could handle the third.

"We'll need a motorcar—I mean a big one, not just a runabout. Do you have a chauffeur's uniform around here?" asked Alice

"Yes," said Peter. "I sometimes work as a substitute driver in the evenings. And there are half a dozen motorcars here no one will miss if I borrow one for an hour or so."

"I've been practicing my driving," said Alice. "Mr. St. Clair, why don't I drive the runabout, and you and Mr. Carlyle can follow in one of these cars, so you can explain the details?"

"Miss Alice, this is already so far beyond what we should be doing. We'll plan it out now. You and I will drive as usual with Peter following, and we'll meet a block away to set things up." She pouted but accepted it. Peter seemed excited about being able to help and quickly changed into a driver's uniform. I realized we could count on him—he was not only a sharp guy, but hauling engine parts around had given him strong muscles and quick reflexes. It would work. Probably.

Peter picked a very nice touring sedan in dark red. It was a beauty, and I made a note to ask him to let me take it around someday. We drove back to the block just beyond the townhouse and all got out. We went over our plan again. I'd have to leave Alice alone for a few minutes, which I didn't like, but it was a safe neighborhood, and she'd be with Peter, who could take care of both of them.

Alice could barely contain her excitement, and Peter looked pretty happy, too. I wish I could've shared their enthusiasm. I made sure my Colt wasn't easily visible, and then I rolled myself a cigarette and started walking toward the brownstone. Out of the corner of my eye, I could see the two men in derbies giving me a look. Yes, they were professionals. My goal was to get them used to me so I wasn't seen as threatening.

In front of the house, I started searching my pockets. "Say, either of you boys have a match?"

"No. Move on, pal," said the older of the two.

"Hey, I'm just being friendly," I said. I pulled out my flask. "Good bourbon. I'll give you each a swallow if you light me up."

"This is private property. Get out of here," he repeated. I just shook my head and continued searching my pockets. It was then that Peter and Alice drove up. She looked great, sitting in the back seat like a queen. Peter pulled up front and ran around to let her out. The two guards headed down the stairs to the sidewalk. Their first mistake.

"Excuse me, this is private property," said younger one, but respectfully, seeing this was a lady of means in a fine motorcar. Meanwhile, I tried to catch a match from Peter.

"Hey buddy, can you help a fellow working man with a light?"

Pete shuffled in his pocket while the older one addressed Alice. "Excuse me, miss, but I think you have the wrong address."

"How on earth could you know which address I was looking for?" asked Alice in a voice full of contempt. "Don't you have any idea who I am?"

He peered at her. "Oh yeah. You're Miss Roosevelt. I'm sorry, miss, but we're not expecting any visitors."

"Clearly, or you would be better behaved. This conversation has grown tedious." With that, she started to head past them. They turned their back on me and Peter to follow her. Their second mistake. I caught Peter's eye, and he jumped the young one in a very neat tackle, considering the guy had a couple of inches and about thirty pounds on Peter.

"Hey—" said the older guy, but by that point, I had my Colt in his back. Alice did as she was told and hopped back into the motorcar to take her out of range of the front door. Then the third guard came through the door to see what the fuss was all about. He reached for his revolver but was too late.

"Don't do that. You'll hit your own men, and we just have a few questions. This is Alice Roosevelt, and she's a little curious about who you've got inside," I said.

"And who are you?" he asked. He still had his hand on his revolver but hadn't pulled it out.

"I'm Secret Service. I know you guys are Pinkertons. You can always spot a Pinkerton. Now, how about you let me in? That way, your boss doesn't find out how easily your men were fooled, and my boss doesn't find out what I've done here today. Deal?"

He didn't like it, but I knew he'd say yes. He was thinking about what his report would look like.

"Either way, could you get this guy off me?" said the guard Peter had tackled, only he used that unpleasant word for colored folk again, and that got Alice worked up.

"Do not use that word. I don't like it. Mr. St. Clair loathes it. He may just shoot you."

"All right. Everyone calm down," said the man at the top. "You and Miss Roosevelt come in. And you two—" He looked at his men. "I'll talk to you later."

Everything wound down quickly. We released the two guards, who looked a little sheepish. Alice and I thanked Peter, who said he had to get the motorcar back to the shop and wished us luck.

Alice couldn't have looked prouder of herself, and I was relieved the whole thing went off without a shot being fired. The man held the door open, and Alice and I walked inside.

CHAPTER 27

He led us into a little parlor off the front. It was pleasant enough inside but not as fancy as most of the places Alice and I visited. The furniture was good but plain, and there were some simple landscapes on the wall. I guessed no one lived here long-term; it was just a basic setup for someone to rent, someone who wanted anonymity and perhaps a sense of hominess you couldn't get from a good hotel. But that didn't explain the armed Pinkertons outside. That outfit had been around since the Civil War, and when you needed serious security, they were the ones you called.

"Jefferson," the guard said, sticking out his hand. He was a little older than I was, with a solid build and a firm handshake. His accent said he was born and raised in New York. "And you're right; we're Pinkerton."

"St. Clair." I showed him my badge. "And this, as you probably know by now, is Miss Roosevelt."

"Your father is a fine man. I'm a great admirer of his," said Jefferson.

"Thank you," she said with a slight nod, accepting the compliment as her due.

"To the matter at hand. You went through a lot of trouble to get in here. Can I ask why?" That was smart of him. He didn't give away what was going on.

"I'm a friend of Abraham Roth," Alice explained. "We know a company he runs owns this house. For reasons we can't discuss, we have to speak to the person you're guarding here. A brief discussion, and we'll leave you alone."

"That'll be his decision, Miss Roosevelt. We provide security. We're not jailers."

"Then tell him that Alice Roosevelt wants to see him. Everyone always wants to see me."

Jefferson shook his head and left the room. We heard him walk upstairs.

"Who is so important they need three armed guards?" asked Alice, looking around the nondescript room. "But the XVII are apparently after the Roths. That's enough to want security." I had to agree.

Jefferson came back down. "Follow me," he said. We'd know soon enough. We proceeded upstairs and into a suite on the second floor. It was the same quality of furniture as downstairs, but quickly, our eyes went to an Oriental gentleman sitting in a comfortable chair. He looked to be in his sixties and was wearing a good black suit. He looked pleasantly curious and stood as we entered. He bowed to us, which is a big deal in the Orient, as we'd found out visiting Chinatown in our last adventure. Alice followed suit and solemnly bowed, too, as did I.

"This is Alice Roosevelt, daughter of President Theodore Roosevelt, and her bodyguard, Mr. St. Clair. And this is Baron Okada, a representative of the Japanese government," said Jefferson. "I'll leave you all to it." He left, closing the door behind him.

"It is a great pleasure to meet the daughter of the famous American president. I am honored," said Okada, and Alice again looked pleased. His English was accented but clear. I had met Chinese over the years; there were plenty of them in New York.

But this was the first time I had met anyone from Japan, and what he was doing as a guest of the Roths was beyond me.

"I understand that you made a great effort to visit me here. I wonder why."

"I wonder why a distinguished visitor from Japan stays here in exclusion, heavily guarded. All I know is that you have business dealings with the Roth family," replied Alice.

"I must assume, Miss Roosevelt, that you are an official representative of your government? I have broken no laws of your country."

"I am not here officially. And I imagine, Baron, that although you were introduced as a representative of the Japanese emperor, you are not official, either. If you were, you wouldn't be hidden away here with visitors sneaking in and out. There is an American expression that describes this: we are in the same boat."

He laughed at that. " 'In the same boat.' I will remember that. I hear what you say, but I need to know what advantage it is to me to tell you."

But before Alice could answer, the door opened, and a man came in. He seemed be one of the Baron's countrymen. He was also wearing a suit, but not as fine as the baron's. He was carrying a tray with three small china cups. The servant put the tray on a little table, and he and Okada spoke briefly in Japanese before he left.

The baron handed us each a cup.

"Allow me to be hospitable. This drink is known as sake, or *nihonshu*. It is made from rice and is traditionally served warm. Please join me."

I have to say that as unusual as it was, I liked it, and if I were offered it again, I would take them up on it.

"It's very good," said Alice. "Thank you." I nodded, too, and Okada seemed pleased.

"You asked me a question," said Alice. "I am not really here about you. I am here about the Roths. Someone has threatened both them and me. I think that is why you are so well guarded. My goal is to try to find out why. I want to know what the Roths' business is with you. It may help me figure out how to safeguard my family and the Roths."

"Do the Roths know about this?"

"About any threats? Yes, although they are reluctant to admit it. About who is attacking them? Probably not. I assume their business with you is too important to want to start an official investigation."

Okada nodded. "Your explanation is excellent. So you want me to relate to you the nature of my business with the Roths?"

"With an understanding that I will keep it confidential, except as necessary to protect myself and the Roths, who may not even be aware of the full extent of the danger. And who might not even believe me. Remember, Baron, that their safety is to your advantage."

"An interesting offer," said Okada. He continued to sip his sake. Alice seemed annoyed. The Orientals looked at the world a little differently, I had found, and Okada was going to consider things for a while.

"Someday, Baron, you are going to want the good opinion of the American president. I can do that for you," Alice prodded.

"Miss Roosevelt, I admire your . . . negotiating ability. I believe that if you thought a little more, you would realize what our business is, and I wouldn't have to break my promise to the Roths to keep it secret. Try to think about what the Roths would have that I would want."

"Money," said Alice. "The Roths have lots of it. And they know plenty of other people with money. So you are borrowing money from the Roths, a great deal of money, on behalf of the Japanese government. That's acceptable, but why do you need the armed guards? Why do you need to be hidden away?"

"Very good, Miss Roosevelt. As for your question, the Roths have said that such a deal as this, with a foreign government, might be subject to curiosity and even . . . harassment from other parties. They asked me to stay here while we concluded our business. The presence of a prominent Japanese citizen in New York could excite conversation. There are those, I am told, who take great exception to business deals of such an enormous size with a nation in the East."

"The next question is: what do you want to buy with all that money? The Roths wouldn't let you have money unless they were sure you were going to give it back. What would be buying with the money to make sure you'd be in a position to pay it back? Factories, ships—"

"Guns, for a war," I said. That got a wide smile from Okada.

"Very good, Mr. St. Clair. Do I assume correctly that you have been a soldier?"

"Mr. St. Clair is a war hero, a sergeant who fought with my father in Cuba," said Alice. "Do I take it, then, that you want Roth's money to finance expansion plans, even war, in the East?"

"It's a pity women are not eligible to serve as president. You'd be a worthy successor to your esteemed father."

I could've told him that Alice didn't need any additional compliments. She was hard enough to control as it was.

"Thank you very much," she said, preening. "So, if I understand you, the Roth syndicate is making a long-term bet on the future of Japan." Okada didn't speak, but his face said everything. "Has Abraham Roth, that is, the younger Mr. Roth, been the representative of the Roth family here?"

"Miss Roosevelt, I want to help you in your quest but cannot fully satisfy your curiosity."

"Fair enough," she said, nodding. I could see the wheels turning in her head. "Baron Okada, I would like to compliment you on your excellent English."

"Thank you. I learned at one of the mission schools established after your Commodore Perry visited us." He was heavy on the "visited." It was before I was born, when the Americans forced

Japan open at gunpoint, and although I knew almost nothing about Japan, I imagined they were still a little sore about it. Like the Georgia boys and General Sherman.

"A Christian mission? Do you know that the Roths are not Christian? They're Jewish. I find that interesting," said Alice.

"I'm sure you do. The distinction was made clear to me. Followers of the Jewish faith, even when they are very wealthy like the Roths, are to a large extent outsiders in America. And so are citizens of the Far East. Perhaps that is why we do business together so well."

Alice nodded thoughtfully. "You have been very fair, Baron. I will ask you one more question and then leave you in peace. Have you heard of a group called the XVII?"

"The seventeen? Like the numerals? The name is not familiar." He paused. "Are they the group threatening us?"

"I'm afraid I cannot satisfy your curiosity," said Alice. Although the baron might've been annoyed that this girl was throwing his words back in his face, he just laughed, and I liked him for it.

We stood to leave, and after some more bowing, Alice and I said our goodbyes. Jefferson was waiting downstairs for us.

"Did you two get what you came for?" he asked.

"I rather think we did," Alice said. "Thank you." He held the door open, and we heard it close behind us as we walked down to the sidewalk. The two other Pinkertons were still on duty and gave us wary looks.

"Come on, guys, no hard feelings. We're all working men here." I took out my flask. "The best bourbon." They looked to see if Jefferson was watching, then they each took a quick slug. With good fellowship restored, Alice and I headed back to the car.

"I'm glad that at least Abraham isn't doing something sordid like keeping a mistress."

"I know he'd be devastated if he thought he had earned your poor opinion."

"I know he would, as well. So where are we? I think we have a sense of what is happening here," said Alice as we headed back into the car. "The XVII have something against foreigners, against anyone who isn't one of the ruling class in this city. Roth was targeted by them because he was powerful but not one of them. Not only are the Roths outsiders themselves, but they are dealing with outsiders, financing an Asian country. I don't see the XVII liking that. Meanwhile, Simon Rutledge is working with Roth for financial reasons, which is why Philly and Abraham have been meeting secretly. Victoria Brackton found out about this—maybe mentioned to Simon that he was betraying the cause. He therefore had her killed. And continues to threaten her, although she's too frightened to admit this."

"Maybe," I said.

"What do you mean 'maybe'?" she said, irritated. "It makes perfect sense."

"Do you see Victoria Brackton challenging Simon Rutledge like that? I see you doing that, Miss Alice, but I doubt if she had the backbone."

"Oh, all right. Maybe she didn't realize what she was saying. She mentioned seeing, or hearing gossip about, what Simon was doing. He heard her and panicked and killed her."

"That's better. But again, I don't see Simon Rutledge doing that, either. He'd have to be a cool hand, faking a break-in and poisoning Mrs. Brackton in his own home at his daughter's debutante ball with a Secret Service agent in his kitchen. Daring and lucky."

"But he succeeded—that's the point. He's a rich and powerful man. He could've manipulated his servants to be in the right place as he planned the poisoning." She waved her hand to indicate she wasn't interested in any more disagreements. "This is a work in progress, Mr. St. Clair. Tomorrow is Thursday, when Mr. Roth and Philly meet. We're going to corner them and pull the information out of them. We have the evidence, even if it's circumstantial. That's evidence—"

"Thanks, Miss Alice. I was a deputy sheriff. I know what circumstantial evidence is," I said.

"It was my understanding that your job was mostly settling fights in the local bordello."

"That wasn't my job. All right, it was part of it, but I was a sworn lawman who testified in court."

"Oh, very well. My apologies. But it's your fault for pretending to be a dim cowboy when you're really quite bright and accomplished. We'll have to work on that. Anyway, tomorrow we're going to take the next steps. Meanwhile, I wish we could get Japanese food in New York."

"What do they eat in Japan, anyway?" I asked. "It's an island, so I'm guessing lots of fish."

"Yes. Apparently, they don't always cook it. They roll it with seaweed and rice and sauces and eat it raw."

"I'll be looking forward to New York's first Japanese restaurant with great excitement," I said dryly. "But I wouldn't mind more of that sake."

Alice agreed and then said there wasn't anything to do until the next day, so we might as well go home. "We'll buy a couple of beers and play cards until dinner."

"Actually, something else is on. In fact—" I consulted my watch. "We need to be going."

"What do you mean, 'we need to be going'? What's happening?"

"You'll find out soon enough," I said.

"Did my aunt tell you something? Why didn't she tell me? If there's a dinner I need to be there for, she usually tells me directly."

I laughed, and Alice sulked as we drove, trying to figure out why she had to be home and why I knew but she didn't.

"I know!" she finally said. She leaned back in her seat and put her feet up the dashboard. "My father is coming to New York."

"Very good, Miss Alice."

"How come you get to know and I don't? And don't you dare make that joke about that's why they call it the *Secret* Service."

I just laughed.

CHAPTER 28

We saw the cops guarding all the entrances at the Caledonia and agents in the lobby, so it was clear the president had already arrived. Alice ran out of the car and into the building. A maid let us into the apartment, and Mr. Roosevelt was right inside waiting for us. Alice ran to him, and he picked her up and spun her around.

"Good to see you again, Baby Lee," he said. He always used her middle name. She was named Alice after his first wife, who died two days after baby Alice was born, and the story was that Mr. Roosevelt couldn't bear to use the name "Alice" ever again. I had never met Alice's mother, but I heard she was a great beauty like her only child. She was only a few years older than Alice was presently when she died, and everyone said Alice took after her, except that Mrs. Roosevelt was cheerful and always well behaved.

"St. Clair, come here and say hello," he said.

"Good to see you again, Mr. President." He gave me a strong handshake and slapped me on the back. "How about this—when we're out of the White House and unofficial, you can call me 'Colonel,' and I'll call you 'Sergeant.'"

"Those were good times—Colonel. That suits me fine." He laughed again.

"Alice, your aunt will be back a little later, and we'll have a family dinner, just the three of us. I have some meetings around the city tomorrow. So tell me, are you and Sergeant St. Clair back in your New York routine?"

"Yes, Father. We've been keeping very busy, meeting all sorts of people. You'd be proud."

"I am. Glad to hear you're keeping busy. I hate few things more than being idle. Meanwhile, I was sorry to hear about the tragedy at the Rutledge ball."

"Mr. St. Clair saved the day, Father. He took a quick look around and called in Captain O'Hara to make sure everything was handled properly—and quietly."

"Good man," said the president.

"And you would have been proud of your daughter, sir. She was the one who saw I was summoned. She kept a cool head. I guess it runs in the family."

Sitting on the couch next to his daughter, the president gave her a squeeze. "That's my girl, not falling to pieces at the first sign of trouble." Alice looked incredibly pleased at that and gave me a look of gratitude. The girl was difficult, but I felt I should give her credit when it was due.

But then Alice, taking advantage of all the good feeling in the room, took us in a new direction.

"Father. I've heard of a group here called the XVII. No one seems to know anything about it. I wondered if you did."

Dear God. It wasn't going to be easy to ask the president about the XVII without going into the details. But as I said, Alice was a Roosevelt, and the Roosevelts didn't fall apart at the first sign of trouble.

The president seemed surprised for a moment. "The XVII? Where did you hear about them?"

"Members seem to wear these signet rings. Rather vulgar, I think, but I noticed and asked, and no one seems to want to discuss it. I'm wondering if it's some sort of secret boys' club, no girls allowed—which isn't very sporting of them."

"Who was wearing one of these rings?" asked Mr. Roosevelt. He was looking at her hard. On the surface, Mr. Roosevelt was an outgoing sporting figure, so some made the serious mistake of thinking that he was one of those dim country gentlemen who did nothing but hunt and drink at their clubs. But he had one of the sharpest minds I'd ever come across, and Alice should have known better than anyone that fooling him was going to be a little harder than playing games with most other members of City Society.

"Oh, Simon Rutledge, if I remember right. I noticed it at the party."

Mr. Roosevelt considered that. "You always did have sharp eyes, my girl. Yes, the XVII. So they've taken to having rings made up? Rather silly."

"But who are they?" persisted Alice.

"As you said, Baby Lee, just a boys' club."

"Surely you know more than that, Father," said Alice.

The president turned to me. "Sergeant St. Clair, New York certainly seems to bring out the curiosity in my daughter."

"If you know a way to curb it, Colonel, I wish you'd share it with me."

"No, properly channeled curiosity is important, a key to knowledge and self-improvement. Oh, very well . . . Simon Rutledge and a few others had some concerns about the considerable growth of New York and a fear, which I think was unfounded, about how the essential character of the city is changing, and not for the better. You know my feeling on immigrants. They have to become one of us, learn the language, and give their new country their full loyalty. But if they do that, they're no less a citizen than I am. From talking to Rutledge and those like him, I gather they disagreed."

"I asked around, and someone said the name references the seventeenth century," said Alice. "That your family has to have been here since then to belong. I think that's ridiculous. What exactly do they do?"

"I suppose they campaign for legal changes, which is their right, even if I do disagree with them."

"Is that all? They haven't been engaging in violence that you know of?" asked Alice. Now that got the president's attention.

"I wouldn't have thought so." His eyes narrowed. "Baby Lee, what is this about? Does this have to do with the Brackton murder? That's been the talk of the city, I understand, and I know you were there. I've also had a report that it may be related to the death of Delilah Linde. Of course, I know all of them, at least slightly." Naturally he would, being part of the same class. Also, the president had scores of people—not the least of whom was his sister—giving him the details of what was going on.

"I admit that it did pique my interest," said Alice coolly. "I was there, after all. There seems to be some question about Mr. Brackton's death, and with enormous pressure on the police to arrest someone—anyone—I thought it would only be right to see if there are any clues among the people the police can't question. Mr. Brackton was in the XVII. So are Simon Rutledge, Marcus Linde, and Miles van Dijk, brother of the late Delilah Linde."

I thought Alice may have overplayed her hand and showed too much interest, more than just idle curiosity. I watched the president lean back and consider what Alice had just said. It could go either way with him, and I could see him considering the seemingly sensible statement his eldest child had made about the police going too far to arrest someone and just how far she might go in involving herself.

"Is this still about your curiosity?" asked the president.

"It's about Booker T. Washington," said Alice. "You had him over for dinner no matter what anyone else thought. And I can be no less brave than you. Do you know who Peter Carlyle is?"

"Should I?" asked the president.

"He's the mechanic who keeps our motorcar in repair, a Negro mechanic. The police have suspected him because he had an argument with Lynley Brackton, but who didn't? And wait until they find out that he recently married a Rutledge house-maid, which supposedly gave him access to the house. It's nonsense, of course, but arrests happen anyway. With Mr. St. Clair's help, we will clear him and anyone else the police arrest may falsely arrest."

"That's quite a speech," said Mr. Roosevelt. He thought. "The Rutledges employ Negro maids?"

"Not to my knowledge. The new Mrs. Carlyle is white—Irish, in fact."

The president nodded. "That could be a problem for them. A mixed-race marriage—that's not even legal in some states. The Carlyles would be easy to convict on murder and conspiracy with only the flimsiest evidence."

"There's more, Father. What about the Jews in this city? We've heard the XVII has been threatening them."

"The Jews? I'm sorry to hear about that. I went with my parents to Jerusalem as a boy and was deeply affected by my visit. St. Clair, you remember we had some Jewish troopers in the regiment. Fine men."

"Yes, sir." I had wondered why so many enlisted. They told me they were still mad at Spain, which had thrown them out of the country some four hundred years ago. Holding a grudge for centuries—now that's impressive.

"Any Jews in particular?"

"We heard about threats against the Roths."

"Reuben Roth? I could see he'd have enemies. He's a good man, and I respect him, but Wall Street is even more rough and tumble than the Dakotas when St. Clair here helped me run the ranch. But I can't imagine why the XVII would be out for him."

"Maybe they don't want Jews pushing into their business?" asked Alice.

"As I said, it's rough and tumble, but financial battles are usually settled in the stock markets, occasionally in courts, but not with threats from mysterious societies. The Roths are powerful, and I've always had the sense they can take care of themselves." He gave his daughter a speculative look. "Are you sure you're not seeing something that isn't there? Letting your imagination get away from you?"

"I'm just trying to help my friend," said Alice, sticking her chin out.

He sighed and turned to me. "I don't imagine I can dissuade my daughter, but you'll keep her safe, Sergeant St. Clair?"

"As well as can be expected, Colonel."

He frowned at that. "It's not like you to not give a straight answer," he said. I saw Alice was watching me closely.

"Colonel, when I picked Miss Alice up at the White House, she was firing a revolver into a mattress in the basement. Despite all the guards and agents in the building, she got herself a revolver and ammunition and had set up a shooting range. Begging your pardon, sir, but safety is always relative with your daughter."

He nodded in agreement. "I hear what you're saying. What was she shooting?"

"One of those old Smith & Wesson single-action revolvers they made after the war."

He turned to his daughter. "Where did you even get something like that?" Alice just shrugged and looked away. "I suppose we could turn her over to Captain O'Hara and have him keep her in the Tombs," said the president.

"She'd probably find a way to break out and take some felons with her," I said, and the president nodded. I could see Alice getting more and more annoyed at the way her father and I were talking about her, but realizing how great the stakes were, she kept quiet.

"Be a good girl, and be guided by Sergeant St. Clair," the president said. "And if you run afoul of my sister, you're both on your own."

At that, we heard someone at the door, and a moment later, Mrs. Cowles entered.

"Theodore, good to see you, as always," she said and gave him a kiss. "We have you for one night?"

"Yes, I'm off in the morning. Has my girl been good?" He was going to get a full range of opinions on Alice.

"All things considered, yes. She's been organizing breakfast meetings. We've been treated to journalists and police officers."

"It's a way to keep watch on what is going on in New York," said Alice. "Isn't that why I'm here?"

"Exactly, my girl," said the president, grateful at least that breakfast at the Caledonia didn't involve firearms.

I thought it was a good time to leave. "If you all are staying in, I'll excuse myself."

"Yes, take the rest of the day off," said the president. "Good seeing you again, St. Clair." He slapped me on my back. I said goodbye to Mrs. Cowles and Alice—who slipped me a quick wink—and headed down to my room.

I lay down on my bed and breathed easily. It had been a near thing, but we were still in operation. Mariah told me she had an afternoon wedding to cook for, but I thought if I came around later, I could get her to cook me something for dinner. For now, I rolled a cigarette and enjoyed the quiet for a while, interrupted by a knock on my door.

I rarely got visitors. My room is not suitable for entertaining, and so I met friends and acquaintances elsewhere. Even if the president went out, I assumed that Alice and Mrs. Cowles would go with him, and his detail would watch over them.

"Come in; it's open," I yelled, too lazy to get up.

It was Alice.

"For heaven's sake, Miss Alice, you know you shouldn't be here, especially with your father and aunt around." I sat up in my bed.

"They're discussing something tedious in my aunt's room, and I said I was just running downstairs to grab a newspaper." She closed the door behind her and sat on the only chair.

"I came to apologize," she said.

"An Alice Roosevelt first. And I was there to see it."

"Do be quiet, and don't make me sorry I came down here. I think we made a splendid case to my father upstairs. I thought you might sell me out, but you turned in a magnificent performance, and I apologize for ever doubting you."

"I just didn't want to have to face you if I hadn't backed your play."

"I know you don't mean that. You just don't want me to think that you trust me so deeply. I am indeed flattered, Mr. St. Clair. Thank you." She got up and turned. "You can be difficult, but when it's important, you're rather a dear. Have a good evening, Cowboy."

"Have a good evening, Princess," I called after her. "Just close the door on your way out."

CHAPTER 29

We didn't have a committee meeting at breakfast the next day, which was just as well, as Mrs. Cowles didn't have any early appointments, so the three of us had breakfast together.

"What are your plans today, Alice? Something a little more useful than associating with reporters from the *Herald*?" asked Mrs. Cowles.

"Nothing much. A little shopping, taking in a museum. Perhaps visiting Philly Rutledge in the afternoon."

"Is she still upset about what happened at her party?" asked Mrs. Cowles.

Alice shrugged. "I don't think so. She didn't know Lynley Brackton very well and didn't much like him. By now I think she's seeing the positive aspects, with everyone talking about it. A little notoriety is always fun."

"A little goes a long way. Anyway, this isn't about your playing police detective again, is it?" asked Mrs. Cowles.

"Of course not. Simply associating with other young people of leading families in New York. Again, isn't that why I was brought back?"

Mrs. Cowles just shook her head and helped herself to more coffee.

★ ★ ★

After breakfast, Alice and I headed to the motorcar.

"She's going to find out eventually," I said.

"I didn't lie to her. We *are* going to visit Philly Rutledge today."

"We're trying to catch her out," I said.

"An unnecessary detail. I didn't see any need to burden my aunt with that," Alice said without even looking embarrassed about it.

The plan was to surprise Philly and Abraham together and get them to reveal the connection between the Rutledges and the Roths.

"You know, Miss Alice, for all we've found out, we still have no idea how Mr. Brackton was poisoned. Who could've done it? How? And are we really sure Mrs. Brackton was the intended target? She may still be hiding something from us."

"I know. I keep going over all of that in my head. I can't get the timing right in my memory. Did Mr. Rutledge look and see something before Brackton got sick? I think he did, but I can't be sure. He was looking at the other side of the punch table. I know he was. Maybe he didn't realize what he was seeing. Or maybe he's protecting someone. Or maybe he just liked looking at the beautiful Delilah Linde. Bit by bit, Mr. St. Clair. There is something here about loyalty and betrayal. Those murders were not coolly arranged. Someone was enraged."

"And lucky," I said. "Breaking into that greenhouse and poisoning a glass without getting caught. They were very lucky . . . unless they had help." Alice nodded, probably still thinking about what Simon Rutledge was looking at. How was he involved?

It was early to start tracking Philly and Abraham, so we did some shopping. Or rather, Alice shopped, and I tagged along. The shopgirls loved serving Alice, and Alice loved being fawned over. She bought some gloves and a new hat.

"Thank you," said Alice. "Please send the account and the packages to the Caledonia."

"Very good, Miss Roosevelt," said the shopgirl.

"Also, I know you don't have men's hats here, but perhaps

you could recommend a haberdasher? I'd like to see my body-guard in something a little more appropriate to New York than his cowboy hat."

"Of course," said the shopgirl, and she spared a quick smile for me. "But everything has to go together—the hat, the coat, the suit. Even the shoes."

"That might be a little ambitious," said Alice, looking me up and down. "Replacing his boots and that coat? We'll think on that. Oh well, thank you anyway."

"I thought you liked the cowboy look," I said as we walked back to the motorcar.

"Oh, I do; I like it just fine. But you'd look so good in some-thing . . . I don't know. You did look awfully good that one time I got you into evening clothes."

"Thank you, but I hope that was the last time."

"Don't you ever want to fit in more?" she asked and looked closely at me for the answer as I prepared to pull into traffic.

"No," I said.

She didn't seem offended at that but did appear thoughtful. We grabbed a couple of hot dogs for lunch before driving down to the Rutledge offices. We parked just beyond the entrance to the building, and after a few minutes' wait, we saw a fine motor-car pull up.

"I think that's the Rutledge motorcar," said Alice excitedly, and she was proved right a moment later when Philly Rutledge came out of the building and the chauffeur let her in.

"Follow her," said Alice. "We have to be sure she's really going to visit Abraham Roth."

"Say a prayer," I said. Following someone in Manhattan traf-fic wasn't all that easy. It could get very crowded downtown, and it was a fine balance to stay close to someone without being recognized.

"This is fun," Alice said, grinning as I steered around other motorcars, carriages, and delivery drays.

"Yes, let's do this again soon," I said.

We were rewarded. The motorcar pulled up to one of the elegant stores the best people go to. Philly said a few words to the driver and then entered the establishment as he drove off. We held our breath—and then Philly, looking cautiously around her, crossed the street quickly and entered the office building belonging to Abraham Roth's business.

"She didn't see us," I said.

"I think she's new to this," said Alice. "She's not as experienced as we are. Now quickly, park the motorcar, and we'll go after her. It's time to end this."

I found a place for the motorcar just off the avenue, and we followed Philly across the street into the small building. Alice practically ran, and it was hard enough to follow her while keeping an eye on the busy afternoon crowds. More than a few people saw Alice Roosevelt running, and I had no doubt they'd have interesting stories to tell to their work mates and families later that afternoon.

The office lobby was about as elegant a room as I had been in. I knew the Roths had deep pockets, and it showed in every inch of the lobby. Marble slabs on the wall made me think we were in a fine bank, but we also saw statues that looked like they came from the Metropolitan Museum of Art, and the carpet was so thick you could comfortably take a nap on it. A well-dressed clerk sat beyond a light wood table that I bet came from Europe because I had never seen anything with that many curlicues made in the States. He stood as we entered.

"May I help you?" he asked. I could see in his eyes that he recognized Alice. Meanwhile, I glanced through an open door that led further into the building. I could see more fine desks and a private office at the end.

"Alice Roosevelt to see Mr. Roth."

"One moment, Miss Roosevelt. He is with a client. If you will take a seat, I'll tell him you're here."

"Don't bother," said Alice, and with a wave of her hand, she took off along the thick carpet down the hall.

"But Miss Roosevelt," said the clerk, his perfectly formed features suddenly changing to a look of absolute dismay. He had no idea what had just happened and no idea how to fix it. He looked to me as if I knew the answer. I just shrugged and followed Alice.

A couple of other men wearing fine suits looked at us . . . and then looked again. It was Alice Roosevelt, and she wasn't accompanied by the clerk, but there was a cowboy on her heels, and like the clerk, no one knew what to make of it. I wondered if Alice would make even a pretense of knocking on the door. She didn't do it at the church, so why should she do it here?

She didn't. She grabbed the doorknob and pushed her way in. Yes, it was just like being at St. Benedict's all over again. Alice knew she wasn't supposed to enter any room first, but if she thought about it—and she probably didn't—she figured that a private office in a Roth building was hardly likely to contain anything dangerous.

It was safe enough. We stepped into an elegant office, not as elaborate as the front room but comfortable and expensive, with a fine Oriental carpet and another blond wood desk and bookshelves. Everything was neat and perfect—*too* neat and perfect. Every time I had seen Mr. Roosevelt's desk—or Mrs. Cowles's for that matter—you could tell from the pens and blotters and piles of paper that people were at work. There was no sign of that here. It may have been called an office, but I think it worked more as a meeting room.

Right now, the two people meeting were Abraham Roth and Philly Rutledge, sitting on a yellow leather couch at the opposite end of the office. We interrupted them sipping coffee from a fancy silver service on a low wood table in front of them. Maybe there was work being done here after all, just not at the desk. But I couldn't tell for sure. If Rutledge and Roth papers were being exchanged, I didn't see them.

"Alice!" said Philly. She looked shocked—and concerned.

"Miss Roosevelt!" said Abraham. He was well mannered because even in his surprise, he stood up. They both looked a little pink in the face, but it wasn't from drink, as there didn't seem to be anything stronger than coffee around.

Usually Alice figured out what was going on before I did, but I think I beat her to it by a about half a minute this time. After all, I was some years older than she was, some years older than anyone in that room. It was exactly like the scene at St. Benedict's, and I suppose I shouldn't have done it, but I couldn't help myself.

I laughed.

Philly and Abraham got even redder, and then the front desk clerk came running in, looking around, not quite knowing what he was supposed to do. I stifled my amusement for a moment as Alice glared at me, and then we all just stood there staring at each other for a few moments in silence, eyes bouncing from one person to the next.

"It's all right," said Abraham to the clerk after about a minute. "Please close the door on your way out, and don't disturb us unless I call."

"Very good, sir," said the clerk, bowing out. By that point, Alice knew what was happening, too, but she wasn't laughing. She remained standing, arms folded across her chest, looking half embarrassed, half annoyed.

"We're really sorry," I said. "Miss Alice was hot on the trail of some big business deal, and all she's done once again is bust up a romance."

Alice just kept tapping her foot in impatience and finally said, "I don't suppose you have anything stronger than coffee here."

"I'm afraid not. But why don't both of you take a seat?" Abraham smiled wryly. "I think we have some things to discuss, and I hope I can count on your discretion."

"Of course," said Alice, and we both pulled up chairs just

opposite the couple. "You remember Mr. St. Clair from the other night."

"Of course," said Abraham, and he reached out and shook my hand.

"What are you doing here? How did you find us?" asked Philly, finally finding her voice.

"Why are you keeping secrets from me?" Alice asked, ignoring Philly's questions. "I should think I'd be trustworthy."

Philly looked a little embarrassed at that, but Abraham was a gentleman.

"That is my fault, Miss Roosevelt. I told Philly she couldn't tell anyone. The penalties for even an accidental revelation would be enormous." Alice glanced at me for a second. We both remembered what Cathleen said at her wedding breakfast. Cathleen and Philly shared a secret about illicit romances, giving them each a strong reason to trust the other.

"What am I doing here? It's a long story, but I'll try to make it short," said Alice. "We're still trying to figure out who killed Lynley Brackton at your party. We thought it was a matter of high finance. We still do. We thought you and Philly were acting as representatives of your fathers."

"But that's ridiculous," said Philly. "My father doesn't share any of his business with me. I just visit with him at the offices once a week and greet his senior employees, and then he buys me lunch."

"And then you meet with Abraham," added Alice, and Philly blushed again.

"We met at a party some months back . . . and then . . ." She couldn't say any more, but Abraham reached out and took her hand, and nothing more was necessary.

"Miss Roosevelt, do I understand that this is the *second* time you've interrupted a romance? This is all part of your . . . investigations?" asked Abraham.

"We've had a few setbacks," she said without a hint of apology in her tone. "But never mind. So you two are having a romance."

"My father would never consent," said Philly. She didn't have to explain. The Roths may be the wealthiest family in New York, but they were Jewish. And Philly's father was apparently a leading member of the XVII.

"I hope it works out for you," said Alice. "But since we're here, we have some questions to ask, and perhaps you can help us"

"Indeed. Miss Roosevelt, whatever made you think that Philly and I had some sort of business relationship?"

"First of all, Philly is a dear friend, and if you're her beloved, it seems appropriate for you to call me Alice," she said. "Second, it's a rather complex situation, and you must bear some of the blame for all this." He raised an eyebrow and glanced at me. A quick look of sympathy passed between us. "There is a small town-house paid for through this office, and we found out something interesting. Its sole occupant is a Japanese nobleman negotiating what appears to be a large and secret deal with your father."

Abraham smiled grimly. "So you stumbled onto that? My father ran it through my business to try to hide it from those who keep a close watch on him. I know about it, although not a lot of details. Anyway, I guess there's no hiding anything from the full weight of the US Secret Service."

"You won't believe this," I said. "But this isn't a Secret Service affair. It's all about Miss Alice here."

Abraham was dead silent for a few moments—and then he burst out laughing.

CHAPTER 30

"Oh, very well," said Abraham, finally controlling himself. "You know some of it, so I might as well tell you all of it. I guess I can trust the president's daughter and the US Secret Service." He looked at his sweetheart. "And you, too, Philly. Perhaps you know what goes on in Russia. Or maybe not. Anyway, it's probably the worst place in the world to be if you're Jewish. Destroying Jewish neighborhoods and killing Jews is practically government policy. My father despises the Russians for that. It's an obsession with him. If you know anything about politics in the East, it's becoming clear that the Russians and the Japanese are due to knock up against each other there. What's kept it from happening is that the Japanese don't have the capital to build a large, modern army and navy. My father is going to give them the money to do that. He's put together a syndicate that's raised a fortune, an amount that can change the balance in the East. And he's doing it because he hates the Russians."

Christ almighty. Imagine having so much money you could buy yourself a war. I don't know if anyone else in that room looked at it that way; I was the only one there who had fought in a war, so maybe not.

Alice digested this. It matched what we heard from Baron Okada. We had known Roth was spending money in Japan but not that it was personal, and that made it different. "Is Simon Rutledge, Philly's father, one of the investors in this syndicate? Philly, did your father mention that?"

She shook her head. "I just meet people. Father never talks business with me, not in detail."

Abraham also shook his head. "I'm only involved in some parts of the family business. This is something personal for Father. He might give me names if I asked." Then he flashed a disarming grin that made it clear why Philly was taken with him. "Men in this city will do business with Jews, but that's as far as it goes. Even if the Rutledges are investing with the Roth syndicate, would that make a difference to our folks regarding Philly and me?"

"Maybe, but fathers can be funny," I said.

"If we can get back to the matter at hand," said Alice a little testily. "It seems that your father was especially anxious to insure the safety of his Japanese partner in this investment deal. I was wondering if there was more to it than just the usual veil of secrecy that men like to put over almost everything they do."

"Alice, what do you know about things like business? My father is an important man of business, and I don't know anything," said Philly. She sounded partly curious and partly jealous.

"I've been in Washington," said Alice grandly. "You have no idea." From the look on Philly's face, she hadn't.

"Since you ask, Father has been a little nervous," said Abraham. "There have been quiet threats. We're used to a certain amount of talk. My father was born in Germany, a Jew. My grandfather was a rabbi. Despite the enormous wealth he made, we are outsiders here. We know that." He said that as a fact without any self-pity. I thought well of him for that. Philly reached her hand for his again and gave him a look of love. I thought well of her for that.

"My father says we're all Americans no matter where we came from," said Alice.

"I wish there were more men like your father," said Abraham.

"But the fact remains that we are not fully members of leading Society here, and in recent months, there's been something else. Not in the mansions of men like my father, in their clubs, and in the dining halls of the important people—"

"But in other neighborhoods," interrupted Alice. "Where the poor Jews live in the Lower East Side, despised immigrants at the mercy of criminal gangs, side by side with the Italians and the Irish and the Chinese and Negroes and so many others. There is someone, some group, who'd rather they never came here at all, is that correct, Abraham?"

Abraham and Philly looked a bit astonished at that little speech. I knew Alice, and even I was impressed.

"Tell me. Have either of you heard of a group called the XVII?" Alice asked.

Philly looked blank. I guess she had never noticed her father's ring. But Abraham nodded. "My father believes there is a group behind the threats and intimidation. He is involved in charitable activities to improve the lot of Jewish immigrants, and he's heard stories. But we've never heard any names. We don't know who they are, but Father is very unhappy about their work and their influence."

"Does this have something to do with Lynley Brackton's murder?" asked Philly.

"Yes. I am sure of it," said Alice. "Lynley Brackton was a member of the XVII, the group behind this. And so is Marcus Linde, whose wife was also recently murdered."

"It's been an open secret that Brackton was killed," said Abraham. "But I thought Delilah Linde died of natural causes. Some sort of sudden illness, the word was."

"It wasn't. Two attacks having to do with the XVII. I don't think it's a coincidence. We thought it had to do with a business arrangement, but it seems it was just a romance." Alice gave me a quick glare to prevent me from laughing at her again. "But I think I was right, if only in a different way. If the XVII don't like foreigners, they certainly won't like immigrant Jewish families making huge business deals with Orientals. There is something there—I haven't figured it out yet, that's all. Philly, think back. We were at the punch bowl with your father when Brackton got sick. Your father was looking at something."

"Alice, don't you think if my father saw something, he would've told someone?"

"But what if he didn't know what he saw? Something out of the corner of his eye, something that seemed wrong but he didn't realize. Let me show you."

The office was in absolutely perfect order, like I said. Nothing out of place. On one of the bookshelves, a half dozen elegant leather volumes stood between a pair of bookends in the shape of beautiful stone lions. The books were centered on the shelf, but Alice grabbed the whole bunch and moved them six inches to the left.

"Doesn't that look wrong?" asked Alice.

"Well, yes," conceded Abraham.

"But not suspicious. Maybe the maid who dusts this room moved them to get to the back of the shelf and forgot to center them again. Maybe one of your clerks needed to borrow some of these books and was careless putting them away. Two likely scenarios. But you wouldn't assume that someone had picked up a bookend and killed someone with it. That's what I mean."

"Alice, that's . . . horrible," said Philly.

"But it makes a lot of sense," said Abraham. "So Mr. Rutledge saw a line of books that was off center, so to speak, and didn't realize it was covering up a murder. You're the lawman, Mr. St. Clair—does that make sense?"

"If anything makes sense here, that certainly does," I said. "But where do we go from here?"

Alice frowned at that and didn't say anything for a moment. The rest of us were quiet, too.

"I don't suppose your parents would be welcoming if the

four of us plus a couple of other guests had a little . . . event, I guess you could call it, in your house," Alice asked Philly.

"What? Why? But no, I don't think my parents want any more . . . events . . . for a while. Mother has hardly been able to get out of bed since that happened, and Father is pretending it didn't happen at all," said Philly. "And it would be awkward enough if Abraham came, too. But why—"

"It doesn't matter. We'll do it in the Caledonia parlor. It'll be good enough. I'll need the two of you and two more, and I'd rather it be people we already know . . ." She gave Philly a quizzical look. "You have a maid in your house, whom we spoke to as a witness. Her name is Cathleen O'Neill."

"Yes, a sweet girl. She's the one who got me ready for the party. You want something of her?" Philly was looking more and more confused, and so was Abraham. I knew Alice better and saw what was coming. I wasn't happy about it, but I knew. "But Cathleen—" said Philly, and then she stopped.

"But what?" asked Alice. "Don't worry. We already know you shared your secret with Cathleen. You would need a maid's help in arranging meetings, and although she didn't give you away, I figured out she knew something about you."

"Really? How . . . surprising," said Abraham.

"Cathleen has a secret, rather likes ours," explained Philly. "She has a fiancé and recently got married. Maids aren't supposed to marry. My mother would fire her in a minute if she knew. As I said, Cathleen takes care of me, and we have an arrangement. I cover for her when she goes out to see her husband, and she covers for me when I visit with you."

Abraham nodded. A single man had more freedom to plan his day than a young woman living under her parents' roof. Alice had me, of course, but I was more obliging than Mr. and Mrs. Rutledge.

"I guessed that was the arrangement," Alice said. "This works out very nicely. We need one more person. We'll have Cathleen's husband join us. He already knows what is happening, as well. Oh, and your sister Mariah," she said to me.

"Miss Alice—"

"She'll be delighted, I'm sure," said Alice, running right over me. I got paid for putting up with her, but Mariah was apparently expected to do it for free.

"It sounds like you already knew about Cathleen's secret, if you know her husband," said Philly. "I don't see how you could—"

Alice was getting annoyed at the interruptions. "It's a long story, and I don't want to go into it now. I know Cathleen is married. I was her maid of honor, and Mr. St. Clair was best man. I'm glad you know, too, as this makes everything much easier to arrange. Now, I want both of you and Cathleen at the Caledonia at eight for breakfast tomorrow. I'm sure you can rearrange Cathleen's schedule accordingly. Mr. St. Clair and I will make the arrangements for his sister, Mariah Flores, and Cathleen's husband, Mr. Carlyle. I think that's all. You can go back to . . ." Alice waved her hand to fill in the blank.

Philly was looking positively dumbfounded with the invasion, Alice's discussions about investigations, the royal summons to appear at her residence, and the final revelation that she and I had stood up for Cathleen and her husband at their wedding. The poor girl looked as if she'd never speak again.

But Abraham found his voice. "Um, Alice . . . What exactly are we going to do at breakfast?"

"Didn't I say? We're going to recreate the murder of Lynley Brackton."

Again, a silence fell on the room.

"Recreate it?" asked Philly in a small voice.

"Philly, you remember what we said. Your father saw something. I'm not saying he ignored a murder, but like I said before by the bookshelf, something happened. I think by recreating the evening by the punch bowl, I can figure it out. I will remember the timing. I have found out everything I can from talking to people, but it always come down to who slipped poison into that glass at your party."

"If you think it will help, Alice, we'll be there," said Philly.

"Good. My aunt will probably have left before we get started, but if you happen to speak with her, don't mention it. I'm rather busy and don't need the extra difficulty of an argument with her." Alice turned to me. "We need to leave now to catch your sister before she leaves for work, and then on to Mr. Carlyle—and if Dulcie doesn't get advance notice about extra guests, she can get quite irritable, and we don't want that, either. Philly, Abraham, see you at eight tomorrow with Cathleen."

Not waiting for a response, Alice made an exit as abrupt as her entrance. Abraham once again gave me a look with a lot of sympathy. I was going to apologize on Alice's behalf but couldn't think of the words, so I just nodded and followed Alice along the heavy carpet.

CHAPTER 31

"Miss Alice," I said as we got into the motorcar. She turned her eyes on me, brimming with innocence.

"Yes, Mr. St. Clair?"

"Don't play the little girl with me. That's quite a crew you've invited to your aunt's dining room tomorrow. You think you can figure out what happened that night?"

"Yes. It was dark then, and I wasn't paying attention, and I had finished a glass of that disgusting punch because it was the only thing they were serving. Now, we have a chance to see what really happened that night. And don't worry about my aunt. She only holds you responsible for my physical safety. Any fuss about my hostessing forays will be between just the two of us."

"You know, Miss Alice, there were times when I wore a badge in Laramie that I had to come between two parties shooting at each other. The fact that they weren't trying to kill me was cold comfort."

Alice looked me curiously. "That was a very clever metaphor, Mr. St. Clair. I didn't expect that from you. You keep showing signs that my aunt is right about you. You're a lot smarter than you let on. Now don't just sit there; drive us to Mariah's."

I shook my head and did as she asked.

★ ★ ★

The rest of the afternoon went well. Mariah was in and let me roll her a cigarette as she leaned back in her kitchen chair and listened to Alice's request with some amusement.

"So we're going to act out the death of this Lynley Brackton?"

"Yes. And you'll get breakfast out of it. I don't want word getting out about what I'm doing, so I'm only asking people who know what this is about, people I can trust."

"I'm honored, hon. Sure, it sounds like fun. See you at eight."

We then drove to the garage where Peter was working. He was under a car and covered in grease and was pleased to see us.

"Breakfast at your place, Miss Roosevelt?" He grinned and shook his head. "Does your aunt want me at your table?"

"Mr. Carlyle, I think we've already established that the Roosevelts invite a wide variety of guests to their table. You're actually a step ahead of Booker T. Washington, as I'm more entertaining than my father and our cook is better than the White House cook." Peter laughed at that and nodded in agreement. "Also, my friend, Philadelphia Rutledge, will be bringing your wife to complete the party."

His face fell. He was counting on our keeping his secret, but Alice quickly reassured him. "Don't worry; Philly already knows you're married, and she is being discreet. She's a good sort. Also, Cathleen is keeping a secret of hers . . . Oh, don't look so surprised, Mr. Carlyle. My father wouldn't do half as well without my aunt, Mr. St. Clair needs me to run this investigation, and now you have Cathleen. Tomorrow at eight. We aren't formal at breakfast."

And that was that.

★ ★ ★

Nothing much happened the rest of that day. Mrs. Cowles told Alice some people would be visiting later, which usually meant Republican worthies and their wives, and "if it isn't too much trouble, could you put on a nice dress and mingle for a while?" Alice sighed and said yes, clearly hoping her aunt would appreciate what a sacrifice she was making, but I don't think Mrs. Cowles did.

Alice did find a minute to go into the kitchen to tell Dulcie that, once again, there would be guests for breakfast the next day—a large group this time. I stayed outside, not brave enough to come between Alice and the cook. I heard voices raised and pots banging, and then Alice emerged, looking smug. "Pancakes and sausages tomorrow, Mr. St. Clair. I do like pancakes."

Since Alice was staying in for the rest of the day, I went downstairs and grabbed some hash for dinner at a place under the El just to the west of the Caledonia. They served it with a fried egg on top. I found a card game in the basement, and I took my winnings early, which bothered the boys, but it was going to be a busy morning, and I needed my sleep.

★ ★ ★

The next morning, I didn't really expect Alice to assemble this particular meeting without Mrs. Cowles noticing. I don't think Alice did, either. Her aunt had always found out about the past breakfast meetings, and now that they had expanded, Mrs. Cowles would be on the lookout. Even though she was an early riser and would already have had her breakfast by eight and be back in her little office making arrangements for the day, I had no doubt that she'd be checking.

Of course, Alice would have to set the stage in the parlor, and that would be a little harder to explain. It was unlikely that Mrs. Cowles would visit that part of the apartment in the morning, and Alice may have warned the maids not to trouble her aunt with what they were doing, so I gave even odds on getting way with that one.

Philly was first, a few minutes early, looking half nervous and half excited. Cathleen came with her, looking entirely nervous.

It wasn't new for her being in a fine residence, but this time she was a guest, not a servant.

Abraham came next, and although Alice had said the Roosevelts weren't formal at breakfast, he wore a very nice suit. My sister followed him a few minutes later, also well turned out. I watched her take everything in, and I knew she was looking forward to telling all her friends and coworkers about what the Roosevelt apartment looked like.

Peter came last, entering the room cautiously. Alice was getting everyone settled in the dining room with the maid, so I answered the door by myself. He wore a suit no better than mine and was looking around as if he couldn't believe this was really happening.

"Yeah, I know what you're thinking," I said, and he just nodded.

"Am I late?" he asked.

"You're fashionably late," I said. "In the better houses, it's politer to come a little late." Peter nodded again.

But Alice made me look like a liar when she stepped into the foyer. "Both of you hurry, and don't sit there gossiping like a pair of kitchen maids. Breakfast is on the table."

The dining room was laid out nicely with piles of pancakes and sausages and plenty of coffee.

"Philly, would you mind moving over so Mr. Carlyle can sit next to his wife? Husbands and wives sit together at events like this until their first anniversary, when presumably they're tired of each other and ready for some fresh faces. Not everyone knows everyone here, so I'll make some introductions."

Then Mrs. Cowles walked in, as I knew she would. The previous evening, I had advised Alice that it might be better to just tell her aunt we were having people over for breakfast, and Mrs. Cowles might be a little more understanding if she wasn't taken by surprise. But Alice said, "I've found that it's easier to apologize for what you've done than to ask permission for what you want to do."

Indeed, Alice wasn't cowed, and if she was dismayed at her aunt's arrival, she kept it to herself. Mrs. Cowles seemed a little stunned, which was unusual for her, considering what Alice had done before. Alice stood, and so did I and the other men.

"Aunt Anna, I am hosting another breakfast meeting, and we continue to outgrow the breakfast room. Your timing is perfect; I was just going to introduce everyone. You know Philly Rutledge, of course. This is Abraham Roth. You probably know, or at least know of, his father, Reuben Roth. This is Cathleen O'Neill—actually, you're Cathleen Carlyle now—who works for Philly, and her new husband Peter Carlyle, who keeps our motorcar in repair, and my friend Mariah Flores, who is Mr. St. Clair's sister. Everyone, this is my aunt, Anna Roosevelt Cowles, my father's sister."

Everyone was quiet for a moment, and then Abraham spoke first. "We haven't met, Mrs. Cowles, but my father spoke with the president at a reception in Washington some months back and is a great admirer of his, as am I."

"Thank you," said Mrs. Cowles tonelessly. She was taking in the crowd and no doubt trying to figure out what we all had in common. After a few moments, she decided what to say. "I'm going out and won't be back until after lunch, Alice. We're having a formal dinner tonight, so be home in plenty of time. We will speak later this afternoon."

"Very good," said Alice coolly, and Mrs. Cowles turned on her heel and left.

"Does your aunt mind us all here?" asked Philly.

Alice just gave her a cheeky smile. "Oh, no. Her concern is not that you're here; it's *why* you're all here. But don't worry—I have several hours to think of a reasonable explanation. Meanwhile, Abraham, that is a lovely motorcar you have, but I assume something that large is your father's. Were you planning to buy your own? Mr. Carlyle knows everything about motorcars, so be sure to take his advice about any purchase. Mrs. Carlyle, I know your people are from Ireland. I know little about Irish cooking, but would you be so good as to discuss it with Mariah, who is an absolute marvel in the kitchen."

That got everyone talking, which pleased Alice. I leaned over to her. "Whoever marries you is going to have his hands full, but he is going to get a great political hostess." It's rare to see Alice blush, but she did then.

★   ★   ★

For a woman built like a longshoreman, Dulcie had a nice light touch with pancakes, and everyone enjoyed them as they spoke. When the breakfast wound down, Alice stood and clapped her hands. "We've all been fed and have had a chance to meet each other. Now to the reason you're all here. As we all know, Lynley Brackton was murdered at the Rutledge ball a few days ago. What you may not know, however, is that Mr. Brackton was not the intended target, but rather it was his wife, Victoria." Eyes got wide at that. "Furthermore, we suspect that Mrs. Linde was Mr. Brackton's mistress and was carrying his child."

That got a reaction. Mariah just grinned slyly, but Cathleen and Philly turned red.

"Miss Roosevelt . . . there are ladies here," ventured Abraham.

"I'm a lady. And this is business. Everyone in this room has a stake in finding his killer. Come with me to the parlor." We all got up and followed her.

The formal parlor was nowhere near as big as the ballroom in the Rutledge house, but Alice had set it up the same way for her purposes. At some point, she had gotten the maids to quietly set up a long table in the middle of the room with a punch bowl and glasses but without that punch I had heard so much about. The table was about fifteen feet long, as long as the one at the Rutledge house.

"One thing we know for sure," Alice said. "At some point, someone broke into the Rutledge greenhouse, stole a poisonous plant, and slipped it into Victoria Brackton's drink. She gave it to her husband, who drank it and died. Something was wrong; something was seen but didn't make any sense at the time. We will see what it is. Mariah, Philly, and Mr. St. Clair—you stand over here. Mariah, you get to be me. Philly, you have an easy job just being yourself. Mr. St. Clair will play Simon Rutledge.

"On this side, Mr. and Mrs. Carlyle get to play Mr. and Mrs. Brackton. Stand here, both of you. Abraham, my apologies, but we're shy one woman. You will be a stand-in for Delilah Linde."

He chuckled. "Happy to serve."

"Good. And as it was dim in the room, I'm closing the drapes." Alice quickly put the room into shadow. Then she viewed the two little groups from several angles. "Mariah—as me—face Simon Rutledge. Philly, you had your back to the wall but were half facing me, away from the punch bowl and not looking at the other side of the table. You, Mr. St. Clair, can see over our heads toward the punch bowl and beyond to the end of the table . . . that's right . . . wait, we all had glasses." She fetched the glasses and handed them around.

I could see the little knot where "Mr. and Mrs. Brackton" and "Mrs. Linde" were standing in their own little group. Alice angled them so "Mrs. Linde" was my mirror image, standing so she could view us, while "the Bracktons" were angled away, so I could only see half their backs.

"Notice I haven't given 'Mr. Brackton' a glass. He had finished his punch earlier. Mrs. Brackton had a glass, though. She then gave it to her husband. Good. Now let me have a look from every angle." She walked around all of us and seemed satisfied. "Can we try it again if Mr. and Mrs. Brackton each had their own glasses?" We did, and Alice shook her head. "No, that's not right. You tend to remember hands, and looking at it now, I would've remembered if each had a separate glass. Also, I didn't see anyone else breaking into the discussion, so unless one of the maids or waiters—"

"I beg your pardon, Miss Roosevelt," said Cathleen a little hesitatingly. "But we were told not to bother the people by the punch bowl. While passing around other refreshments, we were told the guests by the bowl were already helping themselves and to not create a crowd near there. So I don't think it was any of the maids or waiters joining them. There were no servants there, I'm sure."

"Thank you!" said Alice. "These are the kinds of things the police don't find out. They wouldn't have thought to ask, and no one wants to talk with them, anyway. Very good." Cathleen seemed pleased with that, and I saw Peter wink at his wife. "So it's just us then. Now, what did Simon Rutledge see but not realize he had seen?" Alice stepped by me. "Go ahead; pretend you're drinking. Mrs. Carlyle, speak with your husband and hand him your glass. That's what happened with the Bracktons." We all did as asked, and Alice watched . . . and then frowned.

"Philly, do you remember if Delilah Linde was drinking? She had a glass of mineral water, we've been told, to settle her stomach. What if the poisoning had something to do with that? Do you remember the glass?"

"I can't recall," said Philly. "You sort of assumed it. During the evening, everyone came to take one glass of the punch, and then they moved on. If she had punch or mineral water . . . I can't really remember."

"But everyone makes a face when they drink that god-awful punch," Alice said. "I don't remember noticing Delilah. Anyway, we helped ourselves to punch and stepped away from the bowl to give others a chance—if they wanted to—and walked to the ends to talk, and that way we could leave our empty glasses on the table before moving to another part of the room." She paused. "Her hair. Philly, remember that Delilah's hair was rather elaborately styled? She seemed self-conscious about it."

"Yes. Being here like this makes me remember. She was occasionally touching it to make sure it was in place—both sides."

"Which she couldn't do if she had a glass of punch or mineral water in her hand. Is that what your father saw, Philly? That someone was bothering to stay and chat by the punch bowl when they weren't actually drinking anything? Victoria Brackton seemed to remember her with mineral water. Unless she was mistaken or lying. But that seems too subtle. I'm here now and trying to remember your father. It's easier that everyone is in the same position." She stood next to Mariah, who was playing Alice. "Yes, it was just like this. He seemed almost worried. No, not worried. Appalled. Are we sure Delilah didn't have a glass? Mrs. Carlyle, what happened to glasses left on the table?"

"The waiters took them away to the kitchen, where they were washed and dried and then put out again for any other guests," answered Cathleen. "But the waiters wouldn't have done it unless the glasses were clearly left there, not while guests were still standing by them."

"The police said only Brackton's glass was left there, and it was smashed," I said.

"Good. Then Delilah wasn't drinking. She was at the punch table and wasn't drinking. Why?"

"To kill Mrs. Brackton?" asked Philly. "Why? And if my father saw, why didn't he say anything?"

"I don't see why Delilah was having a talk with with the father of her child and his wife," said Alice. "Why commit a murder right then? If anything, it's Victoria who should've been trying to kill Delilah. And even if Delilah was a murderess, we can't forget she was a murder victim, too. Also, if someone was trying to kill her for revenge, she'd be smart enough to be on the lookout for that, not fall for the same murder she had planned herself."

Alice lapsed into thought again. "Delilah. Did she just want to be near Lynley? Was that what this was about? She simply wanted to be near her lover?" Abraham blushed again. "One glass. Victoria changes her mind and gives it to her husband, who dies right there. A quick error, a terrified wife who's threatened again, and a murdered mistress. Let's do this again . . . We need to time this. Abraham, do you have a pocket watch with a second hand?"

"Of course," he said and handed over a beautiful gold watch. Alice timed our interaction, and we ran through it twice more, timing it with both groups talking and Alice watching, watching "Brackton" drinking the poisoned drink and "Rutledge" watching him. When did Rutledge actually see anything?

"Alice, are you sure my father saw something before Mr. Brackton got sick? Maybe he was just concerned that Lynley Brackton was looking unwell. You said there were signs of the poisoning," said Philly.

Alice nodded absently. "Or maybe he was concerned Mrs. Linde was looking unwell. We knew she had some digestive upsets, and they say these are common for women who are expecting a child. Is that what someone noticed? Mr. St. Clair, look worried."

"That's easy. I spend half my time with you looking worried." Everyone found that funny except Alice.

"Be serious. Yes, that's your worried face. But I think Mr. Rutledge was beyond worried. He was horrified. And who the hell is surprised when someone gets sick from overeating or overdrinking at a New York debutante ball? If Mr. Rutledge was horrified, perhaps it was because he saw a poisoning."

"Why would my father suspect someone had poisoned Brackton? Especially if, as we know now, Mrs. Brackton was the target?"

"That's a good question. Everyone hated Brackton. Maybe Mr. Rutledge was looking and thinking someone finally did it. Anyway, running it like this, I think you're right, Philly, about the time. It wasn't what happened in advance. It's what happened at the moment. I saw your father looking upset. But this is working. It's hard to remember how long you were doing something at a party, but when we time it, it helps us recall how long we were talking and at what point in the conversation Mr. Rutledge looked up. I think we have it now. Mr. St. Clair, you have a perfectly clear view of the other side of the table, correct? Good. And Philly, having timed this, are we in agreement that your father's look was timed with Lynley Brackton looking sick?"

"As much as possible. When we recreate it like this, it makes sense. I don't think we could see it at the time, but now I'm realizing that if my father had looked concerned earlier, we'd have seen it."

"Yes. And we'd have noticed it and looked over at Lynley right away. We didn't. By the time we noticed your father and looked at Lynley, he was already looking sick. Mrs. Carlyle, the glasses, if I remember, were hooked on the edge of the punch bowl, right? We all just took them and helped ourselves."

"Yes. We had our instructions most strictly at the start. Whoever brought the clean cups from the kitchen placed them one by one on the rim. The guests ladled their own punch into whichever glass they picked."

"So let's look at our assumptions. One, someone poisoned Mrs. Brackton's glass between the time she filled it and when she joined her husband and Mrs. Linde because otherwise it would've been noticed. Two, Mr. Rutledge saw nothing overt because he would've said something."

"Miss Alice, what did Mr. Rutledge see?" I asked.

Alice smiled. "That's what's interesting. That's why he was surprised. He didn't see a blessed thing."

CHAPTER 32

Alice shook her head but didn't seem upset. "Ladies and gentlemen, you have been immensely helpful. This is what has been bothering me all along—how someone could've poisoned the cup without being noticed. And now I see they couldn't have. It's a negative result, but that doesn't mean it wasn't useful. I now know what could *not* have happened. You have all been patient, and I'm glad we could have breakfast together, and now we're done."

Everyone looked at one another. "Have you reached any conclusions, Alice?" asked Abraham.

"Yes. That this is far more complicated that I realized. I thought this was a simple case, but it involves additional motives, competing motives, and will require more research. What we did today is eliminate the impossible, and that was essential. I will let you know when I know more."

I thought I was the only one there who wasn't fooled. Alice knew something, had concluded something. She was too pleased with herself, too smug. She just didn't want to say it in front of everyone.

"Well, then," said Abraham. "I think I speak for everyone here when I say we are happy we could help in the absence of any official police conclusions." Everyone nodded.

"As I said earlier, you all have a stake in this, so I will keep you informed. But I'm optimistic." If anyone poked around further, they'd find out about the XVII, which Philly didn't know her father belonged to. They'd find out about Philly's relationship with Abraham. And Peter was still the suspect of choice if no one else was picked up.

We saw everyone to the door. "Don't worry—I'm going to work this all out," Alice told the two couples, and they seemed cheered at that. Alice's optimism is infectious, just like her father's. I met Peter's eyes—he had the most to lose here—and gave him a strong handshake.

Mariah hung back for a few moments when the others left. "Thanks, Alice. This was fun. But you aren't fooling me, and I don't think you fooled my brother. You found out something important. You know who did it, don't you?"

Alice looked proud of herself. She seems to value Mariah's opinion. " 'Who' wasn't the really important question. It's about *why*. Now that I know that, I think I'm well on my way."

Mariah laughed. "All right, be proud. You've earned it. But don't be arrogant. You're crossing someone ruthless and desperate."

She turned to go, but then Alice laid a hand on her arm. "Mariah, could you stay for a few more minutes? I have something to ask you, and you're the only one who can help me."

Mariah looked surprised. "Sure, hon. I'm curious, though. I can't imagine what it is, unless you want cooking lessons."

Alice shook her head. "No. It's marriage. I want you to tell me about marriage. You're the only friend I have who's been married. I can hardly ask my father or aunt something like this." She gave me a sidelong glance. "This one would be useless."

Mariah laughed. "I don't suppose we can call on Joey as an expert. So what's this about, Alice? Thinking of getting hitched? You're a little young, but it you've found the right man, I wish you luck."

"No, I have no intention of getting married anytime soon," said Alice quite forcefully. "But I need to understand marriage. For all the politics and secret society nonsense we've seen, I think this is very personal. Two married couples, the Lindes and the Bracktons. It's really all about them; everything else is window dressing—I think. Come, let's sit down in the breakfast room. I've had too much coffee, but perhaps I can persuade Dulcie to make us a pot of tea."

A few minutes later, we were sitting in the breakfast room with a hot pot of tea.

"Here is my problem," said Alice. "First, I understand Delilah Linde. She made a hasty decision to marry a man for his money and then found herself unable to live up to it. She had an affair with an awful man. Very well. It was dishonorable, but not everyone can live up to the ideal."

"You're a hard girl," said Mariah.

Alice looked at her and blinked. She didn't like criticism but accepted it from Mariah because she respected her.

"Things change. You make the best bargain you can. You make a promise. But you're not a very romantic girl, are you, Alice?" said Mariah.

"I . . . I don't think that I am, no. Everyone says I'm outrageous, and I suppose I am, but that's not the same as being romantic. Delilah Linde was romantic. Is that what you're saying?"

"I never met Delilah Linde. But who was this man she was having an affair with, and why was he so awful? I bet he was charming."

"That's what my aunt said. Having made a bad decision on her marriage, Delilah made another one by falling for someone who couldn't give her what she needed, either. That seems . . . foolish."

Mariah laughed at that. "Yes, Alice. Very foolish."

Alice didn't laugh in return, just thought about that very carefully. "How foolish? Foolish enough to kill someone?"

Like me, Mariah has seen a lot and done a lot, so it took a lot to rattle her, but at that, she spilled half her tea into the saucer.

"Dear God, Alice. Women do foolish things, but you have to be desperately in love to kill. I don't know all the details here, and it's fine if you don't want to tell me. But was Delilah desperately in love with this man she was having an affair with?"

"I didn't know either of them. Since they're both dead, there's no way to figure it out. Do women kill the wives of their lovers?"

"Women are practical. Even if they're foolish. Unless she was absolutely insane, she'd have to know that even if her lover was free, she was still married. She'd have to kill her husband, too."

"But she didn't. She died herself. Who could've killed her? Why? Would a married woman kill her lover because he refused to leave his wife for her?"

"Again, not if she was married herself. Do you think she was planning to kill his wife and then her own husband?"

"Perhaps. But then she was killed. And everyone says Delilah was sweet and simple. I don't see her doing that. It's so frustrating." She folded her arms and frowned. "But the other couple. The Bracktons. Lynley treated Victoria horribly, cheated on, her humiliated her. Had affairs with low women, I'm sure. Could she be a killer? But all this is talk because I am sure after our reenactment that Simon Rutledge saw it all. Why is he keeping quiet? And who is still threatening Victoria? It could've been Delilah, who might've had a motive to threaten her lover's wife—but she was already dead." She paused. "Mariah, when there is great love, is there also great hate?"

"Now you're thinking smart, Alice. You can't hate a man you're indifferent to. Only one that you really love."

"That doesn't make any sense," said Alice, almost accusing Mariah. But my sister just smiled.

"No, it doesn't. But it's true, anyway." She sighed. "I don't know how much of a fool this Delilah was, but she'd have to be a great one if she was counting on a married man. That's the thing about married men, hon. If you're having an affair with one, you know right at the beginning he's not reliable."

Alice raised an eyebrow at that. If there was one thing everyone agreed on, it was that Brackton was unreliable. I wondered if they would put that on his tombstone.

"I don't know if there's anything more I can say," said Mariah. "But if you need any more marriage advice, just stop by."

"Thank you, Mariah. You really have been very helpful." Alice suddenly smiled and seemed very pleased with herself again, which made me wonder what she had figured out.

Mariah gave me a light slap on my cheek like she's been doing ever since we were children. "Keep an eye on her. Thanks again for breakfast." With that, she left.

"All right, Miss Alice. I see that look at your face. You've figured something out," I said.

"I think so. After all the politics and the affairs and jealousies, I think it comes down to some very petty things, actually, involving four people: Delilah Linde, Victoria Brackton, Lynley Brackton, and Simon Rutledge. Two of them are dead. One of them might be next. We think we know who was supposed to die, but we can't be sure. There are too many lies, and Mariah showed me there are emotions here I can't really know." She shook her head. "But I'm sure of one thing now—Simon Rutledge saw something. I know that from the reenactment, although I didn't want to say in front of everyone."

"What did he say? If we're sure one of those four is the poisoner, why didn't Rutledge say anything, if not at the time, then to me or the police later on? Especially after the second murder."

"No one saw that as likely to happen. Except the murderer, of course. And something else is interesting, Mr. St. Clair—we don't know if the same person killed Lynley and Delilah. If Delilah committed the first murder—she didn't have a glass, like we had been told, so her hands were free—was she killed in revenge?" Alice just shook her head, and we were quiet for a while. I was used to the words just pouring out of her like a river; Alice tended to speak as quickly as she thought. But when she finally spoke again, it was in a slow, deliberate way. "In the end, Mr. St. Clair, it should be very simple. That's what the reenactment showed me. Three people and one witness. It comes down to three people and one witness."

"He saw the murder, Miss Alice? That would mean he's trying to protect the killer. I don't see why. Why protect someone trying to kill Victoria Brackton? It doesn't make any sense."

"Maybe it wasn't a murder, and maybe Mrs. Brackton was not the target. Let's say it was Lynley all along, and he wasn't murdered as much as he was executed."

I thought about that for a few moments. In Laramie, where I wore a badge, crime was simple. Someone had once used a team of horses to rip the door off of a liquor warehouse, and a day later, the Sennett brothers, who never had a penny in cash between the pair of them, were found passed out drunk with empty bottles of good whiskey hidden in their hayloft.

But here we had a secret society, a Japanese baron, and the biggest man on Wall Street. But most of all, we had the rich. I know Mrs. Cowles said I should've learned something about them while working for the Roosevelts, and I suppose I had, but I also realized that unless you were one of them, you never really understood them. They didn't think the same way as the rest of us.

I didn't like the look in Alice's eye or where she was going with this. "You know something, Miss Alice. Tell me."

CHAPTER 33

"I . . . I just don't know where to go from here," Alice said, not quite answering me. "There is no proof, and no way of getting any. Only four people knew, and two of them are dead. The other two aren't talking. They won't. They can't."

"But you know?" I asked again.

"I might . . . after what Mariah told me . . ." She was lost in thought, as if she'd barely heard me. We stayed quiet for a while, then she seemed to come back from wherever she had gone. She had a glint in her eye when she looked at me, and I should've realized then and there where this would be going.

"Miss Alice, I think you know more than you're saying."

"I don't *know* anything. It's only what I *think*. You're the lawman. You know you have to have to proof to go to court."

Especially for people like this. You didn't need proof for people like Cathleen and Peter, just a suspicion. But you needed a solid witness to get someone in Society sent away. They didn't betray each other, not in public, anyway.

Alice was thinking along the same lines. She suddenly scowled. "I'm not letting this go. I'm not just going to wait for Captain O'Hara to get pushed into picking the wrong person because it's convenient. That's a cowardly way out. You know it is, too. Do you think my father would allow such a . . . a . . . weak solution to something like this, to let killers go free, while poor men paid the price?"

"Of course not, Miss Alice."

"I'll need to think on this. There must be some way we can fix this. I need something to distract me. One day isn't going to make a difference. We'll keep busy this afternoon, and then we'll make some plans over breakfast tomorrow. We'll both give it some thought tonight. Does that sound like a reasonable course?"

Then I made a mistake. Actually, two mistakes. Big ones. First, I trusted her to be sensible, when all I was doing was giving her more time to think of something outlandish. The second mistake was suggesting an activity that I knew would amuse and distract her but in the end, was only going to get her worked up. I wanted to make her happy, but I really should've known better.

"Miss Alice, if you don't have any other plans today, how would you like to learn how to shoot a revolver?"

"Really? Right now?" The aristocratic hostess who had organized that morning's reenactment disappeared, and the little girl came back. She actually jumped up and gave me a hug, then stepped back to give me a serious look. "Just when I am about to despair of you, you come up with something like this. I knew you wouldn't let me down."

I still didn't like the way this was playing out. I suspected she knew more than she was telling me, and I resolved to keep a close eye on her.

★ ★ ★

I drove Alice to an unmarked building near the Hudson—actually, an old warehouse—that Mr. Roosevelt had turned into a shooting range to encourage police officers to improve their marksmanship. I used it myself to keep in practice. There were half a dozen officers there when we entered, and Alice practically skipped in. The men gave us more than a look or two—the cowboy and the girl.

I knew the sergeant on duty, and he had a spare Colt New Police revolver, the weapon Mr. Roosevelt had introduced as standard issue when he was commissioner.

"New recruit, St. Clair?" he asked.

"If she passes the test," I said. I showed Alice how to properly load and handle the revolver so she wouldn't kill anyone. "Now, patience, Miss Alice. This isn't the Wild West. Aim and squeeze." It took a while, but after a few shots, it seemed clear Alice had inherited her father's skill, and with proper guidance, each shot was better than the one before.

Meanwhile, word got around on who she was, and the other cops stopped what they were doing and gathered around her, offering encouragement and cheering her on, which she loved almost as much as the shooting.

"All right, that's enough for one day," I said, seeing her hand was beginning to tire. The cops gave her a round of applause, Alice curtsied, and we headed back outside.

"Imagine if I knew who the murderer was. Or murderers, if there is more than one," she said as we headed back to the motor-car. "If we were out West, I could just shoot them, couldn't I?"

"For God's sake, Miss Alice. What would your father say? He's devoted his whole life to creating and defending proper civil law in this country, and you want to walk up and shoot someone because you think they're a killer?"

"No, not just like that. You know what I mean. Like in Wyoming, where we're both armed and we do a fast draw, only I'd be faster."

"Oh, you would be? Pity you weren't at the O.K. Corral. You've been reading too many dime novels. They make it sound like it's a daily happening. First of all, fast draws have always been a lot less common than Eastern writers would like to think, and second, you can't just pull a gun on someone. You have to wait for the other guy to reach first."

"Why?"

"Because if someone reaches for a gun and the lawman then reaches for his, it's self-defense. But if the lawman reaches first, it's murder, and it doesn't matter if he's wearing a badge."

Alice stopped, her hand on the door of the motorcar. "Thank you. That is a very useful distinction, Mr. St. Clair," she said quietly and looked into the distance.

I should've noticed the look on her face and seen it coming then. Although Alice had been dodging her aunt and father with half-truths and incomplete explanations, I thought I knew what she was up to, but I was only right most of the time.

Not much happened the rest of the day. We had lunch downtown; Alice bought us knishes, which she loved. We talked about things other than the murders, and she was cheerful, so again, my guard was down. She said she was going to spend a quiet evening inside but advised me to be at breakfast at eight sharp. I got myself some dinner under the El and turned in early for a long and untroubled sleep.

★ ★ ★

I felt a little bad the next morning that I hadn't spent one minute thinking about who could've been a poisoner, or how, or why, but I figured that Alice might've have calmed down a bit. When it was really important, Alice saw reason.

She was cheerful enough when she greeted me at the door, not confused and dreamy like she was much of the day before. "Come in, Mr. St. Clair. My aunt and I were just sitting down to breakfast. Eggs and bacon this morning, and toast with orange marmalade."

"Very nice," I said, and I followed her into the breakfast room. "Good morning, ma'am," I said to Mrs. Cowles.

"Good morning, Mr. St. Clair." She gave me one of those quick but deep looks, like she could see into my soul. There was no keeping secrets from her, not in the long term. I carefully sat down and helped myself to coffee. I thought that if Alice was excited about some new plan, she'd be a little more anxious about getting rid of her aunt so we could get started, but she chattered with her aunt about other people in Society, her father's recent visit, a possible visit to the museum—anything but the murders.

And then the doorbell rang. Mrs. Cowles raised an eyebrow. "Another breakfast meeting, Alice? Are you sure I won't be in the way?"

Alice ignored the sarcasm. "Of course not," she said, and I realized from Alice's look that she knew who was on the other side of the door. Had she gone around me and invited Captain O'Hara to join us, after all? As usual, I got up and joined the maid to open the door.

It was Mariah.

I was quiet for a moment before asking, "What are you doing here?"

"Alice invited me. Didn't she tell you? She probably figured it wasn't necessary and wanted to avoid an argument." When I got over my surprise, I noticed she was wearing a good dress, much nicer than you needed at breakfast. A pale rose showed off the black ringlets of her hair.

"Mariah, I'm so glad you could come," said Alice, joining us in the foyer. "Join us at the table while the eggs are still hot."

"Miss Alice, when did this happen?" I asked.

"Yesterday. I sent Mariah a letter with an off-duty porter."

I had a lot of questions, but there was no asking while Mrs. Cowles was around. Now I was the one who wanted her out of the way.

"Aunt Anna, you remember my friend Mariah Flores from yesterday. She's Mr. St. Clair's older sister."

"Of course, a pleasure to see you again," said Mrs. Cowles. "Do take a seat."

I looked around at everyone. Alice and Mariah looked pleased with themselves, and Mrs. Cowles was curious. I cleared my throat.

"My sister is here at Miss Alice's invitation, Mrs. Cowles. I don't want you to think I was presuming," I said.

"Don't be silly," said Alice. "My aunt knows Mariah is my friend and is here at my invitation."

"Alice's friends are always welcome here," said Mrs. Cowles. "I am only sorry that I have morning appointments and am unable to ask Mrs. Flores for the many childhood stories I am sure she has about Mr. St. Clair."

"Another time, perhaps," said Mariah.

"Tell me," continued Mrs. Cowles. "Are you as adept with firearms as your brother?"

I spilled my coffee.

"Who do you think gave him his first lesson?" said Mariah.

"So you have earned the friendship and respect of my niece, and you can handle a revolver? It's a shame the Secret Service doesn't employ women, or we could've engaged you as her bodyguard."

Mariah seemed pleased at the compliment, even as Alice pouted. "But that wouldn't be fair to Mr. St. Clair," she said, laying a hand on my arm. "He'd miss me too much."

"Indeed," said Mrs. Cowles, giving Alice and me meaningful looks. Talk turned to the weather and how the city was changing now that cars were replacing carriages, but I just kept glancing back and forth between Alice and Mariah. After a few minutes of this, Mrs. Cowles stood. "I must go now. Mrs. Flores, a pleasure seeing you again. Alice—we'll talk later." Those last three words weighed heavily, and I knew they'd come back to haunt us. She left the breakfast room, and a few minutes later, we heard her leaving the apartment.

"Finish up. We need to be on our way," said Alice, so pleased with herself I thought she'd kick up her feet. She happily took another piece of bacon and drained her coffee.

"Miss Alice, Mariah, what is going on?" I tried to come down heavy like Mrs. Cowles did, but it wasn't working. I could see from the look on Mariah's face that she knew, even as she was all wide-eyed innocence.

"After giving it some thought," said Alice, "I realized we still don't know enough. This is a case full of emotion. We need to talk some more with Mrs. Brackton, so we're paying another call, and I need another person, another woman, for some insights. Mariah had so many interesting thoughts yesterday. Of course, I can't introduce her as your sister, so she will be Mariah Flores, a dear friend from New Orleans. Now, we really do need to be going because I want to get there early before anyone else calls."

"Miss Alice, I know you. What's going on? This could be dangerous."

"You heard the girl," said Mariah. "Grab your hat and coat."

I realized there was no way out of it, but I had a parting shot. "Mariah, I get paid to do this. What's your angle?"

"It's like Mrs. Cowles said: I want your job."

At least Alice thought that was funny.

★ ★ ★

We squeezed into the motorcar and drove to the Brackton house. Alice continued to look pleased with herself, and I had to remind her to look a little soberer, as we were making a condolence call.

"If I think something is dangerous, I'm dragging you both out of there," I said, but I didn't think either of them were listening.

The butler, still wearing his mourning armband, let us in. He recognized Alice right away.

"Good day, Miss Roosevelt. Mrs. Brackton said you were to be admitted immediately if you called again."

"Very good. I've brought another family friend, and of course, my escort must stay with me."

He showed us into the parlor where Mrs. Brackton was alone, sitting in a comfortable chair. Magazines were tossed carelessly on a side table; she had probably been passing the time leafing through them. When we walked into the room, she practically ran to Alice. "Oh, my dear, you're my one true friend in all of this. Thank you for coming. Please be seated." She looked at Mariah.

"Victoria, I hope you don't mind, I brought an old friend—Mrs. Mariah Flores from Louisiana. She is a widow, too, and knows well the terrible situation you're in."

"A pleasure," said Mrs. Brackton. "I'll have the maid bring some tea." We seated ourselves on a couch, and Mrs. Brackton took a comfortable chair facing us with a low table in between. "I am sorry. You must excuse me, Mrs. Flores, but my mind is a muddle ever since . . . but have we met?"

"Oh, I don't think so," said Mariah, exaggerating her honey-eyed voice. "Nevertheless, Alice told me about the tragic death of your husband, and I said, 'Alice, I must go with you to call on Mrs. Brackton.'"

There was a long pause. Mrs. Brackton didn't say anything but looked curiously at Mariah, as if waiting for something. "Because you're a widow, too?" asked Victoria, perhaps a little disturbed by the enthusiasm from a woman she had never met.

"Oh, well that. But didn't I say? It's because of the deep friendship I developed with your late husband, Lynley, when we met just over a year ago."

Chapter 34

So there was a script. I didn't think Mariah would lie like that without Alice working it out with her first. I looked at Alice, but she gave nothing away.

The maid came in with tea and some plain cookies. I wasn't planning on having anything, as I figured this was dangerous, and I was going to watch every move. Two people were already dead, and Mrs. Brackton had been threatened again.

"You knew my husband?" asked Mrs. Brackton, and I thought her tone was odd, or maybe I was just being too sensitive.

"I was visiting, oh, it was some eighteen months ago," Mariah continued. "I've been a widow for about ten years now. My late husband was in shipping—we have extensive interests in Louisiana and a large house right in the city. Anyway, my husband had a lot of business with your late husband. It had been years since I had visited New York, and while other friends were busy, he took good care of me, showed me the sights. What a gentleman he was. You must feel his loss keenly."

"It's a pity he didn't bring you here to our home. We have an excellent cook," said Victoria. It wasn't my imagination now. Her tone was dead.

Mariah clapped her hand to her mouth. I thought she was overplaying it a bit, but Mrs. Brackton didn't seem to notice.

"I'm so sorry. Perhaps I misunderstood. He told me you were recovering from an illness and needed lots of time to sleep, with plenty of rest and quiet, so he couldn't bring me around."

The room got silent except for the ladies drinking their tea and the crunch of a butter cookie being eaten.

"Oh, yes. I remember now," said Mrs. Brackton. But she was hardly looking at anyone. Alice and Mariah were provoking her, but I didn't know why. It was like the first time I had met her, and I saw she was a woman whose life had been squeezed out of her.

"It's been a tragic few days," said Alice. "Mariah, we lost another good friend recently. I don't think you know the Lindes, but Mrs. Linde also died, shortly after Lynley. She was so young. One of the loveliest young women in New York—wouldn't you say so, Victoria?"

"Hmm? Yes, of course. Very lovely."

"And like you, Mariah, a good friend of Lynley's. It's all so sad." Alice shook her head.

The conversation went on like that for a while. Mariah talked about how wonderful Lynley was, Alice agreed, and Mrs. Brackton just kept disappearing further and further into herself. At one point, Mrs. Brackton rang for her maid and said she had to take some medicine and would be back in a moment. I wanted to talk to the women, but another maid came by to refresh the tea service and put out some more cookies, and by the time she was done, Mrs. Brackton had returned.

She looked a little better now. The doctor had probably given her something to boost her spirits. But Alice and Mariah started in again. I kept watching as the ladies took a cookie or helped themselves to more tea and sugar, as Lynley's praises were sung. Something had to happen. Mrs. Brackton would fall apart, despite her medication. Or someone else would call, and we'd have to make a gracious exit. Or as gracious as we could be after practically convincing Mrs. Brackton that Mariah had been one of her husband's mistresses. Except I could've told them it wouldn't make a difference. Even Mrs. Brackton must've known her husband had other women by the dozen.

And then something happened. Mrs. Brackton leaned back in her chair a little too quickly and overbalanced the tea, which spilled onto her dress. She cried out in surprise and embarrassment, and both Alice and Mariah jumped to her aid and grabbed napkins to help clean her up. Mrs. Brackton flailed a bit and tried to grab another napkin herself from the tea tray, which only made it more difficult for Alice and Mariah.

"Let me summon my maid. I'll need to change, and she can help. You ladies finish your tea," said Mrs. Brackton.

Then I realized I could get back at Alice and my sister. They had surprised me, and now I could surprise them. Alice said we needed a witness, that we needed solid evidence, and she was right.

"In just a minute," I said, and everyone looked at me, a little startled. I had been sitting at the far end of the couch, not saying anything, not drinking or eating anything, just watching the women. I reached over and grabbed Mrs. Brackton's left wrist, which was covered with black lace. She cried out, but I didn't let go, and with my other hand, I reached under her sleeve. I knew I was right. You don't play cards as much as I do without watching what your opponents do with their sleeves.

"Sir, let go! Alice, tell him to stop." But Alice and Mariah were struck dumb as I pulled my hand out with leaves of wolfsbane between my thumb and forefinger.

"How did these get here, Mrs. Brackton? Mariah, don't touch your tea. She just slipped some into your cup. Mrs. Brackton, you're under arrest for attempted murder."

I thought she'd come at me. I hadn't arrested many women, but in my experience, they were more likely to surprise you. When men know it's over, they know it's over. The women often have an extra twist, and Mrs. Brackton was no exception. But she surprised me, anyway—instead of launching herself at me, she went for Mariah. I was also wrong about all life having been snuffed out of her. She had one bit left, and she used it all up right then and there.

Her face twisted in absolute rage. I wouldn't have recognized her, in fact, and she was practically foaming at the mouth as she screamed. "He was mine! Lynley was mine! Stay away stay away—"

But Mariah knew how to take care of herself and moved quickly, sliding away from the madwoman as I grabbed her and forced her facedown onto the couch. She screamed and sobbed as I took my handcuffs out of my jacket, and soon, I had her restrained.

And what was Alice doing? She was standing by with her arms folded, looking absolutely triumphant.

"Do you ladies want to explain why I wasn't involved in your little plan?" I asked.

"You would've said no," said Alice.

"Damn right. What's wrong with you—with both of you? You could both be dead right now."

"Stop fussing. We knew you'd be keeping a lookout, and you were. At some point, if we kept at her, she would break. It was a fast draw, Mr. St. Clair. She made the first move and lost."

But I wasn't going to let her talk her way out of it. "Miss Alice, we have a certain trust. I think I've been fairly good. I've let you get away with a lot. But taunting a murderess until she lashes out . . . that's too much." My heart was pounding, and for a few moments, the only sound was Mrs. Brackton's whimpering. Mariah looked a little amused, and Alice rolled her eyes.

"Like my father said, Mr. St. Clair: 'In any moment of decision, the best thing you can do is the right thing, the next best thing is the wrong thing, and the worst thing you can do is nothing.'"

"We'll see if your aunt agrees," I shot back.

Alice then addressed the prisoner. "Victoria, that wasn't very nice what you did with your maid, Miss Whatley. You were cleverer than I gave you credit for. We questioned Miss Whatley, and she swore under oath you hadn't done anything. But thinking back on her responses, she only said you hadn't done anything. You had her do it for you. When she said *you* hadn't sent a package, she was technically telling the truth because *she* was the one who did it. *You* hadn't left the house, but *she* did on your behalf. My stupid fault for making assumptions and not asking the right questions—only asking about *your* actions, not *hers*. I doubt if she even knew what she was doing, just following orders without question, so I'll excuse her as an unwitting accomplice. But there is no excuse for you."

"Miss Whatley was still lying with her hand on the Bible, Miss Alice," I said. "My mother wouldn't have let me get away with that."

"Oh, but Mr. St. Clair, your mother wasn't assaulted by an employer the way Miss Whatley was. Remember I had said that female servants weren't safe in their house? Miss Whatley probably hated Lynley as much as Victoria did after she had heard about his affair with Mrs. Linde. Victoria, I'm guessing all you had to do was tell Miss Whatley she was helping you take revenge on your husband, and she happily did what you asked even if she didn't know the whys or hows. Right?"

All we got from that was a little sob, which I guess was an agreement. It made perfect sense. But I don't know if much was registering with Mrs. Brackton by that point. She was lost in her own misery by now. Alice shook her head. I was sorry I had misjudged Mrs. Brackton, too. She had found herself married to an unreliable man but had found a reliable servant. In a way, Captain O'Hara had it right. There was a servant involved, although it wasn't a crime of malice, but one of loyalty.

"Mariah, why don't you stay here in case your brother finds restraining his prisoner beyond him. I'm going to find the telephone and summon Captain O'Hara. I hope he can come quickly. We still have another culprit to challenge today, and it'll be lunchtime soon." She strode out the door.

"Another?" I asked, but Alice was already gone. Mrs. Brackton got quieter now, and I hoped she'd just go to sleep after that performance.

"Christ almighty, I wouldn't have thought it, but that plan of hers worked. Joey, that girl of yours is a pistol."

"She's not my girl, but yeah, you're right. She's eighteen and crazy. What the hell is your excuse?"

She shrugged. "Same as yours. I was bored. Don't pretend you weren't." She reached into my jacket pocket, pulled out my flask, and took a long swig.

"You're still a bourbon man," she observed.

"Miss Alice hates bourbon," I said.

"She's young."

It seemed to take forever, but Captain O'Hara showed up eventually with a couple of cops and a capable-looking police matron. He took in the scene.

"St. Clair, are you absolutely sure? If you're not, you know what will happen to both of us."

"Completely sure," I told him. "You can see the wolfsbane in one of the cups there. She killed her cheating husband and his mistress, Delilah Linde."

He sighed. "This isn't going to be pleasant for anyone," he said. "All right, take her away. I have to talk for a few minutes." He nodded at the matron, who firmly but gently lifted Mrs. Brackton up. She seemed a little dazed but willing to cooperate. I took back my cuffs, and the matron, accompanied by one of the cops, led her out of the room.

O'Hara suddenly noticed Mariah. "Who are you, ma'am? A friend of Miss Roosevelt's?"

"Yes, and Mr. St. Clair's sister," said Alice brightly.

"His sister? How about that?" Captain O'Hara laughed. "I'd ask what you're doing here, but I don't want to know."

Mariah smiled. "Believe me, you don't."

"It's rather simple," said Alice. "Mrs. Brackton committed

two murders and pretended that she was the intended victim with that lie about switching glasses. In fact, she poisoned her own glass and gave it to her husband. Then she sent the poison to Delilah. Finally, she pretended someone had sent her the poisoned drink, but she did it herself. We were just having a simple tea when she went crazy and attacked Mrs. Flores."

You didn't get to be a New York City police captain without knowing what was what, and O'Hara knew something was wrong here.

"Miss Roosevelt, you didn't give me the whole story here, but that's all right. As long as I don't get any more surprises."

"Yeah, no more surprises from Alice Roosevelt. I wish you luck," I said. Alice was too pleased with herself to take offense.

That's when we got another surprise—thanks to Alice. Felicia Meadows burst into the room.

"Am I late? I came as soon as I could," she said. "Thanks for your call, Miss Roosevelt."

"I think you two already met at breakfast at the Caledonia. Anyway, Captain O'Hara, this is Miss Meadows of the *New York Herald*," Alice said.

"I have nothing to say," said O'Hara as he started to leave. But Miss Meadows was more than a match.

"Captain, Alice Roosevelt already gave me the basics. I can run this story two ways. Either, 'Heroic Police Captain Solves Society Murder,' or 'Clumsy Cops Finally Stumble Into Right Suspect After Days of Incompetence.'"

"Oh, all right," he grumbled. "If you put it that way." I knew Alice wasn't supposed to give interviews, but she and the captain filled in the details for Miss Meadows, who scribbled furiously. "Front page gold, my friends," she said. "The presses will be running all night turning out extra copies. This will be the biggest issue since they sank the *Maine*. And Captain, you and your men can't talk to any other paper until tomorrow. We own this story, and you owe me your reputation. I'm already Miss Roosevelt's best friend. And now I'm yours."

"All right," said O'Hara, bowing to the reality of the First Amendment. Miss Meadows smiled at me.

"Can I get a quote from you, Cowboy?" she asked me.

"You know the rule. I can't be quoted."

Alice jumped in. "But add that the police department thanks Joseph St. Clair, special agent of the US Secret Service, for his help in apprehending a dangerous criminal."

"Could you leave me out of this?" I asked, but no one listened.

"Good! You have an ear for this, Miss Roosevelt," said Miss Meadows. She looked at Mariah. "Are you a friend of Miss Roosevelt's? Of the arrested woman?"

"This is Mariah Flores, a friend of Alice's and Mr. St. Clair's sister," said O'Hara.

Miss Meadows laughed. I didn't know why having a sister was so funny. "A pleasure. Would love to talk more with you, but I have a taxi waiting downstairs and an impatient editor downtown. Good day to all." She practically ran out of the room.

"Seems like a competent woman," said Mariah, nodding her head.

"Your brother is sweet on her," said Alice.

"For God's sake," I said.

"Really?" said my sister. "Glad to see you're interested in a better class of girl. Alice has been a good influence on you."

Another group of cops showed up, no doubt to talk to the servants and take charge of the poisoned tea. I gave a quick salute to Captain O'Hara as Alice grabbed me by the arm. Mariah followed us as we headed out of the house.

"Now, what's this about another person we have to question?" I asked.

Alice sighed. "You haven't figured it out yet? I'll explain as we drive. Mariah, we'll drive you home first. I can't thank you enough. We really did it!"

"Miss Alice, no more games with poisoned tea," I said.

"Oh, no. I promise. But someone is going to be very angry, so make sure you're ready for a fast draw."

★ ★ ★

Mariah gave Alice a kiss in front of her building, and Alice said she was going to buy us all dinner at the Rathskeller the next night Mariah had off.

"Now, Mr. St. Clair, to the Rutledge house, to speak with Simon Rutledge."

"What does this have to do with him?"

"That's what I couldn't get around, Mr. St. Clair. That's why we couldn't believe Victoria Brackton had committed murder. Because Simon Rutledge was watching her. He knew she was doing it. More than that, he wanted her to. He's just as guilty as she is."

"I know you're excited, but you may be overreaching here. I don't think a court would agree with you," I said.

"The court of public opinion, the Honorable Alice Roosevelt presiding, does agree," she said.

"What if we run into Miss Rutledge?" I said.

"I doubt it. Her mother has probably pulled herself together by now and is having Philly make calls like a good debutante should."

Alice hopped out of the motorcar. "This is going to be fun," she said.

CHAPTER 35

The butler admitted us right away. "I am sorry, Miss Roosevelt, but Miss Rutledge is not at home. You may leave a message, if you'd like."

"I'm not here to see Miss Rutledge. I'm here to see Mr. Rutledge. There has been a tragic development regarding a mutual friend, and it's essential I speak with him immediately."

He showed hardly any emotion as he led us into the same beautiful room with the Mary Cassatt paintings. I stared at them again, still wondering what the women on the canvas were thinking. That was the hard part, wasn't it, knowing the secret loves and fears inside us? What the frightened maid Cathleen was thinking when she interrupted me in this room, what Peter was thinking when he wouldn't tell us where he had been, what Victoria Brackton was thinking when she was at the party, and finally, what Simon Rutledge was thinking when he was watching the trio at the other end of the table.

"Mr. Rutledge will see you in his study," said the butler after he returned, and we followed him upstairs. I was hoping I'd get another one of those cigars but somehow doubted Mr. Rutledge would offer me one by the time we were done.

I had learned something about the way people greeted each other in Alice's world. Even when he was being pleasant to me, like the night of the murder, Mr. Rutledge made it clear I was the help. But Alice was one of his class, so I thought he'd come around to greet her, but he didn't. He stayed behind his desk, that vast expanse of polished wood and leather, and barely rose when we entered.

"Miss Roosevelt? That was a rather odd message you sent me, to say the least. Please explain." With a quick wave of his arm, he invited us to take seats without even giving me a look. "A mutual friend, you say?"

"Victoria Brackton. We just came from her house. She's in the process of being arraigned—I think that's the right word—for the murder of her husband and Delilah Linde. I thought you'd want to know." Alice was looking a little too gleeful in my opinion, but I suppose she had earned it. "I imagine, as you're an interested party, that Captain O'Hara will let you know himself as soon as he's done with the paperwork."

I could see Rutledge had a dozen questions, and I wondered which one he'd ask first.

"How do you know this?" he asked.

"I was there when she fell apart and all but admitted it. She tried to kill a friend of mine out of insane jealousy. But then again, this shouldn't be a surprise to you. I kept wondering why you were watching her talk to her husband and Delilah Linde. But you knew what was happening. You saw what she did. I think you even put her up to it."

I could see Alice had hit home. He was nervous and licked his lips.

"That's . . . extraordinary, Miss Roosevelt," he said and finally acknowledged me with what he clearly hoped was a friendly smile. "Mr. St. Clair—that's the name, right? You're a lawman. You carry a badge. Miss Roosevelt is young. Maybe explain to her about slander laws."

"I suggest you hear her out, sir," I said, and he frowned, not getting the answer he had hoped for.

"This starts with the XVII, that silly little club of yours," said Alice, and I saw his finger absently go to his signet ring.

"I beg your pardon," he said. "How do you even know about it?"

Alice waved away his question. "The organization is ridiculous and your goals offensive—but that's not why I'm here. I'm here about the mistake you made, handing an important job in the XVII to Lynley Brackton. The word people keep using about him is 'unreliable.' You should've known that. I will give you the benefit of the doubt and assume that all you had in mind was some vigorous political organizing, and it was Brackton who began employing an untrained private army for intimidation."

"I don't see what this has to do with any murders—not that I am admitting to anything," he said.

"We're coming to that. Meanwhile, Brackton had recruited Miles van Dijk—Delilah's brother. He was desperate for money, and I'm sure you and your merry band promised to fill his pockets to help run things. Your work in the slums was appalling enough, but what I'm trying to understand is why the Roths? Yes, I know they're 'not one of us,' but they know how to wear evening clothes and use the right forks, so why them?"

He tried to think about that, about what he needed to admit to Alice. "I have nothing against Reuben Roth or his son Abraham. But you must understand that the investments we choose are not only done to enrich ourselves but to improve the long-term health and character of the city and the country. I am not sure the Roths understand that. I'm not sure they care."

"Are we talking about foreign investments?" asked Alice.

"We are talking about the wrong kind of foreign investments. Without going into detail, he and his investors were sending money, enormous sums, into . . . situations that would have long-term implications for the country, far behind the Roth syndicate. Many of us thought that was a mistake. More than a mistake— bordering on tragic."

Alice nodded. She knew what that meant: putting American dollars in the hands of Baron Okada.

"You're a fool. Men like Roth are the future, and so far, I haven't noticed any difference between Christian businessmen and Jewish businessmen—but never mind." She rolled over his protests. "Things started to really get out of hand. Because the unreliable Lynley Brackton was causing more trouble. He preyed on vulnerable Delilah Linde, stuck in an unhappy marriage, even though Marcus was another member of the XVII. What would happen now that his lieutenant was his mistress's brother? The implications were beyond calculation. What a horrible mess you had, Mr. Rutledge."

He was trying to master himself and think about the best defense.

"What of it, Miss Roosevelt? You seem to know so much. Then you must know that Lynley Brackton's poor behavior has been long known. Why would this be a problem now?"

"Because of who he picked. If he had stuck with actresses and chorus girls and artists' models, no one would say anything. No one would care. That's what I've heard—men like Brackton never leave their wives for a common girl. But to cheat among your own set, the wife of a friend, a club member. That was inexcusable. He was truly unreliable."

Alice had paid attention—she had learned about unreliability in all its nasty forms. In the end, it had less to do with the XVII than we had thought. It was Brackton's unreliability as a husband and Delilah's unreliability as a wife that killed them both. I think Alice realized that, too. Did they deserve it? I was glad I was just a simple cowboy and not a preacher.

Rutledge looked more and more unhappy, but that didn't stop Alice. "You had a huge fight with him—yes, I know about that. But he laughed at you. So what did you do? You told Victoria. How much did you tell her? Did you remind her you had poisonous plants in your greenhouse? Did you truly believe she'd go that far that quickly?"

"Of course not. I just hoped she would be angry enough to make it clear he was on the cusp of a major scandal and that fear would be enough to rein him." He was really nervous now.

"Perhaps," said Alice. "Only Victoria knows what she was told, and I don't think we'll get the full story from her. Anyway, I don't think any of us realized just how unhappy she was and how her unhappiness had twisted her. Until that night, when you nervously watched her talking to her husband and her husband's mistress. Delilah was carrying his child. Did you know that? Did you tell Victoria? It must've been frightening, wondering what was happening, seeing Delilah so foolishly cozying up to Brackton that evening, right in front of his wife, no doubt excited for the first time in her life to feel passion for a man. And that night, you watched Victoria put something into her husband's glass. You watched her kill him—right in your house. She really loved him. I know that now. She didn't like his affairs but tolerated them because the women weren't of their class. But when he turned his attentions to one of their friends, the fear and humiliation was too much. Would he leave her for Delilah? That's when her love turned to hate. I learned that."

Yes, from Mariah. And I remembered what I told Alice about marriages I had seen—only the two people in it know what is going on. It was good to know Alice had paid attention.

Philly Rutledge had told us that Victoria Brackton's nickname in school had been "Mouse." That should've told me everything. A mouse tries to run away, but if you corner one, it will fight like a tiger.

"Mr. Rutledge. You allowed her to execute her husband at your party because of all the trouble he was causing you and your club members. What do you have to say to that?"

I didn't think he was very bright. He thought it was all over but wasn't able to see the whole story through to the end. He thought Alice had nothing but guesswork, but I knew her better. I wasn't entirely happy about how this was going to end, but I had become resigned to it.

"You're a smart young woman, and I give you credit for coming to your conclusions. But all you have is theory and a madwoman who will likely, and deservedly, end up on the gallows. I am sorry—"

Alice stood. "Come, Mr. St. Clair. Drive me to the office of District Attorney Jerome. I am going to testify that I saw Mr. Rutledge witness a murder and do nothing. And then there's all that Miles van Dijk told me. You gave him a lot of money, Mr. Rutledge, for his new position? Or just to keep him quiet? Either way, I think Mr. Jerome will be very interested. Good day."

I had one sickening moment thinking about what Mrs. Cowles would say if Alice decided to testify in a murder case. Fortunately, Mr. Rutledge backed down quickly.

"Miss Roosevelt . . . Alice. Please sit. Let's discuss this." Looking smug, she resumed her chair. "I can't bring Lynley Brackton back, as if anyone would want to. I can't undo Victoria's actions. You want to do business. What do you want?"

"Two things," said Alice. "First, Philly has an important new friend in her life. I'd like you to encourage it and invite the friend over. Make him welcome. And if it comes to a marriage proposal, you'll agree."

"Philly is having a romance? That's impossible. But . . . who?" This was not what he was expecting. He looked like someone had hit him with a baseball bat.

"Abraham Roth, Reuben's son. He's delightful, amusing, intelligent, and seems to care for her a lot. I know she's young to marry, so that may not happen, but if it does, she'll be well cared for."

"You're asking the impossible—we're talking about my only daughter," he said, raising his voice.

"I'm not negotiating this," said Alice, raising her voice even higher. "I want to hear about his invitation to dinner with your family within the week. I like Philly a lot, and it's for her benefit I'm not having you arrested."

He took a deep breath to control his temper. "Very well. I promise. But I'll withhold permission to marry until she's twenty-one."

"Fair enough," said Alice. "Now one more thing. This will be easier. You have a maid named Cathleen O'Neill."

"I'll take your word for it," he said. Imagine that—so many servants he didn't know their names.

"I know her. Never mind how. She just married, but to move out of here, she needs money to buy a house. She and her husband need five hundred dollars." They had actually said they needed another three hundred dollars to buy the house, but I guessed Alice wanted to give them something for furniture, too.

"You want me to give five hundred dollars to my maid as a wedding present? That's . . . the oddest request I've ever heard. But very well." He pulled a checkbook out of his drawer, wrote out a check, and handed it to Alice. "Give it to her with my compliments. I think—I hope—that we are done here?"

"Miss Alice might be done, but I have one thing to add, sir. Did you know that the Secret Service is part of the Treasury Department?"

"What of it?"

"We do more than just keep Alice Roosevelt out of trouble. We look into financial crimes. And after I submit my report, I think scores of accountants in Washington will be looking into your ledgers and the financing of the XVII. Don't put away those checks, sir. You'll be writing some more made out to the US Treasury. The XVII is your business, but don't think it's going to be secret after Washington gets through with you."

"Thanks for the warning," he said coldly. Alice reached over and gave my hand a quick squeeze.

"Now, we really are done," said Alice. She stood. "Good day, Mr. Rutledge. And rein in that idiotic society of yours until Mr. St. Clair's friends at the Treasury shut it down for good"

He turned red, and I knew it was time to go. But Mr. Rutledge had a parting shot.

"Someday, you may regret what you've done here," he said. Alice shrugged. When you're eighteen, "someday" is very far away. "Meanwhile, I will give you a piece of advice: don't let this make you arrogant. I was unlucky in my choice of associates, and you were present to take advantage of it. I am still much smarter than you."

It was a combination of my relief and the almost comical seriousness of his tone aimed at a young girl like Alice. I couldn't help it—I laughed. Rutledge turned even redder.

"Did I amuse you, Mr. St. Clair?" he asked.

"I'm sorry, sir. It was just what you said, about being smarter than Miss Alice. Even I'm smarter than you."

Now, Alice laughed.

"That's something from a man in your position," shot back Rutledge. "My butler makes more money than you do."

"I know I'm a poor man and expect to always be poor, sir. But I've never hired someone as unfit as Lynley Brackton for a job. I've never set a wronged woman on a murder spree. And I have certainly never been blackmailed by an eighteen-year-old girl."

That got another laugh out of Alice. She slipped her arm into mine. We left the room and headed downstairs and out the front door.

"Oh, Mr. St. Clair, nicely played. And you were actually witty. In fact, I've decided to forgive you."

"For what? After that stunt you pulled with Mrs. Brackton, you owe me the apology."

"Never mind. I haven't forgotten you laughed at me when I interrupted Abraham and Philly. You told me all I did was interrupt romances. And I did. I actually interrupted three romances, and that was what helped me solve this. Lynley and Victoria. That was the real mistake I made, not just letting her maid fool me. She really loved her husband and would kill him rather than see someone else have him. That was the third love affair—even if it was only one way. Third time's the charm."

I had to admit she was right.

CHAPTER 36

The rest of the day was quiet, but I was waiting for the other shoe to drop. I hadn't forgotten about Felicia Meadows. She and her colleagues would no doubt be writing up all kinds of articles, and there would be no explaining that to Mrs. Cowles.

Alice and I stopped by the garage and gave Peter the good news—and the money.

Peter just started at the check Alice handed over and couldn't even find the words.

"How . . . I don't understand."

"It's a gift from Mr. Rutledge, an attempt to make up for the unfair accusation."

"Come on, Miss Roosevelt. You don't expect me to believe that?" He grinned.

"You don't want to know," I said.

"I suppose I don't," said Peter. "When we get set up, I hope you two will come for dinner." Alice said she'd be delighted.

When we got home, there was already a message from Philly saying her father thought it would be a good idea to invite Abraham Roth for dinner. He had lost no time fulfilling his promise, and I admired him for that. I thought of young Roth, not just invited to a party but to an intimate family dinner, and I also thought of Booker T. Washington dining in the White House, and that made me smile.

★ ★ ★

That night, I had trouble sleeping, stuck thinking about what would happen the next day. I got up at the usual time, however, and joined Alice at breakfast. She seemed very pleased with herself and was eating buttermilk pancakes with an almost celebratory flair. I gingerly helped myself to some coffee while Alice chattered on about some upcoming parties.

Then Mrs. Cowles stormed in. That's the only word for it, and she had a copy of the *Herald* in her hand.

"Alice! What is this? An exclusive interview with Alice Roosevelt regarding the arrest of Victoria Brackton. The rule is that you stick to fashion and parties and complimentary remarks about your father. What were you thinking?"

I'll give it to Alice—she was cool. "Oh, that? I was paying a call on Victoria when the police barged in, and they asked me for a few comments. It wasn't political. I thought it was all right as long as I stayed away from politics. It's not my fault this happened when I was paying an innocent social call."

"Don't you dare try that on me," said Mrs. Cowles, her tone lowering dangerously. "This is bylined by that Felicia Meadows you've gotten close to. What have you been doing? And why has Mr. St. Clair been thanked?" Alice just shrugged.

"You'll want to discuss this in private," I said. I started to stand.

"Sit down," said Mrs. Cowles. So I did.

"Both of you—I know there is more here. This has to do with all those breakfast meetings and your sudden interest in condolence calls. You are sadly mistaken, Alice, if you think I won't find out. Someday. Someday soon." But Alice didn't seem concerned. As I had noted, when you're eighteen, "someday" is far away.

Mrs. Cowles helped herself to some coffee, still glaring at Alice, but Alice wasn't paying attention. She had picked up the paper, joyfully noting the extent of her quotes, when the doorbell rang.

"Another committee meeting?" asked Mrs. Cowles. But it turned out to only be my superior, Mr. Harris.

"Come on in," said Alice, ushering him into the breakfast room. "Buttermilk pancakes this morning."

"Maybe one," he said, helping himself to maple syrup. "Good morning, ma'am," he said to Mrs. Cowles.

"Good morning. Are you here about Mr. St. Clair's mention in the *Herald*?"

"Oh, that? Partly. Glad to see the police appreciate us. Good for public image. Nicely done, St. Clair. You can give me the details later. No, I'm really here, ma'am, because I know from the official schedule that you'll be attending *Aida* tonight, with singer Louise Homer, and as Mr. St. Clair has been so busy, I thought I'd give him a night off and attend to you myself."

"You appreciate classical singing, Mr. Harris? Very good, then. That will be acceptable."

However, that led Alice into a sulk.

"But maybe Mr. St. Clair wants to go," she said.

"I don't mind giving it a miss," I said. I'm not very musical.

"Why doesn't anyone ask what I want?" pouted Alice.

"Yes, Alice. Why would Mr. St. Clair—why would anyone—not want to spend an evening basking in the sun that is Alice Roosevelt?" asked Mrs. Cowles. Alice just rolled her eyes. I, meanwhile, was thinking about what else I might want to do that evening. I had an idea.

★ ★ ★

For the rest of the day, we made a few calls, and Alice got some congratulations, as well as some smirks about her quotes in the *Herald*, which thrilled her.

"What are you going to do tonight? Another card game?" she asked.

"Maybe," I said, and she didn't like that vague answer.

I saw her into her apartment, then went back downstairs. I had shaved earlier but shaved again to look perfect, put a comb through my hair, gave a brushing to my Stetson, and straightened my suit.

It was bad timing, though. I entered the lobby from my room just as Alice, Mrs. Cowles, and Agent Harris were heading toward the hired motorcar that was waiting for them.

Alice looked grand in a fine dress, and her hair was done up nice. But that didn't stop her from looking at me—and looking at me again. She picked up her skirts and practically ran to me, frowning. She ran a hand quickly on my cheek. "You shaved— again. Why, if you're going to a card game?"

"I never said I was going to a card game. I said 'maybe.'"

She sniffed. "Bay rum. You put on bay rum. You never do that."

"Alice!" said Mrs. Cowles. "Can you go an hour without causing embarrassment? Leave Mr. St. Clair alone. The motorcar is waiting."

Alice gave me another look, and I winked at her, which failed to get a smile. The chauffeur saw them into the motorcar, and I walked out and headed to the El. I watched the neighborhoods change as we raced downtown, faster than the traffic below us, and got off near the *Herald*. But here, my timing was good—I didn't have to wait long until Felicia Meadows arrived. She saw me with surprise, and then that lovely mouth curved into a smile.

"Hello, Cowboy. How'd you know when I'd be leaving?"

"I'm Secret Service. We know everything."

"You do? How impressive. What did you think about the article?"

"I loved it. So did Alice. Mrs. Cowles—well, she wasn't so sure."

"I imagine not. But my editor certainly liked it. I made him a very happy man."

"Moving up the ladder?" I asked.

"It seems so. I'll be doing more than Society gossip."

"Want to celebrate your promotion on my dime? I'll buy you dinner."

She raised an eyebrow. "Where would we go?"

"I've come to enjoy Chinese food—I was introduced to it when I started this job. I know a great place."

"I can't use chopsticks."

I reached into my coat pocket. "Two forks," I said.

"I like a man who's prepared."

"And then after dinner, I'll buy you a drink or two at Mezzaluna in Little Italy."

"Mezzaluna? I've heard of it. Glamorous but full of unsavory types."

"Yes, glamorous and colorful. Don't worry—I know the owner, and he owes me and Alice a favor. She got a job for the owner's nephew. I get taken care of there."

"There's a story there, I'm sure. Unfortunately, you can't be quoted."

"Unfortunately." I held out my arm, and after a moment, she took it, and we walked along the sidewalk.

"About Miss Roosevelt," she said. "I've watched her, as a reporter and as a woman. I think she is rather fond of you, Joey."

"I think you're right, Felicia," I said.

"I also think you're rather fond of her, as well," she said with a sidelong glance and another lovely smile.

I had to agree with that, too.

HISTORICAL NOTE

Was Alice as shocking as I portray her here? Although this is a work of fiction, the real Alice Roosevelt was well known for her outrageous statements and behavior throughout her long life. Theodore Roosevelt once commented, "I can either run the country, or I can attend to Alice, but I cannot possibly do both." She really did smoke cigarettes in public and visit bookies.

Alice's aunt, Anna Roosevelt Cowles, is not as famous today as her brother or her nieces—Alice and Eleanor—but she may have been one of the most remarkable members of the family. Intelligent and strong-willed, she was the only one who could manage Alice and was an important influence on her. Anna was also a lifelong confidant of her brother's, and Theodore consulted her on many important decisions throughout his presidency. For the sake of the plot, I have her and Alice in New York during this period, although they spent much of their time in Washington.

Although the Secret Service did start protecting the presidential family around this time, Joseph St. Clair is a fictional creation. He is loosely based on real Rough Rider troopers, but there is no evidence Alice had any kind of friendship with any bodyguard. Mr. Wilkie, who makes a brief appearance at the start of this novel, really was head of the Secret Service at this time. Although this encounter is fictional, I have a feeling Alice drove him to distraction.

The Rutledges, Lindes, and Bracktons and the main plot of the book are my inventions. However, I did base the subplot of the Roths and the Japanese diplomat on a fascinating and yet little-known historical event: Jacob Schiff, a German-Jewish immigrant, was a noted Wall Street figure and philanthropist. He helped fund Japan in its conflict with Russia, motivated largely by his disgust with Russia's anti-Semitic policies. It was a bold move, as no one believed an Asian nation could beat a European one. His investment paid off and had long-term financial implications while changing worldwide attitudes regarding Jews. Interestingly, Theodore Roosevelt was an early supporter of Zionism and spoke out against Russian pogroms. He was the first president to appoint a Jewish cabinet member: Oscar Straus as Secretary of Commerce and Labor.

Alice mentions William T. Jerome, who was in fact the Manhattan district attorney at this time. He would later prosecute Harry K. Thaw for the murder of architect Stanford White, one of the most famous murder cases in the twentieth century. His first cousin was Jennie Jerome, the mother of Winston Churchill.

St. Benedict the Moor Church, where Peter Carlyle and Cathleen O'Neill get married, does exist and was established in the nineteenth century to serve the city's African-American Catholics. It's still a functioning church, staffed by an order of Spanish friars. Many states had strict laws against interracial marriage, which existed until *Loving v. Virginia*. However, New York never had such a law, even though most people probably would've found such a union shocking.

The *New York Herald*, ensconced in its magnificent building (sadly torn down decades ago), was probably the most colorful paper in an era of colorful journalism, when facts were often not as important as a lively story. Felicia Meadows is a fictional character, but female journalists were making their mark even at the turn of the century. The *Herald* merged with its more sedate rival, the *Tribune*, in 1924, and the *Herald-Tribune* continued until 1966.

Finally, a note on Theodore Roosevelt and women: his daughter Alice, niece Eleanor, and sister Anna were all, in their own highly individual ways, outstanding contributors to American political and social life. I think it's no coincidence that Theodore, surrounded by these examples, was one of the first major US political figures to call for women's suffrage, as early as 1912.

ACKNOWLEDGMENTS

The creation of Alice Roosevelt, Agent St. Clair, and their special world was a team effort. As always, major thanks to my agent, Cynthia Zigmund, for years of encouragement, advice, and the staunchest support. The great team at Crooked Lane Books—especially Matt Martz, Sarah Poppe, and Jenny Chen—are a pleasure to work with and make me a better writer with every conversation we have.

So many other authors, especially those at Crooked Lane, have offered insights and good cheer. Who would've thought that people who spend their days plotting murder could be so kind and generous!

Once again, I am grateful beyond words to my family for all their love and support as I bang away on my laptop day after day. My wife Liz, more than anyone, deserves unending thanks for all her encouragement and help over the years and for never doubting I'd be published.